# IN PURSUIT OF PLATINUM

## THE SHOCKING SECRET OF WORLD WAR II

## VIC ROBBIE

# OTHER BOOKS BY VIC ROBBIE

**Ben Peters World War II thriller series**

PARADISE GOLD

THE GIRL with the SILVER STILETTO

Published by Principium Press.

Cover design by Stuart Bache.

Cover photograph: Copyright © Carlo Dapino/Shutterstock.com

Find out more at www.VicRobbie.com

ISBN-13: 978-0-9573464-0-6 (Paperback edition)

au2

❀ Created with Vellum

*In memory of*
*Allan Robbie (1915-1995)*
*and*
*for Christine*

# 1

SHE KNOWS SHE MUST KILL HER BEAUTIFUL SON. THE DECISION WAS MADE IN a moment of ice-cold clarity before panic took over and tears flowed in rivulets of sorrow.

Dressed in a dark blue Chanel suit and a cream silk blouse fastened at the neck by a ruby and gold brooch, Alena lies under filthy hessian sacks on a rough wooden floor. Like a droplet of blood, a rare red diamond ring glints on her left hand, but dirt streaks her blonde hair and her stockings are torn and clothes creased.

Her breath gutters as a candle flame in a breeze as sweat courses down a forehead lined with stress and it tastes bittersweet. Pain squeezes her chest, and she fears the pounding of her heart will betray them. And to her surprise as fear crowds in with a crushing intensity, she realises she is praying although religion has long since deserted her.

Alena had always known it would end this way. As surely as evil follows good, they would never let her go free. Now she accepts flight is futile.

The boy squirms around, his head a Medusa mass of brown curls, and pale blue eyes sparking with a mischief that usually made her smile. And she kisses his lips with a tender passion as her hands encircle his fragile neck.

# 2

He looked out of his office window onto a deserted Voss Strasse and sighed with satisfaction. This was how it should be, not a single person allowed to impede his view unless they wished to incur his wrath.

The morning sunshine streamed through the glass accentuating the deep lines on his face and making his pale blue eyes water, and a weary smile threatened to trouble the corners of his mouth. It was ironic – no matter how high you soared, how powerful you became one small slip and you could fall back to earth with the rest of them. He had an idea what information the young Gestapo officer wanted to share with him. That he had come alone declared his intent. If it had been on the record, Huber would have brought a colleague. He had suspected that it would catch up with him. Many of his enemies would delight in taking advantage of any breach. And just when his plans were going so well. Better now than later he convinced himself.

For Carsten Huber, the intimidating walk through the new Reich Chancellery was the ordeal it was intended to be. Albert Speer designed the monolithic building to reinforce man's insignificance in relation to the authority of the state, and he felt it working on him. Every step of the way he questioned his motives for being a good German, his footsteps echoing like a drumbeat on the red marble floors. What he was about to do was the most audacious action he'd attempted or the most foolish. Only history would tell.

Having driven through the imposing gates, he entered the *ehrenhof*, the court of honour leading to a reception room. Tall double doors opened onto a large hall clad in mosaic. He ran up a couple of steps, passed through a rotunda with a domed ceiling and out into a gallery that stretched for almost five hundred feet. Halfway down, outside the office where they expected him, two thick carpets floated like rafts on a sea of marble. On each, there were several small tables surrounded by chairs on which perched those awaiting an audience with fear and uncertainty shining out of their faces.

Two guards called him forward and, after checking his papers, they opened the high double doors to reveal a cavernous study. The man he had come to see sat behind a large marble-topped table staring out of a window.

Huber hesitated, holding his black fedora in both hands. His legs trembled and the more he thought about it, the more they shook. He wanted to meet his leader, yet the fear of confronting him was threatening to overpower him.

'*Kommen.*' The man swivelled around in his seat to face his visitor.

Huber coughed and took several uncertain steps forward, wondering if he should say something or wait until addressed.

'So?' The man lifted up the corner of a book with an index finger, distracted as if expecting an insect to break cover. He thought the Gestapo officer to be young, possibly in his early twenties. Someone a German father might think suitable for his daughter to marry, but a devious look in his eyes and a smirk betrayed a secret he was eager to share. Huber had mentioned one particular name in his telephone call, requesting to see him face to face. So, Huber knew, but how much?

Determined not to make eye contact, Huber coughed again. 'I have information that I believe is important to the Reich and to you personally.'

He raised his eyebrows as if indicating to the young man he had overestimated the importance of his revelation. 'So, why me?'

'I'm sorry?' Huber wondered if it had been a mistake coming here.

'You should give this information to your superiors. That's the correct procedure.'

The young officer surprised him by breaking into a smile showing a mouth full of white, even teeth. 'This information is for your ears only.'

The man looked away from him. 'Why are you doing this?'

'For my country, for you.' Huber smirked again knowing his reasons were far more personal.

'And a reward, maybe?'

'No, no.' Huber cleared his throat, embarrassed. 'I only want to serve the Reich.'

The man kept staring at him, showing no emotion.

'Well, if you believe I've been of service,' he continued, 'perhaps a promotion, a small elevation?'

Impatient for him to get on with it, the man listened with a concentration that suggested this was new information. Huber knew part of the story, although not all of it, but even that was too much. The revelation at the end shocked him. Something he didn't know, and Huber had seemed reluctant to reveal it. It hit him like a blow to the solar plexus and he wondered what his face showed. The young man's words filled him with a fear he hadn't experienced since he was a small boy. Anger soon replaced it. How had this happened? At first, he thought he himself might be to blame, but that graduated to condemning those around him for failing to protect him. The poison defiled him. He couldn't understand it. It was against everything he stood for, and he couldn't tolerate it. And he was the perpetrator. It was as if he was accused of a crime he hadn't known he'd committed. A sudden desire to wash, to scrub the contamination from his skin and cleanse himself was overwhelming.

Engrossed, he didn't realise Huber had stopped talking, and it took several minutes before the shuffling of the visitor's feet brought him back to the present. He glanced around to confirm no one else was nearby to have heard what Huber had said, then rose to his feet. 'Thank you for this.' His face was even more frightening in repose. 'Who else have you told?'

'No,' Huber stuttered. 'No one.'

'*Das ist gut.*' The man smiled again. They would have to discover how Huber came about this information. And did anyone else know? 'What should I do with you, Huber? If it's true, this information is a personal attack on me –'

'No, I wouldn't –'

He silenced the officer with a raised hand. 'If not, then you are guilty of spreading anti-German propaganda, and that is treason.'

Huber swallowed hard, feeling he might collapse.

'On the other hand, if you are just doing your duty and will let this rest with me so I can investigate its veracity, then perhaps you should get what you deserve.' Not looking at him, he dismissed Huber with a wave of his arm.

Huber nodded in gratitude and saluted and made his way backwards to the safety of the door. Outside, now dizzy, his footsteps appeared to grow louder the farther he progressed towards the exit and fresh air. He'd gone two-thirds of the way down the great gallery when two burly stormtroopers fell in on either side of him and guided him without touching him deeper into the bowels of the building.

As soon as Huber left his office, the man balled a fist and slammed it into the top of the desk. Someone else must know. If it got out, the ramifications would be catastrophic. He must find them.

He picked up a phone and ordered an aide. 'Bring the woman to me. Alive!'

# 3

ALENA STRAINED TO HEAR, BUT SHE COULDN'T DETECT ANYTHING ABOVE the labouring drone of the engine. At least, they were moving.

The boy treated it as if it were a game. Oblivious to their danger, he squealed with delight at every lurch and judder as the van bumped along the gravel drive.

Through the vehicle's rear window, a profusion of pink rhododendron bushes lined the manicured lawns. And her gaze drifted upwards to those obscene flags fluttering from the towers and in the distance in the sharp, clear sunlight of an optimistic June morning the Bavarian Alps were a stain on the horizon.

Whatever the setting, it was still a prison.

'Maman?'

'Sssh.' She kissed his forehead and picked some dried mud from his hair. 'We must be silent, so they don't find us.'

Many a time she'd lain beside him whispering until his eyelids fluttered like the wings of a butterfly and he drifted off into a safe and contented sleep. Then she understood her mother's relationship with her and the unbreakable bond between a child and its mother. She brushed another kiss across his face, holding him so tight she wondered if she might squeeze all the breath from his tiny body. And she hoped the fear in her voice didn't translate to him.

'Lie still.' She attempted a reassuring smile in the dim light.

'*Scheisse!*'

The driver of the van, a small, squat man with a thick moustache, cursed as he coaxed his vehicle into a lower gear. As they approached the grey stone-built gatehouse, he whistled a tuneless sound, betraying his nervousness, and swallowed hard not to vomit.

'Be still now,' he warned them, not taking his eyes off the way ahead. 'Keep as quiet as the dead or before the day's out we will be.' And added in a softer tone as though he'd sounded too harsh. 'Once through these gates you're free.'

She smiled at his optimism. They were coming for her and flight was her only option, but she wouldn't be free until she was far away. And even then? Miles down the road they would switch to a car waiting to take them to a small airfield and then a plane to Paris. In both cases, the engines would be running and if they didn't make their deadline, their transport would leave without them. That was all she knew although she expected they would soon be moved to England. Her secret could change the course of history and only there could she reveal it. She felt an overwhelming gratitude although she accepted the driver and the others weren't risking their lives just for her sake. It was because they feared for their country and wanted to save it from what it had become.

She pulled the sacking back over them and strengthened her grip on her son.

'Sssh.'

The grinding and whining of the van's gears alerted the guards enjoying a game of cards and a bottle of beer. Top buttons undone and caps off, they'd propped their firearms against a wall. When the master was absent discipline was relaxed. When he visited, surrounded by his black-suited bodyguards, they stood to attention, rifles at the ready, and boots so polished they reflected their faces.

It was only the farmer returning having made the weekly delivery of vegetables to the castle. They knew the van was empty, but they had to check everything in and out and be seen doing it. The corporal had discovered what those bodyguards had done to a colleague who hadn't followed orders, beating him with clubs so his legs and arms shattered.

He often queried what he and his fellow soldiers did here. On one hand, they protected the master's whore and her son. On the other, they had to keep her imprisoned in the castle although those thoughts he had to keep inside his head. A word out of place and that would be it. Just do your job, he muttered, rolling a needle-thin cigarette between his fingers as he stepped out of the gatehouse followed by the private who had snatched up his cap and rifle. He felt ridiculous as he raised an arm to bring the van shaking to a halt.

# 4

---

WHISTLING TO HERSELF, LILY SCUTTLED DOWN THE CORRIDOR THAT disappeared into darkness in the distance, and the more nervous she grew, the louder her tuneless melody became. As a drudge, they expected her to carry out any task, and she accepted everything except the long walk every morning to the west wing. She dreaded it and often it gave her nightmares. There was little light save for that which crept through the occasional mullioned window. And in the gloom, the suits of armour, standing at attention on either side with their shields and lances at the ready, appeared to crowd in on her as she advanced. Lily believed she could hear breathing as if there were living bodies trapped inside, and it was tempting to lift a visor to prove it. It took self-control not to run full pelt until she reached the sanctuary of the mistress's suite at the end of the corridor. If it hadn't been for the bucket of cleaning materials, dusters, cloths and sponges she was carrying in one hand and a broom in the other, she might have.

Usually she stared straight ahead, but on this morning, eyes clamped tight shut, she continued, her clogs clacking on the wooden floor. If she'd had a choice, she would have quit the job and got outdoor work. But she knew her employment would be at the castle. There was no alternative.

She exhaled with relief as she arrived unscathed at the apartment and rapped on the heavy oak door, waiting with impatience for a response. When there was no reply, she tried again, harder this time because she imagined the suits were moving closer to her. Again, nothing. The hairs stood up on the back of her neck and she dared not glance over her shoulder. Lily knocked again and also kicked it as panic nibbled at her. No answer.

Convinced no one was inside, she turned the handle, opened the door and let herself in. She called out. Getting no answer, she left her cleaning materials in the small hallway and entered the sitting-room, noticing a tray with a half-eaten breakfast on a coffee table. She frowned. Her mistress, Alena, usually tidied everything away, which was less work for her.

Lily liked her, and Alena smiled when they met and was open and friendly unlike so many who were fearful of every sound and nuance. She even took an interest in her mundane life and sometimes gave her an item of clothing as a gift although Lily worried someone might suspect her of stealing. She liked her son, Freddie. Mischievous as most small boys, he was always happy to see her and often sat on her knee while she recited stories of dragons and princesses, and his eyes widened the more bizarre they became. And Alena appreciated it, looking on with an adoring smile. Lily wondered if maids told stories about princesses, did princesses tell tales about maids.

Her mistress appeared to crave female company, a friend perhaps. For most of the time, she and Freddie were alone, yet when the master visited she noticed the mistress became more withdrawn and there was distrust in her eyes. She couldn't understand their relationship. Alena didn't want for anything and soldiers ringed the castle protecting her from an unknown enemy. Or was she being kept a prisoner like a bird in a gilded cage? There were rumours. All staff and some villagers shared gossip from behind a protective hand after checking to make sure no one else was eavesdropping. Afterwards, they wished they'd said nothing. Even Lily thought the stories fanciful.

Time to go to work. She went into the master bedroom and opened the voluminous brocade curtains and pulled the blankets off the bed.

She threw open the mullioned windows and glanced out at the gardens before gathering up the bedclothes and shaking them out the window.

The rest of the apartment – the sitting-room, dining-room, the boy's bedroom and two bathrooms – had to be checked to assess the amount of work facing her. There was no sign of them, yet she hadn't seen Alena downstairs or heard Freddie's excited squeals and endless chatter reverberating around the place. Maybe the mistress had gone out although she believed Alena had never left the grounds in the time she'd known her.

No matter, for now she might enjoy herself. Who could deny her a quantum of pleasure? She returned to the hall and set the bucket and broom against the door, so anyone entering dislodged them and alerted her. Sitting at the Queen Anne dressing-table, she surveyed her image in the mirror and dabbed perfume on her hand. In an instant, the scent transported her far from her drudgery to a grand ballroom where she was waltzing with the handsomest man there. In a trance, she reached for a hairbrush and ran it through her hair. It was almost the same colour as the mistress's, so she left no visible evidence she'd used the brush. The reflection of the doors to the dressing-room interrupted the rhythm of her brushing. She wondered. Dare I? Excitement made her tingle all over and extinguished the guilt and the fear of what the consequences might be. On occasions when she had time, she selected a gown and put it on and matching shoes and paraded around the apartment in her finery. It was the closest she'd ever get to becoming a princess. Every time she did this, she warned herself never again; it was too risky.

Once again, the temptation proved too great to ignore, and she convinced herself there was nothing wrong in taking one look. The room was an Aladdin's cave of fashion. Clothes hung by sections – summer and winter dresses, ball gowns, suits, casual wear, coats, jackets and above them boxes of hats and to one side endless racks of shoes and boots. She knew her mistress's clothes and at times Alena discussed them with her as if they were equals and occasionally sought her advice. It was at these times she'd do anything for Alena.

She ran a hand along a rack of dresses and suits as a collector might caress works of art and checked them off, pushing them aside one by one, pausing to remove an errant thread or hair or to straighten a garment.

Then Lily realised something was wrong.

# 5

'PAPERS,' THE CORPORAL REQUESTED IN A BORED VOICE WITH A VENEER OF officiousness flitting across his ruddy face. 'What have we here?' He had enlisted to fight for the Fatherland, not to be a gatekeeper, and he believed it gave him the right to bully anyone not wearing a uniform.

'Just delivered vegetables to the castle,' the farmer said repeating what he'd told them when he arrived and had first handed over his papers. He extricated a packet of cigarettes from his jacket pocket and offered one to the corporal who discarded his own roll-up and accepted a real cigarette.

The corporal, throwing the papers to his underling as the farmer flipped open his lighter, leant towards the driver's window to catch the flame. His body stiffened as he stared over the farmer's shoulder into the dark recesses of the van.

The farmer froze, holding his breath as the lighter flame flickered in the breeze.

'What are those?' barked the corporal.

'Just sacks.' The farmer's voice cracked as the words stumbled out.

The soldier turned to face him, his lip curling in disbelief. 'Sacks?'

'For the potatoes...'

The corporal's eyes narrowed to focus on the mound of hessian and he grunted and exhaled a cloud of cigarette smoke into the farmer's face making him cough. 'Why?' He stared as if he might drag a confession out of him.

The farmer laughed nervously. 'Why what?'

'Why should I let you go?'

'I - I don't understand.'

'I could lock you up and have your van impounded. And we could question you – we're very efficient at that – and you'd tell us about your neighbours and so-called friends who are against this war.'

'I've done nothing wrong, sir, I swear it.'

'Since when did innocence make you free of guilt?'

The farmer clenched a fist in an attempt to hold back the panic.

'Get out,' the corporal ordered.

The farmer hesitated.

'Get out, now.'

He almost fell as he climbed out of his cab.

'Why did you offer me a cigarette?'

Unable to lift his eyes to the soldier's enquiring look, he shrugged.

'Something to hide, maybe?' The corporal's eyes never left his face.

'No, no, no.' He bit his tongue and felt blood on his lips.

'Well?' demanded the corporal.

'Nothing, I've done nothing.'

'I know your game.'

'No, no.' He felt the ground disappearing beneath him. 'I –'

The corporal turned away swearing under his breath. He was enjoying exercising his power, but it was wasting time. 'Look in the back,' he ordered the soldier and pointed to his belt. 'Use the bayonet.'

The private handed back the papers to the driver and detached the bayonet from his belt. Fixing it to his rifle, he made his way to the rear of the van, his boots crunching on the gravel.

'We'll see.' The corporal's voice sounded reasonable, and he dragged long and hard on the cigarette until it almost all turned to ash. 'The bayonet will soon tell us. If there's nothing there, you'll just have a few torn sacks, and if you're hiding something, it'll be of no use to you because it'll be damaged beyond repair.' He fixed him with a stare searching for any reaction.

Priming his rifle, the soldier pulled open the double doors. The smell of vegetables and a cloud of dust and dried mud filled his nostrils and forced him to recoil. He cleared his throat with a guttural growl and spat on the gravel, wiping his mouth on a sleeve.

Her training had prepared her for this. They'd told her not to fear death as an enemy but to welcome it as a friend. Death brought an end to suffering. It was some consolation, perhaps, although not for her son whom she'd put in danger. Why should he pay for her mistakes? Anger churned up inside her. And now she had no choice but to end his life. His death would be her final act of love because she feared all the unspeakable things they would do to him if he survived.

# 6

LILY SHOOK HER HEAD AND RETURNED TO THE BEDROOM AND IN THE background the voices of the soldiers at the front gate drifted up to her. Something was missing. She went to the boy's bedroom. Hurrying back to the master bedroom, she opened the jewellery box on the dressing-table, and now she understood. She realised what was missing when she entered the dressing-room. Still she heard raised voices from the front gate and the realisation of what might be happening flooded through her like a drug invading every corner of her body and her stomach cramped and her bowels turned to water. She flopped on the bed, trying to work out a story, a defence. Would they believe it had nothing to do with her? They were like surgeons. If there were a cancer, they'd not just cut out the tumour but everything around it, so it couldn't flare up again. She should finish her cleaning and go home as soon as possible although they would still come for her. They didn't even need to suspect her of having helped the mistress.

Everyone knew what was happening. Why sometimes entire families disappeared overnight. A family would be gone, and the rest carried on with their lives as if nothing had happened, afraid to talk in case they'd be next. They'd still torture her until she'd implicated her fellow innocents. When she was of no further use, they'd shoot her and throw her into a deep pit. And soldiers would return at night for her family. Someone who knew of these things said fathers, mothers, grandparents, brothers and sisters were forced at gunpoint to lie in the pit with their guilty relation before being buried alive in quicklime and earth.

Lily smelled the sweet-sour stench of fear and begged her mistress's forgiveness. She had no choice. She must warn them.

Stumbling to the door, Lily kicked aside the bucket and broom and stepped out into the corridor. Now the suits of armour didn't trouble her. She quickened her step as the panic rose, moving faster and faster before breaking into a desperate run.

'Help.' Her voice echoed along the corridor. 'Help me.'

# 7

Sweat ran down Philippe Bernay's neck, and he didn't like to sweat. The collar of his shirt was damp, and it made him feel dirty forcing him to change into a fresh one. Fear was making him sweat and the realisation that he'd face execution if his plans came to light. Without the hint of a wind to bring relief from the enervating heat of the morning, it felt as if the whole of Paris was holding its breath with the elements a witness to the tragedy about to unfold. He knew the days ahead promised only pain.

As he prepared to leave for his office at the Banque de France, his fellow citizens focused on their own fears. The German army would invade the city within days, and outside on the Rue de Berri people were fleeing, joining the tide of humanity escaping south. Stories of the invading Nazis' atrocities to even women and children added fuel to their panic. Those who stayed had their reasons. Although most viewed the arrival of the Nazis with foreboding, some believed things might not be as bad as expected, but they refrained from sharing those opinions. His plans, which he doubted the more he considered them, compounded his concerns.

As he'd done for twenty years, Stefan, the doorman with a face as red as his uniform, stood at his post outside the elegant apartment building. Some locals called him the '*grande tomate rouge*' although they couldn't deny an upright bearing that proved his military background. He wasn't one to run nor was he the kind to panic. He'd be the last to desert as long as he could still button up his tunic.

Stefan made a final check and was satisfied. The car was in place by the kerbside and, after a glance up and down the street, he saw there were no pedestrians likely to impede Monsieur Bernay's progress.

It was 8.30 am.

As punctual as ever, Bernay stepped out onto the street.

'*Bonjour*, Stefan.' For once he didn't smile. 'So, you're still here?'

Disappointed that Bernay thought he might have considered the option, Stefan touched his cap. 'M'sieu, I'm not running away like so many of our fellow Parisians.'

An acid look flickered across Bernay's face as if he'd touched on an unpalatable truth, and Stefan, regretting he had made the remark, stuttered. 'Sorry, I didn't mean –'

Bernay raised a hand acknowledging the apology. 'My wife and daughters wanted to stay with me, but I sent them away for their safety.'

'Of course.' Stefan turned and with his right hand ushered him to his car.

'M'sieu, the love of your life awaits you.' Stefan bowed with a conspiratorial smile.

It wasn't how a doorman usually addressed a director of the Banque de France. But it had been their ritual for many years and the director more often than not responded with a quip sparking genuine laughter. This morning, though, Bernay was more preoccupied than usual.

They'd got the gold out only days ago. That would anger the Germans and he experienced a gnawing concern as to what the Nazis might do to him once they found out. Under the tightest security, they had removed the country's gold reserves from the bank's underground vaults and smuggled them to Brest on the coast for shipping to Dakar and Canada. Although the Germans would still find gold at the Banque de France, it wouldn't be France's. As they swept through Europe, the Germans were frustrated as the invaded countries had sent their gold to Paris, but for those countries this was the end of the line for their bullion.

His work wasn't finished. There was still one vital task to be completed to thwart the Germans, and it was his responsibility alone. No one else's.

The Derby Bentley was the love of his life after his wife and two daughters, who had left Paris days earlier. The British racing green coachwork gleamed in the morning sunlight attracting admiring glances from passers-by. Just sinking into the pale blue leather seats surrounded by the dark stained burr walnut wood trim and hearing the expensive clunk of the door closing behind him and the rumble of the engine was usually enough to lift his spirits from even the darkest pit of despair. Once behind the wheel anything seemed possible. Here was an extension of his personality and testament to his hard work. Wherever he drove, heads turned, and onlookers knew this was someone at the top of his profession.

Several years earlier on a trip to England he'd driven a Bentley around the Brooklands circuit, marvelling at the smoothness of the ride. Even at 70 mph the car was quiet, earning the soubriquet 'the silent sports car'. He wanted one of his own and as soon as he returned home he instructed the French coachbuilders, Carrosserie Franay, to build his Bentley.

Today, not even the Bentley could raise his spirits. Now what he'd worked for and achieved was of no consequence. Soon he'd part company with the car forever and his own future and everybody else's in the city would be in the hands of whatever gods the Nazis worshipped.

The Bentley's bonnet stretched out before him, a gigantic green phallus, its polished bodywork reflecting the few clouds in the bright blue sky as he pointed the flying mascot at the Champs-Élysées. As he waited for a break in the traffic before turning left, a sudden zephyr caused two attractive women's thin summer dresses to rise above their knees and in their embarrassment, they stopped and turned to look at him. One said something to the other, and they both giggled.

He failed to suppress a smile. In his late fifties, he welcomed any show of interest from the opposite sex although he doubted what he'd do if they ever offered something more than a smile. Unlike many influential men of his age in France, he'd avoided taking a young mistress although there was no harm in fantasising.

He turned east on *La plus belle avenue du monde* as many Parisians believed it to be. The trees were in full bloom and the white flowers of the horse chestnuts acted as a counterpoint to an avenue ablaze with colour. He loved the blossom's scent combining with the aroma of strong coffee. And women in their colourful summer dresses and the pavement cafes with their bright awnings and umbrellas adding to a surreal air that was a last hurrah of defiance. Anticipation of what awaited them was so palpable it swam in the atmosphere as mud in a pond, so thick he could almost part it with his hand. Soon the apparatus of war would overtake this, and the colour be replaced by uniform grey.

The German Army, spearheaded by Rommel's panzer divisions, had torn a hole in the defences of Western Europe with its *Blitzkrieg* tactics. It had taken the Low Countries in a matter of weeks and was flooding through France annexing the crucial coastal towns and even forcing the Allies into retreat from the sands of Dunkirk. Nothing could stop the Wehrmacht's war machine. Days earlier General Weygand, the Commander-in-Chief of the French forces, decreed Paris was not to be defended; it was an open city, so it was only a matter of time before it fell to the invaders. Paris stood before them a naked virgin with nothing to defend her dignity.

For his last drive in his beloved Bentley, and maybe the last of his life, he forced any dark thoughts to the back of his mind. He guided the car along the Champs-Élysées and across the Place de la Concorde. Cleopatra's Needle, the 75-foot tall obelisk taken from the temple of Ramses II at Thebes, dominated the square, its pink granite glinting in the sunshine. And he wondered if the Nazis might ship it to Berlin for Hitler's edification.

Here the French had built a grand statue to Louis XV before dismantling it and using the square for the public guillotining of, among others, Marie Antoinette during the revolution. Could history repeat itself with the Nazis raising a statue to their Führer and using it to stage public executions?

The timeless beauty of his city still aroused him, and he concentrated on locking away every memory. From the square, it was possible to see four great landmarks of Paris and he slowed down to almost walking pace. Twisting around in his seat, he saw to his left, the Madeleine; behind, the Arc de Triomphe; across the Seine, the Palais Bourbon; and ahead the Tuileries.

He veered into the Rue de Rivoli, drove past the Jardin des Tuileries, and opposite the Louvre turned left into Rue de Marengo. Crossing the Rue Saint-Honoré, he arrived at the Banque de France on the Croix des Petits Champs.

Gasping for breath, Pierre, an asthmatic veteran of the First World War, scuttled out to meet him.

'*Bonjour.*' Pierre touched his cap and pointed in the general direction of the North from where could be heard the dull crump of explosions.

'*Le Bosch* are getting closer.' Pierre cocked his head as if hearing the stomping of their boots.

He didn't doubt if Pierre had a gun he'd defend his city against the invaders single-handed.

He looked up at the display of flags above the bank's entrance – five tricolours on either side and two much larger ones in the centre – and wondered how much of France's heritage might survive in the next twenty-four hours. Would they replace them with their swastikas? The Nazis were looting museums and palaces and sending treasures back to Germany. Would they appreciate this impressive building with its abundance of murals, gold leaf and paintings as a prize of war or deface it in an act of vandalism? His staff were preparing for the day's business attempting to stick to their routine with an exaggerated attention to detail as if this might bring order to the surrounding disarray. A wave of depression swept over him and tears welled up in his eyes. It was all so pointless. Whatever remained was not theirs; it belonged to the invaders. His staff may as well go home and await the inevitable. He studied them engrossed in their work as routine supplanted their thoughts, and he squared his shoulders, putting on his most confident smile and mixing amongst them giving a word of encouragement here and advice there. Just a skeleton staff remained, and he noted those who'd fled and those who'd decided they'd no better choice than to stay. Soon the Germans would arrive, and he wondered whether they'd smash the doors and empty the bank's vaults or arrange a more civilised transference of power.

There was still one treasure of France's in the vaults he was determined should not fall into the invaders' hands and he was the only one who could prevent it from happening. Bernay had two choices – do nothing and perhaps survive or do what his conscience dictated and risk punishment.

He could be signing his own death warrant, but he'd decided. He climbed the grand staircase to his first-floor office, admiring the magnificent hanging tapestries on the way, and with a trembling hand picked up the telephone.

'Please put me through to the British Embassy,' he instructed the operator.

# 8

For years, Alena had watched these gates open and close from a distance – the gateway to freedom. Only yards and it would be like stepping over a threshold into a different world. Under her breath, she willed the van to move – closer to freedom – with an intensity so severe she thought she was shouting. And the blood pounded in her brain with such power she imagined it might split apart.

They were going nowhere. The rear doors of the van remained open and the private let the dust settle before, screwing up his eyes, he peered again into the vehicle.

The driver's voice was louder now. He talked about the weather and crop rotation and the price of vegetables. And she wondered whether it was a ploy to help combat any sounds she and the boy might make or whether his nerve was unravelling.

Tears flowed down her cheeks, and she held her son closer with an animal desperation. They couldn't take him no matter what. The pain that had started in her chest was everywhere now like a fever and she sensed herself being crushed into the rough wooden floor. Paralysed by the knowledge that the slightest movement might dislodge the sacks or the whisper of a sound could betray them, she tightened her grip on her son. She clamped a hand over his mouth and nose and pressed hard.

She didn't want to hurt him, only put him to sleep, and she increased the force on his tiny body not wishing to exert an ounce of pressure more than necessary. Guilt flooded her mind, and it linked with the beat of her heart resonating so much her whole body shook to its rhythm.

Struggling for survival, the four-year-old bit into her palm and she wanted to scream as the pain almost caused her to black out. Yet an inner reserve of strength kept her grip tight and her mouth shut and underneath her she felt his wriggling becoming feebler.

Near the doors, sacks had fallen back from the driver's end and lay scattered on the floor. Behind the driver there was another pile of sacking, and the soldier adjusted his grip on the rifle to stab downwards into the hessian.

Her eyes closed tight as she awaited the impact of the blade. The grit from the sacks filled her mouth. Her body knotted causing her legs to cramp, and the pain was excruciating as the muscles contracted and she bit into the fabric of her sleeve to stop herself from shouting out in agony. Attempting to increase the pressure on her son, she wept silent tears of frustration as she realised she couldn't as if an invisible wall was creating a barrier.

The private's downward thrust into the sacks jammed in the wood of the floor. He tugged once, twice and still it didn't come away. He redoubled his efforts and pulled it free sending sacks swirling into the air and spreading out a fine dust, causing him to reel backwards coughing and spluttering.

A discordant jangle from the telephone in the gatehouse demanded an answer.

The private froze looking at the corporal; the corporal glanced at the farmer and turned to answer it.

Alena gasped. *They know.*

After a couple of steps, the corporal, impatient to get back to his game of cards, wheeled and shouted at his soldier 'Get on with it.' And he flicked the glowing cigarette end into the bushes with his forefinger.

She waited. Waited for the steel of the bayonet to rip into her and she moved her body to shield her son from the cutting edge of the blade.

Now two voices whispered to her.

*Turn around. Confront him.*

And

*Don't turn.*

She remembered a night in Berlin walking along a deserted unlit street. A heavy rain drummed on her umbrella and a wind lifted litter high into the air, and she heard footsteps behind her. Although it might have been anyone, a passer-by, a tramp, a thief, she believed she was being followed. She'd wanted to stop and look back to identify the follower, but that would have been dangerous.

*Don't.*

The other voice nagged at her.

*Turn, turn now.*

Was that a breeze on her flesh or the soldier's warm breath? The hairs stood up on the back of her neck and a crackling like electricity rippled across her scalp making her shiver.

*Go on, look.*

*Don't.*

*Don't turn.*

Wiping his mouth on the sleeve of his tunic, the private spat again on the gravel. This time he climbed into the back of the van and it rocked with his weight. He picked up his rifle holding it high above his head for a final lunge at the pile of sacks.

She must.

*Turn.*

She couldn't stop herself.

With a grunt, the soldier started the rifle on its path and as he lifted his gaze, he was transfixed by the terrified stare of a green-eyed woman. Like a tiger with its prey cornered, he bared his teeth in a vicious smile and continued the bayonet downwards in a powerful arc.

# 9

BEN PETERS CIRCLED THE PACKAGE LYING ON A TABLE IN THE SITTING-ROOM of his small apartment on the Rue du Cardinal Lemoine and felt nauseous.

*Damn Bernay!*

Why had he given it to him?

It was still unopened although he realised what was in it by its smell and feel.

*It was evil.*

If there had been any doubt, the small box that accompanied it told him what he needed to know. He'd have to open it sometime, not just yet. Why had his boss involved him? Bernay told him he was going on a special mission and to pack a bag for a short trip. No business attire, clothes as if he were going on vacation. Only it wasn't a vacation.

What did he expect him to do with the package?

On top of his clothes, he laid a lined, yellow notepad and a small leather case holding half-a-dozen pencils and checked the penknife to sharpen them was there. Whatever Bernay wanted him to do, he must still have time for his writing. He didn't want to leave the apartment and wondered if he'd ever return. He'd chosen the location because Ernest Hemingway had once lived in the area. Although four flights up and he could afford something grander, he'd grown to love the place with its rattling pipes and constant creaking like a ship in a storm.

At any other time, this would appeal to his sense of adventure. Not now. Hell, how many chances do you get in a lifetime? Hitler's troops would march into Paris soon and he'd be on the spot to report an episode of history for the New York papers. The Nazis couldn't touch him. As an American citizen, he was a neutral.

If he left Paris, his parents would be overjoyed. He'd received a letter from his mother the previous week, using emotional blackmail to persuade him to leave Paris and France and Europe and get back across the Atlantic where he'd be safe. He could imagine his father, who seldom put pen to paper, looking over her shoulder and adding 'Ben, get your ass over here pronto.' And roaring with laughter. 'Do as your mother says. She's much scarier than that guy Hitler.'

Two years earlier, his manager in Wall Street called him into his office and said they were considering sending him to Paris, France. He'd emphasised 'France' as if it were a distant planet. Ben almost told him to stick it. He didn't enjoy smelly cigarettes and their food to which they did unspeakable things. Wasn't for him.

Amy Ralston changed everything.

He saw her most nights as she worked a couple of blocks away in an insurance office, they'd meet up in a local diner. He always turned up late, and she'd be sitting at the same table with her head resting on her left hand engrossed in a book in front of her. Sometimes he'd stand on the sidewalk for minutes watching her through the big windows, yet she was oblivious to everything around her. Every so often she'd push her hair away from her face and move closer to the page as if climbing back into the story.

He loved the way she'd run her finger down the outside edge of the page before turning it and flattening it with her palm. And always a flicker of a smile anticipating new delights. He'd stand by the table until she'd sense his presence and she'd bend over the corner of the page and close the book before stashing it in her handbag. Getting up, she'd kiss him on the cheek and their date would begin.

He didn't know how often that happened and after a time he resented it. Why was she more interested in her book than him? Why was she not looking out for him, expecting his arrival? He got the feeling if he hadn't turned up at all she'd have kept on reading.

One evening, growing ever more agitated by her behaviour, he grabbed her wrist before she could hide the book in her bag and took it from her. He sat opposite her, checking out the cover, the back, and then turned it over and opened it. He read and forgot she was there.

After a while, she put a hand on the page to stop him.

'Enough!' She smiled as if greeting a newcomer to a secret society. 'Have the book. This is our time now.'

Next night she had a new book for him and so it went on. Until she dumped him for a nerdy guy with glasses and a sports jacket who could apparently recite the opening line of every book that had ever been written.

Paris would be a wonderful experience, the manager said. It would provide an invaluable understanding of how European banks worked as in his words 'we've got to learn how to work with these guys in this new age'.

His parents were overjoyed. Proof that everything they'd done for him in upstate New York had paid off and he was on the ladder to success. Although Paris was farther away than his mother cared to contemplate, it wouldn't be for long and he'd return to promotion. He didn't care about promotion. He'd read what Ernest Hemingway wrote about Paris as if it were an intimate friend and wanted a taste of it. It seemed a magical world full of endless parties, long liquid lunches and elegant women. And when they finished making love in the afternoons, they'd write magnificent prose read by beautiful people and last forever. The French appeared a race so unlike his fellow Americans that he had to experience it. Not only did he dip a toe in the ambience of Paris, he jumped in fully clothed. Wherever possible, he retraced the steps of the author determined he'd make Hemingway's experiences his own. It was not enough to be a spectator. He had to live it so it seeped through his pores and into his core until it flowed through his veins. He committed everything to his lined, yellow notepad believing he was capturing the essence of the great man. If he understood him, perhaps he could write like him. He smelled the same sweet smell of decadence. He ate the same unspeakable food, he drank the wine he'd drunk and some more. Then there were the women who unlike their American sisters didn't avert their eyes when you looked at them. Instead, they sought direct eye contact and when you smiled they smiled back and the introduction was made. The language wasn't a problem. Someone once said the best way to learn a foreign language was in bed – and he was fluent.

He loved the winter best when the first rains came and the smoke from the chimneys above the mansards billowed and blew and changed direction in the wind. He'd miss those afternoons when he wandered, determined to get lost in the city. When he found a new café safe from friends and acquaintances, he'd sit down to write. First, he'd order a café au lait and if the writing was going well, he'd take a cognac.

Oblivious to the comings and goings and the natural hubbub of the café, it provided a comforting rhythm. Every so often, perhaps to sharpen a pencil, he'd look up and observe his companions and again immerse himself in his writing and when he next looked, they'd be gone.

*Damn Bernay!*

This was like running away. Not something Hemingway ever considered. The author had never run away from anything. Even at school Ben faced up to the bully and taken his beating. He didn't want to run away from Paris.

Yet he found it hard to refuse Bernay. The banker had called him into his office and told him in his quiet, persuasive way what was required of him. He respected the director, a good man who cared for the people under his command. He couldn't envisage him ever asking an employee to do something he wouldn't do himself, and that made it harder.

As usual, Bernay had kept the shutters in his office closed so daylight didn't dilute his concentration and a banker's lamp was the only light pouring over his leather-topped desk. He hadn't looked him in the eye at first, instead gazing at a fixed point somewhere above Ben's head. 'Ben,' he said at last. 'I need you to do something for me. For the bank, for France. It's of great importance.'

He hesitated, wondering what was coming next.

'You'll have to leave Paris.'

He groaned. 'I'd planned on sticking around.' He was puzzled and failed to disguise his disappointment. 'Things are just getting interesting.'

Bernay switched his gaze, studying him for several seconds as though questioning whether he'd made the right choice before he smiled and raised both hands in understanding. 'I know. But this is more important.'

'What do you have in mind?' Ben didn't want to hear the answer.

'I can't tell you yet. Just make the necessary arrangements. You'll be away for some time.'

He spread his arms in exasperation. 'At least, tell me where you're sending me.'

The director looked into the distance and a flicker of doubt rippled across his face. 'I can't yet. For your own safety, you understand?'

'Do I have a choice?'

Bernay stared at him.

'What if I say no?'

'I don't think you will when you hear what it is.'

He shook his head, realising it was a futile gesture.

The director got to his feet. 'I'll let you know when I need you. Good man, you won't let me or France down.'

As he reached for the doorknob, Bernay called him back. 'No one must know about this conversation.'

His questioning look demanded an answer.

'It is not without danger. All I can say is that if you succeed France will be in your debt.'

He finished packing the holdall and again checked the notepad and pencils were there. He went over to the table and picked up the small box. Opening it, he counted the contents. There were two missing, and he wondered what had happened to them and whether Bernay had used them.

He couldn't put it off any longer. He opened the oilskin pouch as if it might snap back and took out the heavy object, feeling it cold against his skin. With revulsion, he placed the revolver on the table before him and took a step backwards.

He didn't object to guns, just what they were used for. After all, he was an American. Back home a kid got his first gun around the same time he got his first pair of shoes. It took him back to his childhood when reality became an enduring nightmare, growing more degrading with every visit. He was holidaying with friends, and their fathers took them on a hunting expedition. After hours of tracking, they cornered a wild boar, and the men shot at it and in their excitement only wounding it. The animal sought refuge deeper into the brush and they followed it shooting as they went. And the animal was squealing and grunting every time it was hit. Eventually, it could flee no further and lay on its side and its panting was a long, low sob of pain. Blood pumped out of multiple wounds and, as the men aimed their rifles for the kill because only a death could satiate them, the boar lifted its head in defiance. And then he realised it knew it was dying. And in its eyes there was one last act of pleading aimed at him as if he were responsible for its suffering. He vowed then never to fire a gun.

He pushed a hand through his hair and wondered what he should do with the revolver. Hemingway would've known, he'd have stuck it in the waistband of his trousers.

There again, he thought, I'd shoot off my nuts.

*Damn Bernay!*

# 10

BERNAY BANGED THE TELEPHONE HANDSET ON ITS CRADLE, SURPRISING himself with this unaccustomed show of anger. He tapped the desk with his right hand and exhaled. Pushing back his chair and wincing as it screeched on the wooden floor, he got up and paced his office deep in thought. He'd gone to the British for help. Even they realised the merits of his plan. What he was attempting was risky and dangerous. But there was no alternative. It would have meant giving up without a fight. Now the British were demanding a favour in return for their help – and it complicated matters. It was like a blackmailer. Give him something and he keeps coming back for a bit more. He thought what he'd offered was enough although this was war. He had already discussed his plans with the ambassador who had promised to help although he couldn't contact him on this occasion. Perhaps he'd already left Paris although he suspected he was just avoiding him. Instead, he was put through to someone who gave his name as Brown and said he'd been given the responsibility of finding whatever help he could. Yet even though Brown professed to understand the importance to France of what Bernay was proposing he wasn't making things easy. In these difficult times, Brown explained, it was impossible to get the manpower to carry it out. No matter how deserving the cause.

Bernay felt a desperation creeping over him. This was his last chance.

Brown had heard the disappointment in the director's voice and paused, letting him fill the silence. 'How can I persuade you?'

Brown's intake of breath sounded terminal. 'What have you in mind?'

His mind raced, trying to think of something he could offer.

The Englishman delayed, knowing Bernay had nothing more to offer.

'I'm not sure.' A bead of sweat rolled down his cheek.

Brown could almost smell the banker's desperation.

'Is there anything, Mr Brown?'

Brown hesitated again. There was no rush. He picked the remains of a baguette out of his teeth with a letter opener. The game was boring him. It was time to reel him in. 'Well, now you mention it, there's something you could do for us...' It was vital Bernay should not suspect the importance of what he was going to ask him.

His relief was overwhelming. 'Just name it.'

'One minute.' Brown put the telephone on the desk and went over to a small radio in the corner of his office. He switched it on and turned up the volume until he was sure it would drown out their conversation. The radio whined and crackled as the *Marseillaise* boomed out a despairing protest. He returned to his seat and picked up the telephone. 'M'sieu Bernay, are you still there? Good. This is what you must do.'

Brown let his words sink in. 'Accept and we'll help you. If not... you're on your own, I'm afraid.'

Everything these days came with a price. It was an added complication. What the Englishman had demanded was fraught with danger. Yet without Britain's help, how else could he achieve it? Opening the door to his office, Bernay instructed his secretary: 'Please ask Renard to come up and see me.'

He was still considering his options when there was a light tap on his door.

'Come in, Arnaud, please, enter.'

A small man in overalls, Arnaud Renard, pushed open the door and paused before entering. His boss pointed to a seat in front of his desk. And he picked his way across the polished oak floor on the balls of his feet as if worried he might make a noise or damage the wood. Never had he been allowed to sit on the chair in his oil-stained work clothes, although it didn't seem to matter anymore.

Renard shifted in the seat and noticed two buff-coloured folders on the desk before the director.

'Arnaud.' He smiled his most welcoming smile. 'Is everything going to plan?'

'Yes, M'sieu Bernay. Should be ready to go within the hour.'

'And your assistant?'

'Lefevre,' he reminded him.

'Ah, yes, Lefevre, a good man? What does he know?'

'Nothing. I've done most of the work myself.'

'Good, good, it's better for him the less he knows. This has to be our secret.'

Renard nodded in discomfort wishing he didn't have to be part of any secret.

He smiled at him. 'A drink?'

Renard spluttered. It was one thing to get a summons to the director's office and called by his first name, the first time in all his years at the bank. To be offered a drink and in the morning was unusual.

'Splendid.' He turned away as if his silence meant acceptance and opened a door in his desk taking out a bottle of Armagnac and two crystal glasses.

'I think we deserve this.' He poured two generous measures. 'We might not have the chance to have one later.'

He pushed the full glass across the desk to his worker. He trusted him. Every day when he left the Bentley at the door of the bank, Pierre drove it round and into the underground car park housing the bank's vehicles. Pierre washed it and Renard checked it over and always found something to work on ensuring it was always in the very best condition.

'*Santé!*' he raised his glass and his employee responded and took a larger gulp than he intended almost making him choke. 'Thank you,

Arnaud. This is a historic day. France will salute you. If we succeed, we'll both be heroes. If we fail...'

Putting down his glass, he tapped his fingers on the two buff folders on the desk and pulled them towards him.

'As soon as everything is ready, you must leave the bank. These folders are your and Lefevre's employment records. We will burn these straight away. There must be no record of you having worked here. You understand?'

He waited until his employee agreed before continuing.

'My secretary has an envelope containing money for both of you. Let's say it's severance pay, a very generous amount in recognition of what you've done. I suggest you leave Paris and head as far south as possible.'

The man mumbled his thanks.

'You love this great city as much as I do, don't you, Arnaud?'

Renard replied with a shy smile as if it were a vice to admit it.

'Then it's better for you to leave because once the Nazis have invaded it'll break your heart. What they might...'

His hands fiddled with the folders on his desk.

'... or will do...' His voice trailed off.

'Will you go, monsieur director?'

'No, I have to stay.'

His eyes swept around his office, knowing it would be hard to leave.

'I need to be here when they arrive. Maybe I can lessen the damage. Perhaps save a bit for us when... if ever we win back the city.'

And he thought of the mission Ben Peters was about to undertake and it gave him a quantum of hope. He got to his feet, signalling their meeting was at an end and shook his worker's hand placing his left hand on top as if cementing their agreement.

'Everything will be destroyed; it'll be as if you never existed...'

# 11

―――――――

SMOKE BILLOWED OUT OF A GROUND-FLOOR WINDOW JOINING THAT FROM the bonfire burning in the grounds of the British Embassy on the Rue d'Anjou. A queue of staff lined up to add records, files and papers to the pyre. Those in line waited with impatience to unload their secrets knowing as soon as they had completed the task they would be free to leave. In silence, they watched the fragments of burning paper float upwards from the flames like an armada of tiny ships setting off on an arduous voyage.

Herbert Brown couldn't take it anymore. He had to open the window.

The liaison officer Pickering, dressed in crumpled tweeds and plus-fours and wearing brown brogues, stretched out on a chaise longue with his head on the arm of the seat and his long legs dangling over the end. He puffed on his favourite pipe clenched between his brown-stained teeth as if unaware of the danger they were facing. And he was also oblivious to Brown's discomfort.

Even if Brown had complained he would have received the usual riposte. 'Nothing wrong with a bit of smoke, old boy. The best whisky and the most expensive salmon are smoked so what harm will it do to us?'

Brown often wondered with whom Pickering liaised. He never did much although was ever present at the important meetings picking his goatee beard as if searching for invaders and sucking on his pipe. Now and then he'd remove it from his mouth to add to the discussion and stick it back in as if the idea had deserted him. The word from embassy colleagues was he was 'well connected'.

Pickering had little time for Brown. Not the embassy type, you understand. Pretty ordinary school. Ill-fitting suit. Because of his eyesight couldn't be called up, although he was rather a good shot by all accounts, so they stuck him in Intelligence. Something Brown was devoid of in his opinion. Didn't look the part for embassy circles, close-cropped hair like a convict's and a bony expressionless face.

Brown smiled from time to time and he'd the habit of grinning at Pickering with an irritating expression of superiority. Boy, did that get Pickering's goat. An amused smile but all mouth. No warmth there. He couldn't locate the grey eyes swimming behind the thick lenses of his steel-rimmed spectacles, and that troubled him. When Pickering could see their eyes, he believed he had a chance of anticipating what their next move might be. It would have been better if Maclean had been looking after this, but he'd gone off to marry an American woman and was making his own way back to Blighty.

Pickering seemed unperturbed considering the amount of activity around him as anything that couldn't be taken was being trashed or burned. In a languid movement, he removed his pipe and tapped out the remains in an ashtray. 'So, Brown, what did our man have to say?'

'He wasn't happy.'

Pickering snorted and shook his head in disbelief.

'That's bloody gratitude for you.'

'Well, let's say he was hacked off.'

'Typical French.'

Inserting a new wad of tobacco, Pickering tamped it down as if he were engaged in a work of art before re-lighting the pipe. 'We're over here trying our damnedest to help them.' He took a couple of puffs until the thing smoked like a steam engine. 'Look at our boys being shot up at Dunkirk.'

'It's not –'

'If London weren't so keen on it, I'd have told him where to put his madcap idea.'

'Bernay worried it might make things difficult for them.'

'Without our people he wouldn't be able to deliver a fart, let alone his bloody package.' He wanted to distance himself from Brown, yet he grudgingly admitted Brown had taken up the ball and was running with it although in what direction he wasn't sure.

'I think he accepts that.' Brown gave a wearied nod. 'He thought our arrangement was an added complication.'

Pickering raised his voice in indignation. 'Bloody vital one.'

With a glint in his eye, he unfolded from the chaise longue and lumbered over to a corner of the room. 'Fuck the French,' he roared. 'You're good for nothing but food and fornicating.'

He wheezed with laughter and with his pipe tapped a grille in the wall knowing it concealed the French intelligence services' bug as though it would force them out from their hiding place. He knew where the bugs were. What worried him were the ones he hadn't found.

It was standard procedure. Insult the French snoops and never give them anything of importance. When they discussed confidential details, they moved out to the garden though now there was too much going on out there.

'I doubt anyone's listening now,' said Brown.

He ignored that. 'Well, Brown, I'm sure you'll have everything sorted for him.'

Brown showed satisfaction, feeling everything was going to plan.

'Did you tell Bernay about our arrangement?'

'Good God, no. The fewer who know, the better.'

'Good man, can't trust the froggies. Who's making the delivery?'

'An employee, Ben Peters.' And with distaste added: 'A Yank.'

'Interesting! Quite clever. They're neutral until his government decides to get its finger out, and you're sure he knows nothing about any of this?'

'Nothing, and Bernay still believes his mission to be the important one.'

'Yes, yes.' Pickering coughed, and a flicker of fear danced across his face at the thought of it going wrong. 'What was the phrase he used? Ah, yes... he said it could alter the future of France.' Again, he roared with laughter.

Brown escaped to the door and turned as he opened it.

'And if the Yank delivers our package, it will give Herr Hitler something to rant about.'

Pickering gave no impression he'd heard. He was back on the chaise longue puffing hard on his pipe and staring into the distance.

## 12

BEN RAN INTO THE BANQUE DE FRANCE CARRYING HIS LEATHER OVERNIGHT bag in which he'd hidden the revolver under his clothes. He was met by Pierre, who gave a reproachful expression suggesting he didn't approve of running within the confines of the bank. Pierre raised his eyebrows and gestured over his shoulder with a nod towards the back of the bank's lobby.

'He's waiting for you.'

Bernay was agitated. He kept taking out and opening his gold Hunter pocket watch to check the time as he paced up and down. 'Ah, Ben.' He appeared relieved and clapped a hand on his shoulder.

'Sorry, I'm late.' He wasn't sure if he was.

'Follow me.' Bernay took his arm and led him to a spiral staircase that they descended in silence to the bank's basement.

He'd never been down here before and, although he'd once been told it could house three thousand people, its size surprised him and was emphasised by an empty, echoing coldness. Staff had commandeered the bank's trucks to move their families and possessions away from Paris and out of harm's way.

Empty, apart from in a far corner, two men working on a car up on a ramp. He could just make out in the dim light the garage manager,

Arnaud Renard, a nervous little man in oil-stained overalls, but didn't recognise the other. When he saw them approaching, he dismissed his assistant telling him to go off for a coffee and not to return for at least thirty minutes.

'*Bonjour*, gentlemen,' he said wiping his oily hands with a dirty rag and half turning to the car on the ramp that Ben recognised as Bernay's Bentley. 'She's almost ready for you.'

He'd seen it many times before and admired it and even coveted it although he'd never been this close. It oozed sensuous power and with its shiny body sweeping and curving into the dark looked less like a machine fashioned from steel but more something born of an organic being. And he thought if he touched it he'd find it breathing. Watched by its eyes, five huge chrome headlamps in a cluster, he felt it could pounce and devour him.

Bernay tapped Renard on the back and turned to face Ben before spreading his arms in an extravagant gesture. 'This is your mission.'

He struggled to conceal his disappointment. Surely the banker, whom he took to be a man of the highest integrity, wasn't just concerned about his own possessions with the Germans on the verge of entering the city? It seemed all the director wanted was for him to drive his valuable motorcar far away out of the Germans' reach. That angered him. He'd always wanted to drive a Bentley but not in these circumstances. He could get anyone to drive his damn automobile. Why him? He wanted to do something worthwhile for the war effort. Something he could write about. This was not the material he wanted. Not quite Hemingway. Hemingway at least drove an ambulance in the war and saved lives.

Bernay realised what he was thinking. 'Yes, yes, I need you to drive the Bentley out of Paris. But there's much more.' An impatient edge to his voice. 'This is most important.' He gestured. 'Come.' Lamp in hand, he ducked under the ramp.

He followed and copied his gaze up into the car's innards. Along the entire length of the chassis, canvas bags were strapped by leather belts to the inner rails and Bernay tugged at several of the bags trying and failing to dislodge them.

'A good job, Arnaud, a good job,' he called out and smiled. 'So, there you have it. Ingenious, don't you think?'

His puzzled look was soon answered as Bernay walked over to a trestle table against a wall and foraged in one of the canvas bags extracting an object that appeared heavy.

'There.' He handed it over. 'What do you make of this?'

It glinted silver in the light from the lamp and he nearly dropped it as it was much heavier than he'd anticipated.

'Platinum.' Bernay's voice rose. 'In every bag, ingots of platinum.'

He said nothing. Just stared at the metal.

'You know about platinum?'

'Wealthy women's jewellery.'

'Much more than that. It's the world's most precious metal because it has so many other uses, especially in armaments, and it's in short supply.'

His mind whirled as he tried to make sense of what he was seeing. 'Thought we got the gold out?'

'This is different. The bank holds in its vaults here many treasures for wealthy French citizens. The platinum belongs to four of the most prestigious families in France. They left the country when war broke out and they have instructed me to save their platinum from the Germans, so it can fund France's resistance. All they hope for is one day they will be able to return to a free France.'

His eyes opened wide. 'How much is here?'

'Many, many millions. Doesn't look much. But platinum is so dense you could fit a tonne of it into a large suitcase. The value is more than you could imagine. I won't tell you how much because you might run off to Switzerland with it.' He coughed as if he feared he might do that. 'Enough to fund a war.'

What he was proposing made his hands tremble. 'Oh, no, hang on...'

Bernay watched him.

'What do you expect me to do with it?'

'In a minute.' He laid a hand on his arm. 'Excuse us, Arnaud,' he said to the manager.

The mechanic nodded in understanding.

They walked as far away as possible where they wouldn't be overhead.

'Melodramatic, I'm afraid, yet necessary. The less he knows, the better.'

He barely masked his incredulity. 'You want me to drive your car out of Paris with millions in bullion strapped to its chassis?'

The banker said nothing, just smiled.

'For Christ's sake, what will happen when the Nazis find out what you've done. They'll come after it. We won't be hard to find – a bloody Bentley driving through the French countryside. We'll stick out like a sore thumb.'

Bernay shook his head. 'No reason for them to find out. By the time they did – if they did – you'd be long gone.'

'What if they do, and they catch me?'

The director hesitated.

'They'll shoot me, or worse.'

He nodded as if that wasn't so bad, putting a reassuring hand on his shoulder. 'The more reason you must go now. You must drive the Bentley out of Paris. Make haste and go south and you'll keep ahead of the Nazis. Cross the border into Spain, which will be neutral for I don't know how much longer. Head for Portugal and on to Estoril where you'll rendezvous with a British agent. It'll be his task to get you and the platinum to England. In the car are maps, directions, and food and drink for several days. I'll also give you money to help smooth your path.'

'And the gun?' He hoped he would change his mind and reclaim the weapon.

'I'm sorry, Ben, rather large and unwieldy. A Lebel eight millimetre, my old officer's pistol from the last war. The only gun I could get my hands on. It's there in case you encounter problems.' And he shrugged as if it were unlikely.

'I don't know if I can do it, Philippe, it's crazy and you'll just lose your platinum,' he snapped and felt ashamed of what he'd said. 'Anyway, the car probably wouldn't make it, carrying the extra weight.'

Bernay flashed him a reproachful look. 'Don't you think we've thought of that? Renard has already made certain modifications, including strengthening the chassis.'

There was a determination in the man's eyes he hadn't seen before. 'There are no problems with the car. I wouldn't be asking you to do this, Ben, if it weren't important.'

He turned away. He wanted to get out and keep walking.

But the director pulled him back. 'The British have promised to give us any help they can. If we get the platinum to England, it'll be sold to raise funds for France's freedom fighters. Better we have it than the Nazis. It's imperative you make it. You've an advantage being an American. No one will suspect you... you must go now. I don't know how much more time we have.' And he glanced over his shoulder.

He wavered.

'If you succeed, you'll be a hero.'

'If I don't?'

'You'll still be a hero.'

'Maybe... a dead one.'

It was crazy. The director was a careful man, measured in thought and action. He'd taken leave of his senses. He shook his head several times in an attempt to erase the images flooding through his brain, and they were of him lying with a bullet wound between the eyes. It was crazy. Yet there was something appealing about it in a perverse way. He'd been looking for some action, something to make his mark on this war. Perhaps this was it.

'You'll do it?' Bernay was almost pleading, and he felt sorry for him. Sticking his hands in his pockets because he couldn't be sure what he might do with them, Ben found he was nodding in agreement.

Overcome, the banker paused before embracing him and kissing him on the cheek. '*Mon brave*, you're the only man I could trust with this task.'

Now he realised why Bernay had given him the revolver.

ACROSS THE RIVER on the Left Bank in the corner of a nondescript café, a man in overalls was on a public telephone and sipped his café noir as he waited for his call to be picked up.

'Yes?' a man's guttural voice answered, eventually.

'I have something of interest for you.'

# 13

A SHARP PAIN IN THE PRISONER'S SIDE AND A SMELL OF BURNING JOLTED HIM back to reality every time he drifted into unconsciousness. Stripped to the waist, he sat in a straight-backed wooden chair with his wrists fastened to the armrests by a coarse rope cutting deep into the skin, and his bare feet were also tied to the chair legs.

How long had he been in this room? He didn't know whether it was hours or days and every time he slipped away they brought him round. They were in a long, narrow room with a stone-flagged floor and limestone walls. A heavy wooden door with iron studs was at one end; at the other, sandbags, stained red in places, lined the wall. Above the sandbags diffused light crept through a grille and he heard the occasional muffled thud, footsteps running and screams although he wasn't sure whether they were outside or his own.

A single bulb flickered the room with light. And he could just make out the two men who'd stripped off their black jackets and rolled up the sleeves of their khaki shirts before they beat him with their hands and rubber truncheons. They chain-smoked vile smelling cigarettes and when not interrogating him spoke to each other in German laughing at their own jokes. Each time he drifted into sleep they jabbed a lighted cigarette into his side just below the rib cage to revive him.

They asked the same thing repeatedly, but he didn't understand the questions because he didn't know the answers. He wasn't a brave man. He would tell them anything and everything except what he told them didn't appear to satisfy them. At first, the pain ripped through him as they switched from one area of torture to the next, all the time laughing. Now the pain was constant. After they had beaten him so that his face became a congealed mass of blood and flesh, the tearing out of his toenails turning them into bloodied stumps made little difference. Occasionally, they offered water to lubricate his answers, but his lips were so swollen he couldn't force his tongue through them to get at it.

'*Heil* Hitler!'

He was aware of the two men straightening up and raising their arms in the Nazi salute as the door creaked open.

The newcomer looked with disdain at the troopers and didn't return the salute. Hitler was not his Führer. Tall, at least several inches over six feet, he stooped as if embarrassed by his height and his thinning grey hair and grey stubble made him appear older. In a different situation, he might have been a university professor although the look in his grey eyes and unsmiling face brooked no familiarity and for the first time the prisoner felt real fear.

The troopers waited for him to talk. Members of the *SS Einsatzgruppen*, they followed the conquering soldiers and, with a relish for brutality, they cultivated the vanquished. Those who might cause the Nazis trouble were executed, those with information tortured, and others who could smooth their paths used.

In some villages, they denied inhabitants food and to eat they had to serve their new masters in any way deemed fit. Others of no use to the Germans starved or scavenged for food often excavating fresh graves to boil the corpses before eating them.

The newcomer reached into the inside pocket of his long black leather coat and pulled out a gold cigarette case with the initials LW.

Ludwig Weber extracted a Russian cigarette and tapped it several times on the case while taking in everything in the room. He hated these apes. They gloried in this war and the violence. It was not his war. He would have preferred to remain at home with his family.

The men said nothing, waiting for him to break the silence. Instead, he made a play of lighting his cigarette and inhaling so the warm, comforting smoke penetrated every corner of his lungs. It was important to keep them in their place like guard dogs. One slip, show an ounce of compassion and he'd end up in the chair.

He didn't approve of their methods for extracting information, yet his team had their work to do and he couldn't interrogate every prisoner. His way, while more thorough and with the minimum spilling of blood, took longer.

'Well, has he told you what we need to know?'

'No, Herr Weber,' one man answered and shook his head.

He said nothing, just stared at him until the trooper dropped his gaze. He turned and pulled a chair in front of the prisoner and sat.

'So, what have we here, m'sieu?' He spoke in perfect French and smiled at him in an almost apologetic way as if sympathising with the prisoner's misfortune at getting into such a predicament.

There was no response.

'Just tell us what you know, and you'll be free.'

Again, the prisoner said nothing.

'Your silence is futile.' His voice grew harsher. 'No one can help you now. We can make it so you just disappear off the face of the earth.'

Still there was no reaction.

'Very well.'

He pushed back his chair and got to his feet. He studied the prisoner, his eyes dwelling on his bloodied feet.

The prisoner watched him with his one remaining eye.

'Tell us what we need to know.'

He moved closer to him.

'No more pain, it's straightforward.'

Still no response. He crossed his arms and waited.

'Talk now and we'll let you die with no more pain.'

This time he didn't wait for an answer. With all his power, he stamped on the man's unprotected feet.

The man catapulted backward in the chair and attempted to shout, a bubble of red coming out of what had been his mouth.

The fools had gone too far this time.

He studied the prisoner not sure he wanted to do what he'd do next.

'Very well,' he said in resignation and signalled to another black-suited trooper to come forward through the doorway.

The soldier pulled behind him a small boy who stumbled, and the trooper continued to drag him until he regained his feet. He gestured to the soldier and took the whimpering boy's hand and guided him until he was standing in front of the man shackled to the chair. Although the prisoner tried to smile, it was that of a gargoyle and so horrific the boy pulled away.

He spoke in a hushed tone as if it were a secret between them. 'I don't wish to harm the child, but if you won't tell me what I need to know I must hand him over to your two friends.' He looked in the troopers' direction.

Again, the man struggled in his chair, which almost fell over, and the boy recoiled in fear not recognising his father, and a loud moaning noise came from deep in the prisoner's chest. The pain inflamed the man's mind and everything concentrated on the seat of his excruciating suffering. Weber moved in close and put his ear to the man's mouth. Words tumbled out unedited, between sobs, and without meaning, and Weber nodded in understanding several times as a priest taking a confession.

He was adept at extricating the truth from pain-crazed ramblings and, with a sigh and a shake of his head, he straightened up and stared at the two soldiers until they shuffled nervously.

'You've been wasting my time here,' he accused them and turned on his heel, releasing the now hysterical boy's hand.

He left the room slamming the door behind him. He was sick of battlefields and battle songs and broken people and misery. Tomorrow they would be in the City of Light. Civilisation. The French had declared Paris an open city whether out of cowardice or good sense he didn't know and didn't care. Instead of desolation, there would be restaurants and plenty of food and good wine. And he could sleep in a comfortable bed with clean white sheets of linen and bathe in hot water and have a shave.

'Herr Weber?' The soldier stood by a small table on which there was a brown Bakelite box. 'I have a telephone call for you.'

The soldier's face was white, and he appeared to tremble. 'Please.' He proffered the handset of the *Feldfernsprecher 33* field telephone as if he no longer wanted it.

'No, not now.' He waved a dismissive hand at the soldier. 'Not now.'

The soldier was insistent. 'You must, Herr Weber, it's very important.'

He detected fear in the soldier's eyes. 'Who is it?' he asked.

The soldier croaked a nervous response.

'Oh, very well.' He snatched the handset from the soldier and barked down the phone. 'Yes?'

The voice at the other end sounded as if it were underwater. 'Herr Weber, please wait.'

After a series of clicks and intermittent crackling, a new voice came on the line, a high-pitched effeminate voice and Weber had known before he said his name to whom he was talking. And he felt thousands of ants crawling across his body.

The soldier exhaled and allowed his shoulders to relax relieved the call was no longer his responsibility.

Weber had pulled over a chair and sat with his elbow on the table and his head resting on a hand and he listened deep in concentration. He'd heard it all before. First would come the compliments then the underlying threat that if he didn't achieve the task he was being set, there would be severe repercussions. With growing trepidation, he listened. The Führer himself asked for him to undertake this task. All means would be put at his disposal to track down an enemy who had the power to endanger the Fatherland's war effort.

The soldier watched, convinced the longer the call lasted, the more Weber appeared to age.

After what seemed an eternity, although it was only a matter of minutes, he removed the phone from his ear and sat staring at the wall.

'Herr Weber, is everything okay?'

He lurched to his feet and threw the handset onto the table and without a word left the room. Walking up the stairs, he made his way out into the daylight. Everywhere there was destruction, demolished buildings, fires burning, clouds of smoke and the smell of cordite yet the air was fresh compared to the stench of hopelessness in the cellar.

Even the landscape was depressing. Not just featureless, but also interminably flat as if nature had created it on an off day, too weary to fashion an undulation far less a hillock or a ravine or river. Or it had passed over this barren land in a hurry to create a masterpiece elsewhere, and it was forgotten as it had been by everyone who had trodden this sorry earth since.

He sat on what remained of a wall. Across the way was a gutted building resembling a blackened skull with the empty upstairs windows eye sockets and its mouth the hole that had been a door. As he lit a cigarette, the muffled crack of a pistol shot from within the building and the sound of a man shouting made him start.

Paris was now nothing more than a dream. 'First, I have to find someone,' he muttered knowing he had no time to finish his smoke and ground out the cigarette under his heel.

Crack! A second pistol shot rang out deep in the cellar.

Reichsführer Heinrich Himmler had been emphatic. 'Find them,' he'd warned, 'or your family will be held to account.'

# 14

---

Bernay thanked Renard and even hugged him. 'We'll meet again in better times, *mon ami*.' And Ben was sure there were tears in his eyes.

'Please have the car ready in 30 minutes.' Bernay waved an imperious hand. 'Time is pressing. The Nazis are close.'

Renard nodded and went back to his work with renewed vigour.

Bernay led the way to the stairs. 'Come to my office, Ben, there's one other thing we need to discuss.'

In the gloom of his inner sanctum, Ben saw no one else at first. Then to his left a slight movement and a rustle caught his attention. He focused his eyes in the dim light and saw a woman sitting with her legs crossed on an upright chair against the wall. Her shoulder length blonde hair cut close to her cheek fell like a veil over her right eye, so he couldn't make out her features.

'Ah, Madame,' said Bernay. And she wheeled around as if awakened and her eyes shone jade green like a cat's in the light from the lamp.

'It's a pleasure to meet you.' The director stepped forward and, still sitting, she extended a gloved hand.

'If you please, Ben,' He called him forward. 'Ben Peters, let me introduce Madame...'

'My name is of no importance.' A frown flitted across her face.

He offered his hand, but she ignored it and turned to Bernay. 'Is everything ready?'

His confident smile was the answer she needed. 'Then we must go now.'

'There's no problem,' he reassured her. 'You'll be on your way within thirty minutes, I promise...'

'Why the delay?' She pushed her hair from her face with a gesture of impatience, glancing at the door as if looking for an escape route.

'Ben has agreed to drive you to safety, the car's waiting downstairs.'

A scrambling noise from under the banker's desk interrupted Ben as he started to speak. Bernay froze and doubt slipped across his face as he stooped to determine from where the noise emanated.

A small boy with a mass of brown curls crawled out from under his desk dragging a worn teddy bear. 'I've found him, *maman*, he was hiding. He's a naughty teddy.'

She laughed, a warm, deep-throated chuckle filling the room and softening the edge to the atmosphere, and he wondered if he could ever make her laugh. 'Good, Freddie, come on. We're going for a ride in a car.'

He turned questioning the director, who shrugged.

Apparently, Bernay had known this and anger built up inside him. He'd agreed to drive the Bentley and the platinum out of France. Crazy enough. But to be a babysitter to this woman and her child was ludicrous and even more dangerous.

'I can't do this,' he said. Perhaps it wouldn't be too late to catch a train to the coast and a boat over to England if he decided not to stay in Paris. 'It's impossible. Surely your friend can find a safer way to get out of Paris, Philippe?'

Aware of movement, they both turned. The woman had stood and was smoothing down her black and white houndstooth suit. She started towards them with a determination in her step. Shoulders back, she walked with the confidence of someone used to being watched and her heels beat a tattoo on the wooden floor.

For the first time, she acknowledged his presence and close up she was even more fascinating with high Slavic cheekbones and clear skin that glowed with a light tan. A dimple like a perfect scar marked her right cheek and she smiled at him with her full red lips open, showing she knew what he was thinking, and he found it disconcerting.

'Mr Peters,' she said, using his name not out of respect, more as if dealing with a servant. 'This woman and child aren't afraid to make the journey, surely a big man isn't afraid?' He noted the hint of a tremor in her voice.

He stood his ground, shaking his head.

'We were prisoners of the Nazis before we escaped. We've something they want and if they find us, they'll torture and kill us.'

He watched her mouth and wondered what it would feel like to kiss. 'Slip away to the country and find somewhere to hide.' He felt he was being backed into a corner.

Her hair reflected the light from the lamp and kinked over her right eye, touching her curled eyelashes and making them flicker.

'You don't know the Nazis, you don't understand what they're capable of.'

He was finding it difficult to concentrate. Like dark pools of hypnotic green, one moment her eyes shone with a haughty arrogance and the next were so haunted it was as if two separate personalities were battling each other for dominance of her psyche. And it betrayed a vulnerability and he wanted to reach out and touch her.

'They'll find you. Even in their country they've set up a system of informers. Everyone tells on each other, it's the only way to survive. Brothers against brothers. Sisters against sisters. They even indoctrinate children to report their parents.'

Pushing back her hair, she smiled although it was more an appeal for help. 'We've no other options; you're our last hope...'

This wasn't a great idea. The more he thought about it, the more complicated it became burrowing into his conscience like the roots of an unwelcome tree. He looked away from her to the director, hoping to break the spell and for common sense to prevail.

He had never seen Bernay so agitated. The banker stepped between them and, grabbing both arms, propelled him backwards and up against a wall dropping his grip when he realised what he'd done.

'For God's sake, Ben, if not for me or for France, please help this woman and the child. If you don't, it will be on your conscience for the rest of time. The British asked me to arrange her safe passage. All is lost if you don't. She's very important.'

The small boy looked up at Ben, uncertainty in his pale blue eyes.

Ben glanced around as if expecting someone to come to the rescue but realised he was outnumbered. Instinct told him to walk away, yet he almost welcomed an adventure. Bernay was playing on his conscience and he knew he was about to make the wrong decision and would pay for it. He smiled at the boy. 'Right, come on Freddie, we've a car to catch.' And took his hand.

The woman gasped with relief and grabbed his sleeve. 'Do you have a gun?' She tugged at it. 'You'll need one.'

'Oh, boy, do I have a gun.' He looked accusingly at Bernay and realised there was no point in saying he'd never fired one.

'Promise one thing.' She fixed him with a desperate stare. 'If the Nazis are about to capture us, shoot Freddie first then me. Don't let them take us alive. Promise!'

'I promise.'

## 15

AT FIRST, HE DIDN'T NOTICE. SHE'D TURNED HER HEAD AWAY FROM HIM and the hissing of the tyres on the tarmacadam and the whistling of the wind through the Bentley's open windows muffled the sound of her sobbing.

They'd packed Freddie into the back seat under a travel rug. But as Ben nosed the Bentley out of the bank's car park, the boy was up on his knees with his nose pressed to the small rear window taking in the pandemonium on the streets. To get out onto the roadway took forever as the entire population of Paris appeared to be fleeing. By now, the railway stations had closed their gates as they were being besieged by Parisians desperate to catch a train south. And only the more athletic could get into the stations by climbing over the high railings. Fear of the unknown hung over the city like an enormous, dark immovable cloud and the thousands of refugees knew the big boot of the Nazis could crush them at any moment.

It was a parade of despair. They used any means of transport available to them – cars, motorcycles, vans, trucks, bicycles and horse-drawn carts piled high with possessions with women and children sitting precariously atop everything. And the horses were skittish adding to the mayhem. Others without transport walked carrying a few essential possessions on their backs and even the youngest children wore back-packs. Cripples, knowing they would be the first on the Nazis' list for extermination, hobbled along on crutches and when they fell, no one came to their aid. Some ran in a blind panic with no sense of direction, scrambling to escape a ruthless army that was only a matter of hours away.

As they sat becalmed by this mass of humanity, she became increasingly agitated and kept glancing at her watch as if she knew when the Germans were expected.

'If we're going to share this car over the next few days, I should at least know your name,' insisted Ben with what he hoped was a reassuring smile.

She studied him for several seconds debating whether to give away any more information than necessary.

'It's Alena.' She glanced away as if her eyes might reveal more.

'Alena?'

'Until we get to Estoril, it's Alena Peters.' There was an edge to her voice. 'It will be better if they believe we're a family.'

He thought it made sense if they ever got moving. Bernay had planned a route south heading for Orléans, Tours, Poitiers, Bordeaux and crossing the border into Spain near Hendaye on the coast. But getting out of the city would be more of a problem than he'd expected. His misgivings about accepting Bernay's mission were mounting. Alone, he could have coped. Now he had a car, a woman and boy to babysit.

She interrupted his thoughts. 'Get out of the driver's seat.'

'Why?'

'I was brought up in Paris. I know my way around.'

He did as he was told and walked around to the passenger's side as she slid over into the driver's seat.

'Right,' she said. 'Let's go.'

She glanced at him with a determined smile.

'Hold on, Freddie,' she shouted, and he squealed in excitement.

He couldn't see any way for her to break out of the jam, but she pointed to a narrow opening about fifty yards along the road.

'If we can make it to that alley I know a way.' And she gripped the steering wheel tighter.

She pulled hard on the wheel and reversed mounting the pavement and knocking over a dustbin and he winced at the thought of the damage to the Bentley's expensive bodywork. The car made a horrendous mechanical grinding noise as she slammed it into first gear and it shot forward along the pavement scattering everyone in its path. He was convinced she was driving with her eyes closed because anyone with any sympathy for humanity would pull up faced with a mass of bodies.

Somehow, they reached the opening. Again, she pulled hard on the wheel lurching off the kerb and into the traffic. The Bentley's nose parted a clump of screaming people in danger of falling beneath its wheels and they scraped through a gap between two cars.

'Sors de la voie, salauds,' she shouted at them and he glanced at her in surprise.

Horns blared and people shouted in anger as they crossed the road and entered an empty alleyway that appeared to be a dead end. But a hundred yards farther on it turned sharp right and, crossing another road, they sped down another narrow alley.

'For Christ's sake,' he shouted gripping the dashboard. 'It's one way and we're going the wrong way.'

Pushing her hair away from her eyes, she turned with a defiant smile. 'So what? We're all going one way.'

They wound their way through alleys and alongside streets in a blur and emerged onto the Rue du Pont Neuf where the traffic was now crawling. Law and order no longer existed. The few traffic police still on duty gave up, and all courtesies were ignored as cars aimed for wherever there was a gap to put a few yards more between them and the advancing enemy. As they approached the Seine, the traffic groaned to a halt. Their path appeared to be blocked.

'We'll take the quais and try to cross the Seine at Bercy where it might be quieter,' shouted Alena swinging the car left. And in his ignorance, he nodded his agreement with a sharp intake of breath. He'd thought the Coney Island Cyclone roller-coaster with its 85-foot sixty-degree drop was the scariest ride he'd survived – it was nothing compared to Alena's driving. She showed no quarter to either man or machine and after a series of unusual manoeuvres that forced him to close his eyes, they were running free in the outskirts of the city.

'Take over,' she ordered bringing the car to a gradual halt. 'You're the one who's supposed to be driving.'

It had been one of his fantasies to drive this Bentley and even better with a stunning woman by his side, but not in these circumstances. The smoothness of the ride was nothing like his old Ford convertible back home. That was driving a biscuit tin compared to this beauty, and it lulled him into a relaxed state almost diminishing the imminent danger.

He'd never worked out whether Hemingway was into cars. The writer loved his boats and his game fishing. Ben couldn't handle them. He couldn't even swim. As soon as he stepped onto a boat, the movement made him queasy and when his parents took him on boat rides as a kid, he spent most of his time being sick. No, give me a Bentley, he thought, and he'd be a happy man.

Her sobbing was now becoming louder, and her shoulders shook the more the southern suburbs receded.

'Don't worry, we'll make it.' He placed a hand on her arm and she stiffened at his touch and pulled away.

'I'm okay, okay.' She pushed her hair back from her forehead and her eyes were red with the tears. 'It's just a relief getting out of Paris.'

'The Nazis must have reasons to want you?'

She gulped and cut off his questioning by turning to adjust the rug covering the now sleeping Freddie.

He wondered why they were pursuing her and why the British were so desperate to get her to England. Where was the father of her child? Lurid permutations flashed through his mind and the responsibilities on his shoulders grew heavier with every mile. They had escaped Paris unscathed, but what lay ahead?

# 16

THE WHOLE OF FRANCE APPEARED TO BE ON THE MOVE LIKE AN ANTS' NEST disturbed.

They passed convoys of cars and trucks, including one with twenty nuns in the back, sitting prim and upright and singing hymns, and horse-drawn carts and groups of refugees trudging along the side of the road weighed down by possessions as heavy as their thoughts. Items once important were discarded for the sake of speed and littered the roadside, and vehicles lay abandoned because they'd run out of fuel or ceased to function. A potent mix of despair and fear swirled in the air. And Ben knew if the Bentley should fail this would be their fate, so he listened to the note of the engine for an early warning of any mechanical problems.

Side by side the aged and infirm struggled with the able-bodied but failed to keep up. Haunted by the image, he suggested they allow some to cling to the car, standing on the running boards, at least until the next village. The vehemence of her answer surprised him. 'If we do, every time we slow or stop we'll have them jumping on us.' She frowned at his stupidity. 'How long would we last?'

He gritted his teeth and concentrated on the road ahead. They made slow progress, but they were putting distance between them and the

Germans and with every mile she seemed to relax a little more, although he thought a coiled cobra might have been more relaxed. Any attempts at conversation were futile. Now awake, Freddie jumped about in the back seat, taking in everything he saw and asking interminable questions, and only when she answered them with a concerned patience did she show her human side.

The main highway had become more than just the tarred road and the endless convoy branched off wherever it appeared suitable for a vehicle. With the zeal of pathfinders, they took any gap helping them leapfrog the vehicles in front. When congestion blocked the way, several broke free from the cavalcade, as a tributary from a river, going cross-country until they found a path to rejoin the road. Occasionally, this tactic backfired when investing their trust in the leader they'd find themselves at a dead end and had to stop and reverse and manoeuvre their way back with much shouting and honking of horns.

Like an unwelcome visitor in the night, every so often the suggestion slipped into his mind. At first, he dismissed it before it could get a hold, but after a while he listened to it and it had an appeal. Why not keep the car and the bullion of course? Perhaps he could persuade her to live with him somewhere in Spain or Portugal. Then he could write every day and when this blew over they'd return to America and...

'Ben, BEN.' She shouted at him and shook his arm to get his attention making the car swerve. 'Where's your gun?'

'Why?' There was no danger and the longer he could put off handling it again the better.

'What would you do if we came upon a German patrol?'

'They're not supposed to be here.'

'We've no idea where they are. For all we know we might be heading straight into their lines.'

He shrugged without thinking.

'These people kill for fun; they'd shoot you like a stray dog. They don't value human life. And these...' She gestured at the refugees. 'Any of them could ambush us and steal the car.'

'They aren't our enemies; they're trying to escape the Germans as we are.'

'Don't be naïve.' She brushed her hair out of her eyes in exasperation. 'They're more desperate than our enemies and possibly more dangerous. When trying to get out of Germany, I'd have done anything – even kill – to escape.'

He looked across at her and didn't doubt her for one minute.

'It's in my bag,' he said.

'Your gun's in the trunk?' She screwed up her face in disbelief. 'Jesus, you're supposed to be protecting us.'

He nodded.

'It's no use to you there,' she shouted slamming both hands hard on the dashboard. 'Stop the car now.'

He stamped on the brakes and the car screeched as the tyres burned rubber and fishtailed to a halt.

'Go on, get the gun.'

Drivers of following vehicles shouted and cursed him to keep moving, but he ignored them and retrieved the gun. When he returned to the car, she took it from him and he noted she loaded it and expertly checked it before placing it in the glove box as he got the car rolling again.

They'd been watched by two youths sitting by the roadside and now they jumped on the running boards either side of the car and hung on. The one on Alena's side stuck his head through the open window and almost into her face.

'Thanks for the ride,' he chuckled enjoying the innuendo.

'Get off,' she ordered him.

He glanced at the youths on either side but had to concentrate on taking evasive action to miss a horse fallen on the road.

'No way, we're coming with you.'

What struck him most was the way Alena handled herself. She was in control as if she'd been in difficult situations before. 'If you don't get off now, I will shoot you,' she warned the youth, reaching into the glove box and removing the revolver and pointing it at him in one smooth movement. 'I know how to use this.'

Doubt swept across the youth's face and he glanced at the moving road below. 'I can't. I'll break my neck.'

'That's your problem.'

'No, I can't, I won't.'

'Let me help you.' She slammed the butt of the revolver hard on his fingers clinging to the frame of the door.

With a scream of pain, he released his grip and fell backwards onto the road rolling over and over like tumbleweed.

She swung round to face the other youth and pointed the gun at him so that it was now in front of Ben's nose. 'Get off.'

'I'm going, I'm going,' he shouted, watching for a spot to soften his fall and then leapt onto the grass verge. Ben glanced in his mirror and was relieved that both youths were sitting up in the road shaking their fists at the disappearing car.

She leant back closing her eyes. Whether asleep or just warding off any attempts at conversation, she kept them closed as they skirted Joan of Arc's city of Orleans. Perhaps she was the modern equivalent of Joan of Arc. He chuckled. The city's spectacular Sainte-Croix Cathedral and its Gothic spire, which he could just make out in the distance, sparkled untouched in the afternoon sunshine. Even here a stream of refugees made its way out of the city heading south.

A couple of miles on as they rounded a bend he saw men in the road. His mouth dried up and he felt his pulse racing. Soldiers.

As he braked, she opened her eyes. 'What's happening?' And he detected panic in her voice.

'That.' He pointed at a soldier holding a rifle and standing in the middle of the road with a raised hand ordering them to stop.

'Oh, *merde!*' She gripped the sides of her leather seat.

From behind Freddie chirruped. 'Look, *maman*, soldiers with guns.' And he made the childish sound of a gun firing.

They came to a halt just feet from the soldier who walked around to Ben's window and peered in checking his passengers. The officer in his early twenties, yet with the strained face of a middle-aged man, was hatless, and the two top buttons of his jacket undone.

'M'sieu, pardon,' he said. 'A convoy is coming, and I need you to pull over so my trucks can get through.'

Alena put a hand on Ben's arm. 'Where are you headed, *mon capitaine?*'

'North to engage the Germans, our defences are being overrun.' He shrugged his shoulders and sounded beaten already. 'The Nazis have taken Rouen and Reims, Paris is next, then … what does it matter now?'

'We're heading south to Spain. What's up ahead?'

He gave a weary smile as if he'd been asked the question many times.

'You must be careful,' warned the officer. 'Much damage. Many casualties. There's nothing we can do. German planes are bombing the roads and shooting women and children. Don't let the boy see. We got our trucks through though I don't know about your car.'

He gave a perfunctory salute and what he thought was a smile although it was more of a painful grimace. '*Bonne chance*! *Vive la France*!'

The trucks thundered by much to Freddie's delight, but the troops they carried knew there was no hope.

# 17

LUCIEN AND NATALIE SAT HUNCHED BY THE SIDE OF THE ROAD. LUCIEN WAS ten and Natalie seven. Terror sculpted Lucien's pale and narrow face, his red-rimmed eyes unseeing and his sister numbed by shock.

They'd been riding in the back of their father's truck and playing amongst the family's possessions while their parents sat up front in the cabin. Oblivious to the human tragedy unfolding around them, the children thought it an adventure and their parents not wishing to burden them with their fears said nothing to dissuade them.

It came without warning, a hurricane of destruction. A screaming noise exploded from the sky like an aggravated banshee. The plane diving perpendicularly on the column, releasing bombs that whistled on their descent, then flattening out and raking the fleeing refugees with its machine guns. Explosives made contact with a concussive thud, first one and another close behind followed by screams. A column of humanity strewn by the roadside. Broken people and horses, with their huge stomachs torn apart and their innards spilling out, lay side by side, and refugees died where they'd hidden in ditches as if they were ready-made graves. Cars, trucks and carts lifted up and twisted into strange shapes and deposited in fields. The Stuka flew low over their truck and Lucien was convinced he saw the face of the pilot surveying his day's work.

And then it departed and there was just the low sobbing and moaning of the injured. A young mother carrying her baby had been cut down and spilled the infant now lying alone and crying on the road. Those who'd escaped the massacre got to their feet to help the others.

Lucien watched the Stuka climb high in the azure sky and on reaching its zenith there was no sound as if the pilot had switched off the engine, and it looked a thing of beauty. It rolled on its back and started another steep dive and he realised the pilot was coming back for them. Sirens screamed its intent as it released two more bombs and he saw flashes coming from the plane's machine guns before everything went black. Those who'd survived the first run died then.

Almost all did. Lucien and Natalie were protected by the bundles of clothes in the back of the shattered truck, now lying half on the road and half in a field. The truck's cabin was ripped open and their father had disappeared. One minute he was there, the next gone. They came across their mother face down yards from their truck and with considerable effort pulled her up into a sitting position. No amount of cajoling could bring her back even though Natalie cradled her mother's bloodied head and appealed over and over to her.

'Wake up, *maman*, wake up.'

In their grief, the children didn't notice a car appear amongst the carnage and mayhem. Its driver peered through the windscreen at the black smoke as he steered around the debris and bomb craters. Sitting beside him, a blonde woman looked out of her window with a mixture of shock and anger spreading across her face.

'Stop, Ben, stop,' she shouted.

'Not here. The plane might come back. Got to get out of here as fast as we can.'

'No, no, we must stop.' Her voice crackled with emotion. 'The children. We must save the children.'

# 18

Paris belonged to Renard, or so he'd always believed. Whenever he needed to reinforce his feeling of ownership, he'd stand on the steps in front of the Sacré Coeur, its travertine stone sparkling white in the sunshine, on the hill of Montmartre. And he looked out over his city and marvelled at its size, its substance, its majesty. Occasionally, he climbed the 234 spiral steps up to the dome from where you could see forever. Today with the imminent arrival of the Germans he wasn't sure if there was a forever.

From there, he made his way up the cobbled lanes and across the Place du Tertre, where artists exhibited their colourful paintings to sell to tourists. It always made him smile seeing the paintings on display on their easels. The tourists never realised if they returned the next day they could just as likely see an exact copy of the picture they'd bought the day before on the same easel. Not all were artists. Some just owned the pitch and bought in paintings from wherever they could and stood around with paint-smeared smocks to add credence to their fiction. This was a village within a village and although there were now no visitors to buy their paintings, the artists were still out in force as if to show the strength of their community.

In times of trouble, he headed for his bolthole a short distance away in a side street where he whiled away his spare time. A place of refuge to exclude the outside world. Therefore, it was no surprise Renard came here after he left the bank for the last time. He felt safe here. His usual table was at the back of the café near the urinals. The smell didn't bother him or the other regulars, and in winter when the café was warm and the air thick with tobacco smoke misting up the windows it added to its familiarity. In summer, the aroma was its first line of defence and the look on the faces of newcomers as they entered amused him. Their noses twitched, and they left without buying anything giving the impression they'd stumbled in by accident and it was another bar they'd intended to visit. Good! He didn't want his café overrun by tourists. This was for locals.

He'd been a regular for many years, and the patron knew him by his first name, as did most of the other regulars yet they never engaged him in conversation. Arrivals raised an arm in welcome and shouted 'Bonjour, Arnaud' although never more than that. He always sat alone often listening into conversations at other tables, nodding and smiling in agreement, or shaking his head in disagreement as if part of their debate. And when they raised their glasses to drink he did, too. A long time ago he'd realised he could talk to cats and engines. People were a little more difficult.

Bernay had advised him to get out of Paris and as far away as possible. But to where? And how? His cats needed constant care. He couldn't take them with him and the neighbours who may have looked after them had fled the city. He experienced a growing stubbornness, anyway. This was his town why should he let the Nazis drive him out? Surely, they'd have more pressing things to take care of. He was too old to be a threat to them and he wasn't a Jew, and if he kept his head down, they'd probably not notice he was there.

He was well into his second bottle of Bordeaux, a better quality and much more expensive than his usual. The director had given him money so why not spend it? He hadn't seen the newcomer come into the café and now noticed him sitting across the room at a table against the wall. Tall with grey hair, he wore a black leather coat and looked out of place amongst the locals. His first instinct was that he was German although the man conversed with the patron in perfect French, so Renard thought no more of it. Before the man was a cognac and a *café noir* and he'd spread a copy of *Le Matin* out on the table and seemed oblivious to those around him.

The Bentley had left the bank after he'd given it one last loving polish so that it gleamed like never before. It would be the last time he'd see it and it was as if saying goodbye to a child or one of his cats. They hadn't allowed him back in the basement garage although he'd managed to get to an upstairs window with a good view of the exit. From there, he had watched it lurch out onto the street and come to a halt in the tide of refugees.

The American, Ben, was at the wheel and he saw the profile of a woman sitting beside him and there also appeared to be the face of a child pressed up against the rear window.

His table being jolted interrupted his thoughts and his bottle of Bordeaux, now almost empty, toppled over onto the floor in slow motion. He looked up into the eyes of the outsider and thought the man was observing him as if storing in his memory every line and blemish of his face. It was a fleeting feeling and the warming glow of the wine took over.

'*Pardon, m'sieu, pardon.*' The man looked upset to have spilled his wine. 'Please...' He put out a hand and turned to the patron. '*Encore, s'il vous plaît.*'

The patron uncorked another bottle and placed it in front of him with two fresh glasses before, irritated by the extra work, sweeping up the broken glass from the wine bottle.

'May I?' The man gestured to the empty chair.

'A pleasure,' Renard said, pleased he wanted to join him. In his years of using the café, no one had ever sat with him.

'Ludwig Weber.' The man offered his hand.

He paused as he filled the glasses and his eyes narrowed. 'German?'

Weber put up his hands in mock horror. 'No, no, my father was a musician and loved Beethoven.'

'Dah, dah, dah, DAAH!' Renard beat out the tune with his fist on the table.

They both laughed.

Weber extended his hand again and he took it and was reassured by the strength of the grip.

'Arnaud Renard.'

'*Santé!*'

They both took a couple of gulps of the Bordeaux before Renard broke the silence.

'Are you from around here?'

'No, from out of town. Many years ago, I lived in Paris.'

'It's changing now.'

'For better or worse?'

He shrugged. 'Who knows? I've always believed it makes no difference to someone like me. Keep your head down. Communists, fascists they're just labels, they don't affect ordinary people...'

'Germans?'

'Who knows, look at the Catholic Church they think they'd be good for us.'

'Ah, the Church, it always goes with what it thinks is the winning side.'

'I don't know, I just get on with my job...' He looked pained as he remembered he no longer had the job he loved.

Weber put out a hand and touched his sleeve. 'What's wrong, my friend?'

He gave an unconvincing laugh. 'Just remembered I don't have a job. Retired now. No longer work at the bank.'

He couldn't quite make out the look on Weber's face whether it was one of envy or sympathy for him. It was in that split second that he realised he should leave. The wine may have dulled his senses, but he saw a warning sign blinking at him in the fog. Bernay had warned him not to talk about his job. What did they say? Walls have ears. There's a time when you've drunk a lot that you know there's a point of no return and one more drink could have you stumbling across the threshold. If he stayed, everything he'd done in the garage and his own safety, not to mention Bernay's, would be in danger. He lurched to his feet and summoned the patron. '*L'addition*.' he requested and fumbled in his jacket pocket for the francs.

'Excuse me.' Weber pointed towards the toilet doors.

The toilets were empty. Weber went into a cubicle and closed the door behind him. He reached into his coat pocket and extricated a metal object and pressed a button so that its blade shot out reflecting the light from the bulb above his head. He ran a finger along the edge and felt its cold sharpness and touched the end of it pricking his finger and drawing blood. Sucking his finger dry, he folded the knife again and replaced it in his pocket.

He'd waited for Weber to reappear and shook his hand trying to show it was not because of him he was making a hasty departure. 'It's been a pleasure, Ludwig, but I must go. Things to attend to...'

'The pleasure has been all mine,' Weber replied.

As he left, Weber ordered another cognac.

The fresh air took him by surprise as he stepped down the steps of the café into the street, and he wobbled.

Within seconds of his departure, Weber got to his feet, threw down more than enough francs on the table to meet his bill and headed for the door.

Renard had gone only a hundred yards when he realised he was being followed.

# 19

THEY STOPPED. NO MATTER THE DANGER FROM THE SKIES OR ELSEWHERE they couldn't leave the two children sitting alone with their dead mother by the roadside.

As soon as Ben brought the car to a halt, Alena was out and running towards them with Freddie following. The children didn't acknowledge their presence as the boy was immersed in a world of his own while the girl was still talking and staring at her mother's body.

Alena placed a hand on Lucien's shoulder and with the other stroked Natalie's head. There was no acknowledgement from either and not even Freddie's efforts to engage them distracted them.

'Get food and drink,' Alena ordered, and Ben went back to the car to fetch provisions.

When he returned Alena had coaxed the girl onto her knee and whispered in her ear while stroking her hair, caked with dust and blood from her mother. Freddie, copying his mother, massaged the boy's head. Natalie was now responding to Alena's ministrations and Alena persuaded her to take water that she sipped warily. She offered her bread, but Natalie shook her head and began to cry again, whimpering like a wounded animal.

As if he were awakening from a deep sleep, Lucien's eyes focused.

He looked around, remembering the terror of before, and asked, his face full of suspicion: 'Who are you?'

'We were just passing.' Alena offered her hand, which the boy took. 'We can take you away from here.'

'My *maman...*'

'I know, I know. Sssh...' She pulled his head to her breast. 'We're here to help you.'

'Are you angels?' Natalie's eyes were wide in wonder.

Alena gave a throaty chuckle, and the boy joined in, hesitant at first and then moving to the edge of hysteria.

Ben took Freddie away and wandered into an adjoining field. He found a broken spade and with it dug a shallow trench. The earth was soft, and he made good progress.

'What are you doing?' asked Freddie picking up a stick and endeavouring to help.

Ben put a finger to his lips. 'Sssh, it's a secret.' He winked at Freddie.

When it was deep enough, he gathered rocks from the roadside and took them over to the trench. He found two long sticks and used some long grasses to fashion them together into a cross.

On seeing what he'd done, Alena talked to the children and hugged each one in turn. Bending over, she took from the dead woman's body a gold ring and a necklace and she gave them to the children. She glanced at Ben, signalling she was ready. He picked up the woman's body and, as he prepared to take her into the field, the children stopped him and first Natalie and then Lucien kissed their mother on the lips. And Lucien hung onto her body until Alena prised him away. Ben laid their mother out in the trench and with the children watching built the rocks around her before putting the cross in place.

Natalie pulled her hand away from Alena and ran back to the roadside scrambling in the dirt as if looking for something and returned with a green silk scarf she draped over the cross.

'Why is their *maman* hiding?' Freddie asked thinking it was a game.

Alena looked at Ben and he nodded.

'Come on, Freddie,' he said. 'Let's see if the car is still there.'

Back in the Bentley he offered Freddie water and bread and ham, and it diverted him from asking difficult questions. And he felt guilty burying the children's mother and not the other poor souls scattered across the road who were attracting the attention of hungry birds. Didn't they deserve a decent burial, too? He averted his eyes from the carnage, and from his seat he could see a back view of Alena holding hands with the children, one on either side of her. And, looking down on the grave, she turned her head, talking to each of them in turn.

Beyond them, the fields of France looked peaceful in the diffused afternoon sunlight that glanced off the blonde of her hair and appeared to present a halo around her head.

# 20

LUCIEN RODE ON THE RUNNING BOARD WITH ALENA'S ARM AROUND HIM, and the wind in his face helped to diffuse memories of the attack. And Natalie hunkered down on the back seat with Freddie, allowing him to distract her with his incessant chatter.

When they had returned to the car after the burial, Alena reached over, and her lips brushed Ben's cheek and she smiled, sending his spirits soaring. The flotsam and jetsam of the refugees' desperate flight still littered the road ahead and Alena did her best to divert the children's attention. Gradually, the sights of destruction petered out, and the road cleared. The growl of the Bentley's engine was encouraging him to put his foot down and Alena placed a hand on his arm reminding him to slow so that they didn't lose Lucien.

'I'll keep a watch out for German planes,' the boy shouted using one hand to hang onto the door frame and the other to shield his eyes from the sun as he searched high into the sky.

'Where are you taking us?' Natalie piped up from the back of the car.

They didn't know. They couldn't take them across the border and into Spain and onto England. Perhaps when they came to the next village, they'd find some good-hearted souls who would care for the children until they contacted the rest of their family.

'We're taking you away from all this.' Alena turned and smiled at the little girl and leant behind to squeeze her hand. 'Somewhere you'll be safe.'

'And *maman* and papa, too?'

Alena smiled and there were tears in her eyes when she turned back.

'Ben,' Lucien ducked his head through Alena's window. 'War is shit, isn't it?'

He nodded.

'Why do people do it?'

Ben shrugged, but the boy kept on staring at him demanding an answer.

'I don't think it's the people, they have no say,' he began and kept his eyes on the road. 'It's the politicians. They become greedy and power mad and you can never trust politicians.'

'Are they our bosses?'

'They like to think so even though in some countries the people vote for them.'

The boy digested it for a few seconds before continuing. 'If we vote them in, can't we tell them what to do?'

'Watch out,' Alena's cry interrupted the questioning, and he pulled hard left on the wheel to avoid a crater that would have ripped off the undercarriage. Although the car lurched, Lucien hung on and it diverted him from his questioning and he went back to searching the skies for Stukas.

Again, Alena smiled at Ben. Not the hard, suspicious smile of earlier, a genuine full smile with open lips as she brushed her hair away from her eyes.

'Doesn't it bother you?' he asked.

'Does what bother me?'

'Your hair?'

'I like it.'

'No.'

'No, what?'

'I meant the hair falling over your eye, does it bother you?'

'Not at all, only when men like you ask me that? Does it bother you?'

'Does what bother me?'

'That I'm not bothered that you're bothered about my hair.'

They both laughed as did the children and the road was clearer now although Lucien kept watching for enemy planes. Occasionally a vehicle drove past going in the opposite direction and its occupants shouted and waved and they reciprocated, and the children enjoyed it and looked for more.

Bernay's instructions had been specific. They had to be in Estoril in time to rendezvous with an RAF flying boat on Monday and there was no second chance. The British attaché Rafe Cooper there would help to get them and the platinum aboard the plane.

He had no idea where the Germans were and whether they knew what the Bentley was carrying? Did they know Alena was travelling with him? Were they in pursuit? Any delay meant the Nazis would be closer to catching them. As much as he concentrated on the road ahead he glanced in his mirror expecting to see a pursuing vehicle coming around the corner. Alena kept looking at her wristwatch comparing their progress to her own deadlines as they'd lost valuable time stopping to help the children. Ordering Lucien back into the car, he was determined to press on and cross into Spain as soon as possible.

He had to make sure they'd enough fuel because there was no way of telling what was available farther south. At the first opportunity, he stopped at a small garage to fill up the tank and purchased a couple of jerry cans of fuel as backup and wedged them in the trunk.

Several miles after the garage, they entered a small village comprising a few houses and shops clustered around a church on the main road. He slowed looking for a spot to stop and, while he checked the map of the rest of the route, the children could eat and drink. They drove on past the *boulangerie*, a *charcuterie* and a café with tables and chairs set out on the pavement. It was an eerie quiet. No inhabitants were to be seen as if they had got up and walked away. Halfway through the village a small square with a gravel *boulodrome* was surrounded by benches under a canopy of trees, and he turned in.

The children explored free from the confines of the car and Freddie found a set of boules lying in the dirt and threw them so that the balls made a regular metallic clicking. He pulled food out of the car and Alena prepared a meal.

Ben took the maps Bernay had given him and sought a level area of ground under the canopy of an old oak tree's luxuriant branches. He placed a stone at each corner and got on his hands and knees and traced their progress from Paris calculating the distance to the Spanish border.

So engrossed was he, he didn't realise the chatter of the children and the clicking of the boules had stopped.

# 21

RAFE COOPER AWOKE IN STAGES. HE OPENED HIS EYES WITH DIFFICULTY AS if the lids had stuck to his eyeballs. It took time and effort to determine his location. Afternoon sunshine slanted through the shutters and gradually he recognised the large crack on the ceiling he always imagined looked like a relief map of the Amazon. He sighed. He was safe. Too often he awoke in a strange bed and suffered the obvious inconveniences caused by that uncertainty.

He tried to keep his head on the pillow so as not to make any sudden movements that would aggravate the deep-seated pain emanating from somewhere behind his eyes and stretching to the back of his head. He reached out with his right hand and made contact with a whisky bottle which rolled off the table and shattered on the tiled floor.

'Fuck it!' he muttered and regretted having spoken.

With his left hand, he felt a mass of hair. He grasped the sheet and pulled it back. Out of the corner of an eye, he saw a naked brown body lying face down on the bed, her buttocks quivering as they moved in unison with her heavy breathing.

'Shit!'

He stroked them not out of passion, instead in an attempt to trigger a memory as to who she was and how they'd arrived at this point.

Recollections came to him in flashes, each painful, and just when he thought he'd grasped a strand of the truth it disappeared as a mist in a breeze. One thing he'd learned was any movement was counter-productive. From experience, he knew it was better to lie still and let the thoughts creep into his mind and build a picture.

He'd plenty of time. Everything was in hand. They wouldn't be here for days yet and by then his head might have healed. The British attaché stationed in Lisbon sighed and settled deeper into the bed. The message from Paris excited him. This was real agent's work.

He spent most of his days at Estoril's Hotel Palácio gleaning infor-mation from the other agents who frequented the bar. They'd gossip like old women, tell each other tales and each of them would go back and report it to their HQs and let them sort out the lies from the half-truths. Sometimes when people double bluffed or even treble bluffed, they let some of the truth escape. It could be worse; he might have been stuck behind enemy lines without a drink for days on end. Now that would be making a sacrifice for your country.

Getting the woman and child and American aboard the flying boat should be straightforward as long as there weren't any Nazis around. The platinum was a different matter altogether. He'd arranged a garage where they could take the car and strip it before transporting the bullion to the harbour and loading it onto the plane. It was tricky work. If the Germans caught wind of it, it would be nigh on impossible to get it off to England. Then there were the locals. While they wouldn't care a fig about his human cargo, a fortune in bullion was another matter. The sweeteners had been arranged. Still, he had to be ultra careful. If the local gangsters learned of it, they'd want a piece of the action, if not all of it.

His instructions were simple. The woman and child must be on the plane. If necessary, the American and the platinum could be left behind. And he was certain he wouldn't be allowed home again if he failed.

## 22

---

ALENA DAREN'T SPEAK. SHE DAREN'T BREATHE. ALTHOUGH THE MAN'S GRIP had immobilised her, it wasn't what stopped her from shouting a warning to Ben.

It was the gun pointed at Freddie's head.

Two brigands held Lucien and Natalie, whose eyes were wide open in terror, and everyone watched the leader of the brigands, a slight man wearing rimless spectacles and with his long fair hair flecked with grey tied in a ponytail. Days of stubble covered his chin and stress lined his face. His dark jacket was white with dust in places and he carried a bandoleer of ammunition around his shoulders. The leader observed Ben with an amused smile playing around his mouth.

Eventually, Ben realised something was wrong and lifted his head from the map. Alena willed him not to make any sudden movement because two more of the group waited behind with their carbines trained on him. She sighed with relief and relaxed. He hadn't reacted as she'd feared. Instead, he appeared to take in the whole scene around him evaluating what course of action if any was left to him.

At first, she'd believed Bernay was providing a driver, now she realised there was more to him, and she found she appreciated his company making the journey less arduous. His pleasant, strong face was framed by dark hair brushed back from his forehead. His quiet voice was reassuring, and a hint of a smile played around the corners of his mouth. If times had been different, she would have wanted to get to know him.

'So, you are with us,' the leader said, resting his rifle on his shoulder.

'Is that necessary?' Ben struggled to control his voice and pointed at the brigand holding Freddie.

'Aha, an *Américain*.' The leader turned to his men and pointed to him. 'An *Américain*.'

There was a rumble of assent.

'So how goes your war, *Américain*?'

He ignored the question. 'We're no threat to you; please take the gun away from the boy's head.'

The leader stared at him as if he were not used to being challenged, and his eyes flashed an order to the man holding Freddie who holstered his pistol.

'Where are the villagers?'

'Why? Why should you care?'

'If you've harmed them, you're no better than the Nazis,' he persisted, his voice rising, realising it was the wrong thing to say.

The leader exploded into action and within a few strides was on him grabbing him by the hair and pulling him forward into the dirt. His men cowered anticipating what might follow.

'Here, you answer my questions. Understand?'

'I understand,' he said choking on the grit clogging his mouth.

Immediately, the leader's tone changed, and he offered an apologetic smile, helping him back onto a bench and dusting him down.

'If I ask the questions, it will be better for us all. Why are you here?'

'We're on our way to Spain.'

He gestured towards the car and wished he hadn't.

The brigand studied the Bentley, his eyes running up and down the length of the machine and he knew what the leader was thinking.

'Ah, more dogs running from the Germans with their tails between their legs although you're doing it in style, eh?'

He bit his lip, annoyed he'd brought attention to the Bentley.

'To get to Spain will be difficult, no *Américain*?' And he spread his
arms wide.

'Why?'

'Because you are donating the car to our cause. I'll sit in the back
and be driven around with my ladies and everyone will say I'm a
prince.'

His men roared with laughter.

'Why would I do that?'

'Generosity. You are helping us. While you run, we will stay
and fight.'

'Yours is not a cause, you're a thief and you'll get caught.'

'I'm no thief,' he growled. 'To be fair, in exchange we'll give you a
strong horse and cart to transport your family.'

Again, his men roared with laughter and made neighing sounds.

'You can't.'

The leader shook his head and looked around as if searching for
Ben's allies.

'Who will stop me? You?' An amused expression spread across his
face. 'I don't think so. The police?' The leader raised both arms and
shrugged. 'They've run away. The villagers?' He shook his head.
'They're locked up.' And he waved a dismissive hand in the direction
of the church.

'The Germans? I think not. They'll find us hard to catch, and we'll
niggle away at their supply lines. When this war is over, we'll all be
very rich.'

His men shouted their approval.

'I've got to get them to safety,' said Ben wondering if that was still a
possibility. 'Please, we're not a danger to you.'

The leader swivelled and from the hip fired a round from his rifle at
a mongrel entering the square. With a yelp, it fell to the ground.

'That's what we do to stray dogs. Because you have children – and I
like children, I used to teach them – I will allow you safe passage on
your horse and cart. Take my offer while you can.'

He said nothing. If he argued with the brigands, they'd shoot them,
and if they left the car, the Nazis would catch them and their fate at
German hands might be a lot worse.

The leader stared at him, angered his message didn't appear to be understood, and barked an order to one of his men who scuttled off. The leader walked over to two of his men engaging them in conversation.

Striding back to where a colleague held Alena, he stopped in front of her and gave a small bow. 'Madame.' He smiled. 'It's a pleasure to make your acquaintance.'

He reached out and grabbed her by the chin forcing open her mouth.

'Good teeth, now if she were a horse I'd get a good price for her.'

'Leave her alone,' he shouted.

'You are lucky I'm not taking your woman as well.'

The men returned with a long, thick rope. The leader searched out a strong bough and instructed the men to throw the rope over it and one fashioned a noose.

## 23

THE BRIGAND'S MEN RETURNED TO THE SQUARE PULLING BEHIND THEM A middle-aged man dressed in a shiny suit. His head was on his chest and he watched his steps as he shuffled. There were traces of blood on a face contorted with fright, and his hands were tied together in front of him.

'Ah, m'sieu mayor.' The leader turned to Ben. 'He's the No.1 man in this village, or he was.'

'Please, sir,' the mayor's voice faltered. 'We've women and children in the church. Have mercy.'

'Mercy, eh?' The leader's lip curled, and he marched over to him and screamed in his face. 'You showed me no mercy. You had me kicked out of the school and my home because you believed me to be a communist just for challenging the status quo. I'd taught your children yet there was no mercy for me.'

'We made a mistake.'

'I know your kind. You use the office of mayor to line your own pockets. It's because of people like you France is in this mess. This country is an old woman, who although she's past her best plasters on her powder and rouge still thinking she's the pick of the bunch. There's no equality, no socialism. The Germans are overrunning us because we're led by geriatric generals and politicians who are too busy gorging on their greed. This is what France has become. There's now no law that isn't corrupted and so we must take it upon ourselves to be judge and jury.'

The leader spat in the dirt at Ben's feet. 'In fact, you can be the judge here and decide the fate of this criminal.'

He shrugged unsure how to answer and glanced at Alena, who was now holding a bewildered Freddie.

'It's time to confess, m'sieu mayor.'

'Confess to what?'

The leader didn't answer and instead just stared at him awaiting an answer.

Turning to Ben, the mayor pleaded. 'Please help us, m'sieu?'

'Did you not instruct the school to end my employment?' The leader interrupted.

'That's not the case.' The mayor's eyes bulged so much it looked as if they would pop out.

'Did you not tell them I was a communist?'

The mayor's gaze swept around looking for help from the crowd. 'No, but –'

'Okay, I'll give you a choice, m'sieu mayor.' The leader stamped his foot. 'Deny it and I'll shoot you between the eyes before the words leave your mouth. Confess and this court, or rather the *Américain* judge here, will sentence you to a punishment befitting your crime.'

The mayor babbled something Ben couldn't hear.

'Well, speak up man, guilty or not?' The leader sighed as if he couldn't understand why he was hesitating. 'For the time being, this is a democratic country. The choice is yours.'

Uncertain how to answer, the mayor's eyes darted between them, and as if to help him decide the leader raised his rifle.

'I'm guilty, yes guilty,' the mayor blurted out and dropped to his knees begging forgiveness and dissolving in tears.

Smiling, the leader clapped a hand on Ben's shoulder. 'If courts operated this way, we'd have a more law-abiding population.'

The mayor screamed in pain as a brigand planted a boot in his ribcage.

'There's no need for that,' the leader admonished his colleague. 'It's okay, m'sieu mayor, I'll not shoot you.'

A grimace of relief spread across the mayor's crumpled face before turning to doubt as he wondered what other things they might do to him.

'What should be his penalty, what would you suggest?'

'Make him step down as mayor and make an example of him.' He didn't know what to say. 'And let them all go.'

The leader wheeled on the shaking mayor. 'There you have it. The *Américain* is a wise judge; he has saved you from shooting. He says you have to resign as mayor.'

'Gladly, gladly,' the mayor whispered.

The leader looked doubtful. 'In this war there will be those who resist and die and those they imprison. And us who will be a continual irritant to them. Then people like you who will collaborate and give them everything they want – food, drink, drugs, women and information. When the Germans march in, you'll be up their arses and selling your own people for favours.'

'No,' the mayor protested. 'No.'

'Let him go, you've got what you wanted.' Ben went over to the mayor and pushed away his guard.

The leader moved fast and within a few steps was on him hitting him across the side of the head with the butt of his rifle. He went down fast, blood oozing from the gash, and before he blacked out, he heard Alena and Freddie screaming.

'Right,' the leader shouted. 'String him up.'

# 24

REGAINING CONSCIOUSNESS AND RUBBING BLOOD FROM HIS EYES, BEN watched as two brigands stepped forward dragging the mayor to his feet and marching him beneath the tree the leader had selected. One man found a wooden box, and they lifted the mayor, his hands still tied together in front of him, up on to it while another placed the noose over his head. A brigand held him in position and when the mayor tried to say something punched his stomach to silence him. Two others grabbed the end of the rope and waited for their leader's order.

A nod of the head delivered the sentence and the two men hauled hard on the rope, their biceps bulging and straining the cloth of their shirts. The mayor tried to keep contact with the box and was now standing on his toes. The men exerted more power pulling free his legs, which were spinning as they tried to regain the support of the platform. Then the men gave a powerful final heave and lifted the body by several feet. A cracking noise, whether it was the mayor's neck or the tree, rang out like a rifle shot breaking the silence in the square. They let go of the rope and the body dropped and the rope rasped back across the bough of the tree like an angry snake before coiling up in a heap on the body of the former mayor.

He snatched a glance at Alena, who was white-faced and shielding

Freddie's eyes from the scene, and both Lucien and Natalie stood open-mouthed in shock. Brigands dragged away the body and others milled around their leader talking in loud voices and laughing as if they had something to celebrate.

None of them heard it. It was as if the plane had switched off its engines. It exploded into sight above the rooftops, flying low and the flashes from its cannons signalling its intent. Shells spat up sand and earth as it traversed the square. The leader who'd been standing in the middle of the square watching the execution, was hit in the leg and as he fell another round thumped into his chest. Two of his men fleeing along the path of the gunfire were cut down and others dived under trees and behind walls and pointed their rifles in a token response as the plane disappeared over the roofs.

He glanced at Alena and the children to make sure they hadn't been hit and felt a surge of hope. This was their opportunity to escape. When the plane returned for more blood like a hungry vampire, the brigands would be distracted trying to repel the attack. They had a chance if they could make it to the car.

'Alena,' he called. 'Quick, over here.'

He gestured to her, and she rounded up the children and led them across to him. The brigands paid no attention now; all eyes fixed on the sky waiting for the reappearance of the plane. Dazed and frightened, the children allowed themselves to be shepherded into the relative safety of a doorway. Almost immediately an angry drone announced the return of the plane. It swooped low over the square spraying death. Bullets flew everywhere and if they didn't hit their intended target, the ricochets off the brickwork did.

It was chaos and above the sound of exploding shells and the agonising screams of the wounded and dying he shouted: 'Keep your heads down. As soon as the plane goes over, run for the car. Don't look back, just run.'

The fighter cleared the red rooftops and banked in the distance preparing for another attack. It was now or never. He pushed Alena and Freddie out towards the car and they started a stumbling run, Alena half-carrying and half pulling Freddie as if he were a rag doll.

'Come on, kids.' He took Lucien and Natalie by the hand.

Across the square, a brigand lifted a bazooka to his shoulder ready for the next attack. He had never fired the weapon and as he tried to line up the sites he accidentally pulled the trigger and fell back in surprise as it launched its rocket.

It hissed along its path towards them and Ben threw the children face down in the dirt. The shell slammed into the wall behind and the blast showered them with stonework, throwing them into the air with such force it tore off some of the children's clothes. He couldn't tell if he'd been hit although he was seeing double. The drone of the plane signalled another attack, and this was his last chance to get them to the safety of the car which Alena and Freddie had reached and were screaming at them to run.

Almost losing his balance, he struggled to his feet. 'Let's go.'

The children lay still, and he knelt and tried to pull them upright, but they didn't respond. He turned Natalie over. Her eyes were closed as if in a deep sleep. Lucien had sustained a heavy head wound and the empty eyes stared back at him.

He didn't want to leave them there, but he had to and sprinted the rest of the distance to the car and threw himself in behind the wheel.

'The children, the children,' wailed Alena. 'Don't leave them.'

'We can't do anything.' He fired the ignition as the plane began its descent again on the square.

'We must, we must.' Alena grabbed the steering wheel.

With one hand, he wrestled back control of the wheel and with the other pushed her so hard she fell backwards against the door, her eyes burning with something close to hatred.

He slammed the car into gear and they launched out onto the road away from the square. Seconds later a salvo of cannon fire ripped into the spot where the car had stood.

# 25

Alena didn't speak, she just stared out of her side window with unseeing eyes. Even Freddie was silenced by the experience. Ben didn't know how long they drove, and he remembered nothing of the route, it all passing in a blur.

He blamed himself for the deaths of Lucien and Natalie. Could he have saved their lives? If they'd sought cover until the attacks passed, would they be alive? The brigands might have spared the children. Even if they'd let them go, they would have kept the Bentley and the platinum and ended Alena and Freddie's hopes of getting to England. All he saw in the windscreen were the images of the children lying lifeless in the dirt. And anger welled up in him as he cursed this godforsaken war that destroyed the lives of the innocent.

Although he kept glancing over at Alena, her gaze was locked on the passing fields as a glorious red sunset dipped below the horizon. Exhausted and frightened, Freddie drifted into sleep on the back seat. He'd wake in the morning, and Ben hoped time would cloud the memory of the day.

What else lay in store for them? Events were coming at them so fast he reckoned they were stumbling from one crisis to another, and he was no longer in control of his life, which troubled him more than he cared to admit. Consumed with guilt, he stole another glance at Alena regretting he'd used force to quieten her.

'Alena,' he whispered, so as not to wake Freddie from his deep sleep and touched her sleeve.

'Don't.' She pulled farther away from him and so hard against the window if the door hadn't been shut tight she might have fallen out. In the deepening darkness, he couldn't make out her face although he guessed her features were set dead against him.

He peered in the mirror for a sign of headlamps confirming their pursuers were making ground on them. And he knew he must drive through the night if they were to get out of France. The driving and the adrenalin rush of the escape had taken much more out of him than he'd imagined, and he felt more tired than ever and he struggled to stay awake.

'I'm sorry about the children,' he said, not knowing whether she was listening. He had to say it aloud if only for his own satisfaction. 'There was nothing I could do for them. They were dead, I wouldn't have left them otherwise, believe me.'

She shifted her position with a rustle of her clothes.

'Sorry I pushed you, but we had to get out of there. If it's the last thing I do, I'm determined to get you to England.' And he thought it just might be.

Alena gave no sign of having heard.

Not a light showed anywhere. The only illumination was from their headlamps and he wondered if it might give away their position. He switched them off, but only for a moment because it made it impossible to see in the moonless night. The roads were empty, and they passed ghostly images of villages. The rhythmic purring of the engine was his only companion and the singing of the tyres on soft, warm tar and the swish of the car brushing roadside foliage whispered at his concentration. It dragged him deeper, deeper. The headlights picked up what he thought were shadows crossing the road, but it was just a trick of the light. His eyes closed, and his head dropped, yet just on the edge of the pit of sleep he pulled himself back to consciousness and opened his eyes and gripped the steering wheel all the tighter.

Until the next time.

Perhaps he should have opened the window, but he didn't want to disturb Freddie and Alena. So he licked his fingers and wet his eyes and blew cool air upwards from his lips. In his head, he repeated an old song and worked through Hemingway's novels and tried to remember the opening lines of his books.

Sleep.

It swooped down like a guillotine, blinding him to a sharp left-hand bend coming up fast. He awoke too late to the danger and braked hard forcing the car to careen straight through the bend and into some bushes. The collision sent them spinning back across the road hitting a tree with a glancing blow, slowing the car and gouging a long groove in its sleekness.

Alena was shouting and Freddie screaming from the back before the instinct of self-preservation kicked in. Pulling hard on the wheel, caused a horrible rending sound as the Bentley shuddered back onto the roadway and slid sideways. The car stuttered as if about to come to a halt before finding some purchase and continuing on its way.

Ben opened his window and stuck his head out and gulped in the cold night air and let it play over his eyes. In the darkness, Alena's hand reached for his arm and squeezed it. 'Let's find somewhere to stop, you must sleep.'

## 26

LOW CLOUDS ROLLED IN FROM THE OCEAN IN THE OBSIDIAN NIGHT AND they saw nothing apart from that which came within the compass of the Bentley's headlamps. Far off to the right, pinpricks of light flickered like distant stars although it was impossible to tell whether they came from houses or from boats fishing out on the ocean.

As they rounded a bend, Ben spotted a break in a stone wall and, taking a chance, drove through it. They entered what appeared to be a paddock but there was no sign of a farm or houses. It was perfect. The walls hid them from the road.

Alena had fallen into a deep sleep holding Freddie, who hugged his teddy bear for comfort and was oblivious to everything around him. She had covered them both with her jacket and her head rested on the side window and they breathed as one.

Trying to surrender to fatigue, every time he descended into sleep a mental alarm jerked him back to wakefulness. It was as if they were still driving and if he gave in they'd wander off the road and into trouble. So he admitted defeat and sat behind the wheel staring out into the darkness piecing together the steps they had taken on route to this point. The platinum shouldn't be his problem. That was down to Bernay. Why hadn't the British arranged Alena and Freddie's escape?

He felt like a swimmer being carried along by a strong current, and he had neither the strength nor the wit to save himself.

With a sigh, Alena awakened and rubbed her head as if to activate her brain and her hair covering her face like a mask. She turned to him although he couldn't figure her mood in the dark.

'Have you slept?' Her voice thick with sleep.

'Afraid not,' he replied, feeling aggrieved.

'That's not good.' He detected the irritation in her voice.

She placed Freddie on the back seat so that he wouldn't be disturbed, and smiled at Ben, opening her door and getting out, and it clicked shut behind her.

He heard her walk around the back of the car, and the trunk open and close with a dull thud. She'd been gone several minutes before he realised she wasn't coming back in, so he joined her in the cool night air. A bottle and two glasses filled with wine stood on the roof of the car.

'I wondered when you'd come.' She cupped her hands against a whisper of a breeze as she lit a cigarette. Reaching up, she took a glass and pushed it into his hand.

'Look at those stars.' She leant back on the car and tilted her head to get a better look through a gap in the cloud cover and her veil of blonde hair fell away showing a perfect profile. 'Do you imagine someday man will travel out there?'

His grunt didn't do the question justice.

'They say the light from the stars comes from long ago. Imagine if we travelled for ages and arrived to find no one there? And we were all alone in the universe.'

She took a long drag on the cigarette and screwed up her eyes as if that made it easier to see.

He was so tired he couldn't think of anything to say. 'I didn't know you smoked,' was all he could muster.

'Now and again.' She glanced at him, amused by his interest. 'Only when I'm relaxed or when I'm stressed.'

'Which is it?'

'Sorry?' she asked as if she'd used the line so many times before as a reflex and hadn't realised she'd said it.

'Relaxed or stressed?'

'I think you know the answer.' She laughed. 'Drink your wine, it'll help you sleep.'

'I'm beyond sleep. I just want to get out of this damn country.'

They touched glasses in agreement and he took a gulp of the wine and realised it was a white and winced at its sharpness as it hit the back of his throat.

'You must rest. Otherwise, we'll end up in a ditch.' She stared at the stars and puffed hard on the cigarette lighting her face. 'And that will be the end of your mission.'

'What mission?'

'Why would an American risk his life in this crazy war by driving this car out of France?'

Although he shrugged away the question, she persisted. 'Why didn't Bernay do it and try to save his own skin?'

'Can't answer for him, but I like helping damsels in distress.'

'Bullshit.' She laughed cynically. 'You'd already agreed before you met me. You were surprised when you realised you had to drive us as well. I saw it in your face.'

'Perhaps I just have a love of beautiful cars.'

She laughed again. 'Is it money?'

He winced, knowing she was closer to the truth than she realised. 'No, it's not money.'

'Don't be offended.' The tone of her voice became softer. 'That's hard to believe.'

'Okay, if you think I'm hiding a secret, I'll trade it for yours.'

She poured more wine and took another long pull on her cigarette and exhaled the smoke so that it rose in the night air making a galaxy of its own. For a moment, he thought she was on the verge of revealing something, some secret, before she recovered her composure. 'I've no secrets. What you see is what you get.'

'I see a beautiful woman.'

She flicked him a smile.

'A frightened woman and her son desperate to get out of this country.'

'True.' There was a weariness in her voice.

'What I can't understand is what's so special about you?'

'What do you mean?'

'You say the Nazis are after you and your life is in danger...'

'It is, and if they find us, they'll kill us.'

'Why?'

'Because...'

'What?'

'Because of what happened...'

'What's happened? Why are they chasing you?'

'I-I...'

'There's no reason for the Nazis to be chasing me.' He hoped they weren't. 'They've got more to worry about than Bernay's car, so why you?'

He took another swig of the wine to stop saying more, realising his persistence was closing a door that had been ajar. About to say something, instead she suppressed a sob. Maybe he should have put an arm around her, but he didn't want another rejection.

'I was a prisoner of the Nazis in Germany.' She spoke so softly he strained to hear. 'People put their own lives at risk to help us escape. We made it back to Paris then everything happened so fast we had to get out of France. Perhaps in England we will be safe, for how long I don't know.'

'Many other French people are trying to escape from the Nazis. What makes you so special? Are you a spy?'

She snorted and stamped out the cigarette on the ground to signal their conversation had ended.

'Why are the British so keen to help you escape?'

She shrugged. 'Maybe I can be of use to them.'

'I take it your husband has influence?'

'I've no husband, we're alone.'

'The boy's father?'

'He wants the boy, perhaps he wants to kill him, I don't know.' She shrugged again. 'As for me, I don't matter in his eyes. I can't expect you to trust me now.' Her hand brushed his cheek. 'When we get to England, you'll understand.'

She threw the remains of her glass on the grass and put the bottle and glasses back into the trunk. 'Come,' she ordered, 'you must rest or this magnificent car of yours will never make it to Portugal.'

She led him to her side of the car and told him to lie back with his head against the window and resting on the cushion she'd made with her jacket. As he closed his eyes, her soft hands stroked his face and her body nestled into his and he drifted into the deepest sleep.

# 27

HER TONGUE MOVED OVER HIS CHEEK AND INTO HIS MOUTH AND IT WAS rough and corpulent and very wet. He felt her face on his and the hot air from her nostrils, but the sleep was too good to give up.

'Don't,' he mumbled and averted his head as the tongue followed. 'Don't, Alena, leave me alone.' Not sure he wanted her to stop.

From somewhere, he heard a shrieking, and it came closer. He didn't want to open his eyes, and he knew if the tongue went away so would the shrieking and both continued probing at his subconscious. The noise grew in intensity and, as he was emerging from his deep sleep, he recognised the sound of hysterical laughter, not something caused by pain. With difficulty, he opened one eye and saw both Alena and Freddie, tears streaming down their cheeks, holding their sides as if the laughter might split them open.

So, who'd been kissing him? If it wasn't Alena, who was it? Or could it have been a dream?

He turned the other way and came face to face with the largest brown eyes he'd ever seen. The cow had its head through the open window of the car and was intent on washing his face again.

'Get outa here.' He rubbed his lips on the back of his hand in disgust, and it pulled back and cantered a few steps away and gazed at him with the mournful eyes of a jilted lover.

Again, Alena and Freddie roared with laughter.

'Sorry,' she said chuckling at her co-conspirator. 'I opened the window to give you air. It looks as if you've made a good friend there.'

He didn't know whether he'd called her name in his sleep or out loud and she gave no hint of having heard his indiscretion. He got out of the car and shooed the cow away and it broke into a trot and hurdled a low fence to join a group of relatives.

It was one of those crisp, cold mornings when heavy dew covered the fields like icing on a cake so that everything appeared fresh and untouched. A low mist on the horizon wrapped them in their own world and not even birds disturbed the silence. They were alone, at least for now.

He could see his choice for their overnight stop had been perfect. They were hidden behind stone walls and there were no houses or farm buildings in the vicinity. While he explored the perimeter of their camp, Alena and Freddie removed the rest of the food and water from the car and set up a spread on the Bentley's bonnet.

In the distance through the mist, he could just make out the Pyrenees, the path to their freedom. Once over the border, they'd be in Spain and, he hoped, safer. Or maybe he was deluding himself. While hidden behind these walls, they'd have been out of sight of anyone following them. It was also possible during the night their pursuers had passed them and gone on ahead. Now, apart from keeping watch behind them, there was the possibility they could be ahead and waiting to ambush them anywhere along the route or at the border crossing into Spain. There again, he tried to reassure himself, they would have to know where they were headed. He'd no reason to think the Nazis could have found out the Bentley was carrying the platinum.

Unless?

As he understood it, apart from British Intelligence, only two other people, Bernay and Renard, knew the plan. And even Renard didn't know the whole story. He'd been sent away when they discussed details and he didn't know the route. Surely Bernay wouldn't have waited around for the Nazis to invade because if they got their hands on the director they'd soon get the information needed to track them down. No, he tried to convince himself, he must have gone into hiding.

And there was Alena. He wasn't sure whether he believed her story. Why were the Nazis wasting time looking for a runaway mother and her child? According to Bernay, the British were very keen to get her out of the country. Or was it just a smokescreen to hide the fact British Intelligence were more interested in the platinum than they made out?

Although he wished he could just walk off over the fields and keep on walking, he knew Bernay had handed him a poisoned chalice he couldn't let go. He glanced back at the Bentley and for the first time wished he was driving an ordinary Citroen.

Alena and Freddie's chatter over their makeshift breakfast broke into his thoughts and the need for them to get moving again spurred him into action.

'Come on.' He clapped his hands to bring them back to reality. 'We must get going, the sooner we get to Spain the better.'

Alena looked at him in surprise as if she'd forgotten why they were there. 'Come on,' she shouted at Freddie springing to her feet. 'You can finish it in the car.' And she bundled him into the back seat and gathered up the remains of the breakfast and put them in the trunk.

As he sat behind the wheel, Ben broke out in a sweat so much that his shirt was wet against his back. What if the car didn't start? They'd be stranded and sitting ducks. He'd often found machines were unreliable and always when you most needed them to perform. He could have written a book about how often his old Ford had failed to fire.

The Bentley was now showing the scars of its journey. In escaping the brigands, gunfire had raked the sleek bonnet leaving gouges in the bodywork and, he feared, possible internal damage. Holding his breath, he flicked the ignition switch, set the advance/retard lever on the steering wheel and coaxed it into life with the choke. She coughed with the growl of a heavy smoker. Coughed again. And then the massive engine found its voice making the whole car vibrate.

They lurched out onto the road and as the morning wore on the sun burned away the mist, and in the sunshine, everything was fresh and new and the war and the Germans seemed a million miles away. They passed through villages getting ready for the day and villagers waved and stopped to stare as they drove through. Some even offered wine and cheese, rather giving it to travellers than letting it fall into German hands. They waved their thanks and pressed on. He kept his foot to the floor wherever possible always aware he needed to nurse the Bentley. Once in Spain, they still had a long road ahead of them and he'd no idea just how much strain the weight of the platinum was putting on the car's chassis.

Alena was more relaxed as she chatted with her son, pointing out sights of interest and answering questions coming in an endless stream. In contrast, Ben was becoming more concerned. Had the Germans entered Paris yet? What if Bernay, through a mistaken sense of duty, had stayed on at the bank? What if they'd tortured the truth out of him? With a kaleidoscope of thoughts and consequences running through his mind, he kept watching for pursuers and concentrating on trying to spot an ambush ahead.

Outside the coastal town of Hendaye and close to the Spanish border, what he had feared happened. A slow-moving convoy of a variety of modes of transport clogged the road ahead, their occupants all with the same aim of getting out of France. They stopped and started for a few feet at a time and he slammed his hands on the steering wheel in exasperation. Pushing her hair back from her face, she gave him one of those smiles telling him not to worry. *We'll get there.*

Gradually they ground to a stop and from where they sat on a slight hill they looked into a dip before the road rose to the border. Spanish flags fluttered in the light breeze and the Spanish police, the Guardia Civil, and gendarmes were checking cars and their occupants.

'Oh no,' she gasped and glanced back over her shoulder as if expecting to see the Germans emerge behind her.

'What's wrong, *maman?*' Worried by the anxiety in her voice, Freddie leant over and put his arms around his mother's neck for reassurance.

She half turned and smiled. 'It's all those cars, so many of them, it's like being in Paris.'

Freddie giggled. 'Paris with cows.'

The halt was terminal. No one was going anywhere, at least not for some time. Up ahead, people got out of their cars and were talking with much shouting, waving and shrugging of shoulders. They climbed out of the Bentley, joining their fellow refugees in an attempt to glean what information they could. A man walking back along the line of cars told them he'd been waiting for at least several hours.

She shook her head in frustration and again looked at her wristwatch. 'You stay with Freddie. I'll walk on ahead and try to find out what's happening. It'll be better if I go alone.'

Freddie grabbed his arm. 'Don't worry, Ben, you stay with me. I'll look after you.'

He ruffled the boy's hair, and they both laughed as they watched Alena progress along the line of vehicles, stopping every so often to become engrossed in conversation until they lost sight of her. Freddie stood in the front passenger seat jumping up and down and pulling knobs and twisting dials on the dashboard always asking 'What's this for, Ben? What does this do?'

Seeing he was preoccupied with his thoughts, he turned and pushed his face close to Ben's. 'Why did you ask *maman* to stop it?'

'Stop what?' Ben asked with one eye watching out for Alena.

'I don't know, you just said it before you woke up,' Freddie said with mischief shining in his pale blue eyes.

He felt his cheeks burning with embarrassment and before he could reply Alena's face, showing a mixture of concern and defeat, appeared in the car window. She was out of breath as if she'd been running and she blurted out. 'Gendarmes. They're coming. Along the line. Checking people's papers.'

'Just what we don't want?'

'It's a big problem,' she said regaining her composure. 'They've closed the border unless your Spanish.'

'Oh, God, what'll we do now?'

'People are saying Paris has fallen.' Her face crumpled, and she was near to tears.

He looked past her and up to the northern slopes of the Pyrenees lined with forests of beech trees and above them the dark brown granite of the mountains. And he wondered if this would be the end of the road.

## 28

THEY CAME ON THE MORNING OF FRIDAY, JUNE 14TH, 1940. THE GERMANS entered the city by the Aubervilliers Gate and marched through the north-western suburbs and on until they paraded down the Champs-Élysées. It was low key at first with just a few motorcycles with sidecars reconnoitring the route into the city. Then trucks followed and stopped at street corners and soldiers jumped out to set up machine-gun posts all the time cracking jokes to each other in guttural voices. Tanks squeaked and rattled and pumped out an evil-smelling black smoke. Armoured reconnaissance cars, anti-tank units, and trucks full of soldiers, followed by more soldiers on horseback. Finally, the rest of the army swaying as one and the tramp, tramp, tramp of their boots setting a rhythm the whole city moved and shook to.

Millions had already fled the invaders, and Paris was almost empty. Yet those remaining attempted to carry on with a semblance of normality as though this was their stubborn protest at what was about to befall them. Although many of the shops were boarded up, house-wives still shopped while others sat out at café tables determined to have one last drink while still free to do so. There was even laughter although the forced hilarity sounded more like mourners at a wake celebrating that for now they were at least alive.

On several streets, particularly the Champs-Élysées, Parisians lined the roadway. Some dressed in their Sunday finery; some crying, even men. The adults watched in defiant and sullen acceptance. They had no choice. This was an army sweeping all before it; no one could stand up to its power. There was a crushing inevitability that they'd become slaves in their own land and no one could help them. They were deserted yet their silence gave a message of protest to the invaders. To let the Germans know they were witnesses to an act of barbarity and desecration.

As the convoy rattled by, children jumped around and shrieked. Dogs chased the vehicles and ran back whimpering with their tails between their legs when they got too close. Although older children shouted abuse and made rude gestures, the soldiers never acknowledged them. Once defeated, they'd ceased to exist as human beings. It didn't change even when a group of youths became more adventurous pelting the soldiers with vegetables. The Germans just sat in their trucks looking straight ahead holding their rifles.

At the tail end of the procession followed by a black Citroen saloon car, came more trucks of soldiers different from those who had preceded them. They wore black uniforms instead of the grey of the army. While some troops had looked almost boyish, these were more mature with thickset heads and brutal faces. They laughed and joked and looked around and when one spotted an attractive woman he'd shout and wave to the crowd. Sometimes, someone would wave back, but they were forced to drop their arm by the disapproving looks of their neighbours.

Growing in confidence, the youths had replenished their stocks of vegetables and now renewed their attacks on these black-uniformed soldiers. A large potato flew out of the mob and through the open window of a truck catching a soldier on the nose knocking his helmet off his head. The truck swerved out of the line and screeched to a halt and six of the black-suited, black-booted troopers, carrying rifles, jumped down. A soldier wearing the black uniform of an SS officer with a khaki shirt and a black tie with a swastika pin and a skull and crossbones on his cap appeared from behind the truck and shouted at the youths.

'*Kommen.*' He gestured with a gloved hand and smirked. 'Come here.'

The youths' ringleader stepped towards him and his mates crowded in behind him. The officer barked a command, and the troopers lifted their rifles to their shoulders and each fired several times. The youths fell together in a heap and for seconds there was no sound as if the Parisians were holding their breath in disbelief. With a sneer on his lips, the officer unclipped his pistol from its holster and pointed it at the head of the twitching ringleader and fired. The crowd gasped as one.

The officer was heading back to his truck when a piercing scream caused him to pause. A small girl ran out of the crowd and knelt by the fallen youth. She cradled his head in her arms and her tears mingled with the blood from his wounds. The officer stepped forward and pulled her away with his left arm and raised his Luger to her head.

'Let this be a lesson to you,' he shouted at the crowd. 'You mustn't insult soldiers of the Reich.'

He returned his attention to the girl.

'Halt!'

The Citroen had pulled in beside the truck and Ludwig Weber climbed out.

'Put away your gun,' he ordered as he walked over to the officer and removed the soldier's hand from the girl's shoulder.

'We're here to occupy Paris not to exterminate them,' he whispered so no one could hear.

Weber was smiling at him and the officer pondered whether to shoot him although there was something about his eyes that made him think better of it, and he snapped to attention.

'*Heil*, Hitler.' He saluted and swivelled on his heel before climbing back aboard the truck. '*Gehen wir, schnell,*' he shouted at the driver and the truck lurched away.

Weber stroked the girl's head and spoke to her before leading her back to the pavement and sending her on her way with a gentle shove.

Somewhere deep in the crowd someone clapped, then another, and another until there were perhaps twenty clapping in unison. It was a slow handclap, and from far away, came the strains of *La Marseillaise*.

## 29

ALTHOUGH IT WAS JUNE, THE RAGGED PEAKS OF THE PYRENEES TO THE EAST were dusted with snow that hadn't succumbed to the warm winds sweeping up from Spain to the south. And Ben cursed their size and their grandeur because these mountains might prove to be the walls of their prison.

The gendarmes made their way along the line of waiting vehicles occasionally pulling one out of the queue to be searched and its occupants interrogated. It was only a matter of time before they got to them and once they saw their papers they'd face many difficult questions. At best, they'd have to turn back and at worst, if the police discovered the platinum, they'd face arrest. They needed no more delays if they were to rendezvous in Estoril. Bernay had been emphatic the flying boat wouldn't wait for them. They had only one chance.

From what Alena gleaned, there was no way through to Spain on this road today or in the foreseeable future. Turning around wouldn't improve the situation because they would risk falling into the clutches of their pursuers. And even if they travelled farther east to find another crossing, the detour could mean missing their deadline.

As he gazed up at the mountains marvelling at their rugged beauty, his eyes drifted downwards to the wooded foothills where smoke from farmhouses drifted in the morning sky.

It was an idea. Not a great one. But perhaps their only chance.

Twenty yards on the left, a lane ran through fields of nodding, yellow sunflowers, complementing the lazy blue of the sky. He traced its path all the way up into the foothills. Not much more than a farm track and about the width of the Bentley, presumably used by farmers' cars and wagons.

'Hold on, guys,' he said to Freddie and Alena and fired the engine. 'We're leaving.'

'For God's sake, where are we going?' Alena dug her fingers into the leather of her seat.

With just enough space between them and the car in front, he pulled onto the verge to an angry chorus as they drove down the grass scattering those sitting and enjoying the sunshine. Horns blared as they turned into the lane and the noise attracted the gendarmes who called up a van which they sent in pursuit, its klaxon blaring. He couldn't risk going faster. The rutted path with a raised grassy section in the middle might pull off the bags of platinum or worse still rip out the exhaust. The pursuing police van had no such worries and gained on them with a gendarme hanging out of the passenger door gesticulating and shouting.

The farther they progressed, the narrower the lane became and as they rounded a bend bushes and brambles encroached from either side scraping along the sides of the car. And he winced at what it was doing to the Bentley's bodywork. The vegetation forced the gendarme to retreat into the cab and, as it was being buffeted from either side, the van had to slow. With no way through, the gendarmes switched off the klaxon and reversed back along the lane.

Freddie, who was on his knees watching the pursuit through the rear window, shouted and clapped his hands. 'We're winning, we're winning.' And he shrieked with laughter.

# 30

BERNAY SAT ALONE IN HIS HIGH-CEILINGED, WOOD-PANELLED OFFICE WITH A glass of Armagnac in front of him and looked around it with affection. He'd enjoyed his time here. He had achieved some of his greatest moments in business in this room and he was sad it had to end in this way. A photograph of his wife and two daughters in a heavy silver frame sat on his desk and he picked it up looking at each in turn. He wished for once he'd put personal matters before business and had gone with them to the south of France.

Earlier, he'd received news of Renard, found in an alleyway with his throat cut and his wallet stolen. He wondered if Renard had been carrying the brown envelope containing his pay-off. That must have been why the murderer had targeted him.

The bank was much quieter today. Some staff went out to watch the Germans entering the city; others walked away and kept on walking. He questioned why he should await the arrival of the Germans. He supposed he'd always had problems delegating and his sense of responsibility was all-consuming. Any other person might have put his own safety first, yet he found it hard to desert his post no matter the consequences to him. Someone in a senior position should be at the helm when the Nazis arrived at the bank.

The sound of vehicles coming to an abrupt halt outside the bank shook him out of his reverie and he moved over to the window and opened a shutter. Two trucks of German troops and two cars flying swastikas from their bonnets had pulled up outside. There was a deafening clattering of boots on marble as soldiers ran into the building and up the stairs taking up positions at strategic points. The remaining staff cowered behind their desks and some women wept, and for once Pierre was nowhere to be seen.

He sat back behind his desk, lifted the glass to his lips and drained it in one. Refilling it, he rested his elbows on the desk and steepled his fingers in front of him and waited. Surprised they showed him the courtesy of knocking, he hesitated long enough to prevent them breaking it down. *'Entrez,'* he said with resignation. Two troopers pushed open the doors and entered with rifles at the ready. Their gaze swept around the room before they nodded to figures behind them. Two men in grey suits – one older than him and the other much younger – followed them into the room and sat on the two chairs before Bernay's desk without being asked. Behind them came a stout army officer who looked as if he was about to burst out of his uniform. The troopers guarded the door.

The older man had a few strands of grey hair plastered to his scalp and rimless spectacles. And he had the careworn look of someone who had been here before and didn't want to be again. 'Good morning, Monsieur Bernay, my name is Müller and I represent the Reichsbank in Berlin,' he said. 'This is my colleague.' He gestured to the younger man although he didn't give his name. The younger man didn't acknowledge Bernay and just stared at him with an intensity he found disturbing.

Müller continued: 'We must carry out an audit of your resources...'

'You will be expected to help.' The younger man interrupted him and moved forward in his chair to emphasise his point.

Müller appeared embarrassed. 'I am sure the director will give us every assistance.'

'He has no option,' said the younger man determined to have the last word.

'Yes, you're right,' agreed a chastened Müller.

The officer's boots were making an unwelcome noise on the wooden floor. 'It's too dark in here,' he snapped. And he stomped around the room opening up the shutters to let in the daylight.

Müller flashed him a look of irritation before continuing. 'Let's conduct this as bankers. May I?' He pulled his chair closer to the desk.

Bernay stared, wary of the German's civility. 'This is pointless. What's in this bank is the property of France and its people...'

'Please.' Müller glanced sideways at his colleague as if asking his permission. 'We're not barbarians intent on ransacking your bank. We will not fill our pockets and go off with your money. Everything will be done under the new order in the country.'

He said nothing as he felt everything slipping away from him.

'We must arrange the paperwork of course. There will be a daily charge made to the French government to cover our costs to occupy Paris.'

'I'm not authorised by the government to make any such payments.'

Trying to insert a finger between his red neck and the collar of his shirt, the officer interjected. 'I'm surprised you know who your government is. They've run off to the south like mongrel dogs.'

The intensity of Müller's glare silenced him. 'As I said, the paperwork will be completed and I'm sure you realise it's in your own best interests to co-operate with us fully.'

Bernay's eyes blazed. 'However you do it, it won't be legal.'

The younger man stood up and leant both hands on the desk. 'You are not in a position to dictate. The High Command believes banks are vulnerable to all sorts of renegades in a time of war, so my orders are to instigate the immediate transportation of France's reserves – gold etcetera – to Berlin for safe-keeping.'

The director nearly choked.

As if ready to squash an irritating insect, the younger man said: 'Be careful, Bernay. If we find a problem, it won't be good for you...'

A noise at the door made him swivel with impatience.

A tall man with greying hair and wearing a long black leather coat had entered the room. He walked past the guards before they had time to raise their rifles and stopped to have a whispered conversation with the officer.

Agitated, the officer stood to attention and gave the salute and clicked his heels. 'Gentlemen,' he said. 'We must postpone this meeting. Herr Weber is on urgent business on the orders of Reichsführer Himmler.'

Müller got to his feet, fear contorting his face.

Bernay felt pain in the pit of his stomach as if someone had reached in and was wringing his intestines and nausea washed over him with the force of a wave.

'Not you.' The officer leered at Bernay. 'Herr Weber will talk to you in private.'

# 31

THEY CLIMBED LEAVING BEHIND THE NOISE OF THE CROWDS AND HONKING horns and the road wound left and right as it found the easiest way up the foothills, often doubling back on itself. It rose all the way from the Atlantic in the shadow of those majestic peaks and the slopes were so wooded they couldn't see what they'd left behind.

The Bentley bucked and twisted, and he worried the weight of the platinum and the bumping and grinding could cause the chassis to collapse. Although it was holding up for now, it must be causing a severe strain on the engine and might surrender, at probably the most crucial moment.

With only trees to look at, Freddie became bored and kept on asking 'Are we there yet?' and complained of feeling sick, and Alena pulled him over and sat him on her lap and that quietened him.

He had no idea where 'there' was.

As if reading his thoughts, she asked with a look growing more intense by the second. 'Do you think this is going somewhere?'

'Somewhere, yes. Whether it'll be where we want to be is another matter.' He shrugged, annoyed he didn't sound more positive.

The higher they climbed the more his great idea looked to be heading for a dead end although he couldn't admit it just yet. The track here was even more rutted and under the grass and mud were boulders causing the Bentley to spring from rock to rock and judder into the gaps. This might be passable for animals or perhaps a cart drawn by donkeys, but he doubted whether a vehicle had ever been here before. It became monotonous. Turn a bend and another stretch of rutted track hemmed in by trees stretched out before them and then another and another. And Freddie's mood grew darker.

As they rounded yet another bend, the track petered out and before them stood an inn displaying years of neglect. In the middle of a clearing, it faced out across the Bay of Biscay. Built in the traditional Basque style with its timbers stained ox-blood red, tiles had slipped from its roof and the shutters were broken and a wooden sign with the word *Etchegarry* engraved on it hung on one chain and swung in the breeze.

Ben summoned his most upbeat voice, glad to get out from behind the wheel 'Let's get out and see if there are signs of life.'

Freddie whooped with delight and ran off to explore. Alena, however, clasped her arms to her body in a defensive posture and looked up in despair at the dilapidated building. As he approached the inn, it was obvious it hadn't been inhabited for years. Some time ago a part of the clearing was turned into a garden, now overgrown, and in it were rickety wooden tables and benches that would have collapsed had anyone sat on them. From the back of the inn came a dull rhythmic thud of the chopping of wood.

She went off ahead, knocking several times on the inn's large oak door and, getting no answer, pushing on it. It made a tired creaking noise as it swung open, and he followed her into what must have been the inn's main room with several tables and benches and chairs hewn out of tree trunks. Dust carpeted everything in the room and the musty atmosphere caused them to gag and cobwebs hung from the ceiling like a forest of ferns.

'Hello, hello,' she shouted, and louder. 'Is there anyone here?'

There was no response and Ben noted the chopping had stopped and in the silence a breeze appeared to make the house sigh as if weary with age.

'What now?' She flopped on a leather couch in front of a massive inglenook fireplace, sending a cloud of dust into the air. Freddie had followed them in and went around the room chattering to his teddy bear.

Once this had been a thriving inn serving walkers and climbers on their way to the peaks. Their last chance of a meal and refreshment before facing the challenge ahead and later they might return to the inn for a celebratory banquet. But customers had stopped coming long ago.

'Where do we go from here?' She turned to him, demanding an answer.

He shrugged. 'It's a dead end.' He ran a hand through his hair.

'Will we have to go back?' Her voice broke as she fought back tears.

He didn't answer and wondered what he could say to stop her worrying more.

'We have to get to England,' she said.

'Who are you?' A man's gruff voice boomed out behind them. 'What are you doing here?'

His bulk filled the doorframe and even Freddie stopped chattering and watched him in awe. Stripped to the waist, he carried a large axe over a shoulder and his muscles and chest glistened with sweat. His long unkempt hair, black as a crow's wing, tumbled over his shoulders and his eyes burned with suspicion.

'No one comes here,' he said throwing down his axe.

'We're sorry,' Alena said. 'We didn't mean –'

'Not since my wife died.'

'– to intrude.'

'What do you want here?'

'We're trying to get over the border into Spain,' Ben said, 'and wondered if there was –'

'No chance,' the man snorted, picking up a rag and wiping the sweat from his face. 'The way to Spain is back down the mountain.'

'I know –'

'There's a road that will take you.'

'We can't, we can't get through,' Alena said.

The man showed no interest in their problem and spread his arms as if it was all he could offer. 'So, bad luck.'

'With the Germans invading your country we have to get away,' persisted Ben.

The man glowered at him and spat on the ground and turned away muttering 'La Pays Basque.'

She grabbed Ben's arm and whispered. 'He's Basque. They believe they are a separate country neither French nor Spanish with their own customs and language.'

'Pardon, monsieur,' he apologised. 'I can pay for your help?'

The man turned back and squinted at them trying to evaluate their worth.

'What good's money in this hole? Now that's a car you have there. Give it to me and maybe we can talk.'

'I can't.' He shook his head. 'It goes with us.'

The man roared with laughter, looking at him as if he were an imbecile.

'Only mountain goats go up there.'

'Look, I know refugees are smuggled across the border into Spain,' he said.

The man's face was impassive and if he knew of smuggling, he was making sure he gave nothing away.

'We're desperate and our lives are in danger.'

The man stared at him and Ben reached into his jacket and pulled out a wad of notes, not knowing how much was there, and threw it on the table in front of him.

'Will that do?'

The man pondered, suggesting it was a possibility although it would require more negotiation.

'Maybe I can find someone to guide you.' He picked up the money. 'It needs all of this though.'

'So?'

'Once in Spain, your problems are just beginning. The Spanish are imprisoning refugees in camps before sending them back to France. You need help on the other side, but this is not enough.'

The man threw the money back down on the table as if he'd been insulted. Ben reached into another pocket and removed the rest of the money Bernay had given him and placed it on the table. Picking up the new bundle, the man put it together with the first one, licked his fingers and counted the money. When he'd done, he stuck it in his back pocket.

With a cursory nod of his head to Alena, he said 'You'll find bread and some *fromage de brebis* and coffee in the kitchen.'

'Ewes cheese,' Alena explained.

'Stay here. I have someone to see although I can't promise anything.'

And he went out muttering.

## 32

WEBER ORDERED MÜLLER AND HIS SIDEKICK AND THE SOLDIERS TO LEAVE the room and waited until they'd closed the doors behind them. He approached the desk and offered his hand to Bernay who shook it as if he were being presented with a wet fish.

'My name's Ludwig Weber, I'll call you Philippe if I may.'

Noting Weber spoke with a regional French accent, he said nothing knowing it wouldn't make any difference if he had. Weber sat in the seat Müller had vacated, scanning the office, trying to empathise with the man he would destroy.

'Do you mind if I smoke?' Weber had already reached inside his coat and pulled out a gold cigarette case. He opened it and offered him one.

Determined the German wouldn't lull him into a false sense of security, he waved away the offer.

Weber tapped the cigarette on the case before lighting up and letting the smoke creep into his lungs and exhaled long and hard. 'Let's be civilised,' he said, knowing civilised was the last thing he intended. 'These are crazy times, my friend.'

*Don't call me friend.*

'In fact, we might have been friends, you and me, but for all this.'

And he looked around the room as Bernay wondered what he meant. 'Because circumstances are beyond our control we find ourselves on different sides of the fence. I don't enjoy what's going on any more than you do – one thing we can't do is dictate the course of life. You know in Germany many believe Adolf Hitler to be a genius, even a messiah.' He shrugged his shoulders as if it were unthinkable and turned down the corners of his mouth to show he wasn't one of them. 'And there are just as many who think him to be a madman. They can't voice their opinions in public of course, not even in private to the ones nearest and dearest to them.'

Weber paused and frowned. 'I can say this to you, but if those people out there –' he waved an arm towards the door '– heard what I was saying they'd shoot me.' He gave a weak attempt at a smile, but the grey eyes didn't join in.

He allowed the German to talk because for every minute wasted the Bentley would be closer to safety. 'What did you do before the war?' he asked, not caring for one minute what Weber did.

'I was in newspapers, an investigative reporter.'

'Couldn't you have continued covering the war? Rewriting history?'

'No,' he appeared amused. 'In Germany, we are told what we must do for the Fatherland. We've no choice.'

'Not good.' The director shook his head.

'I, too, have a family, and it's my Achilles heel.'

A dead weight grew heavier in his gut and a shiver rippled down his spine.

'Each time they want me to do something, they ask after the well-being of my relatives. Although they do it with a smile, the inference is there.'

The German paused. 'How is your family, Philippe?'

The mention of family flustered him, and he swallowed hard and mumbled something Weber didn't understand.

'I need information from you. The quicker you tell me, the better for everyone.'

He had no reason to believe Weber was aware of the platinum and he was convinced he was on a fishing expedition. 'I doubt if I can help you.' He hoped his face didn't betray his secrets.

Ignoring the remark, Weber continued. 'I understand, and we can sort this out with no need for –' He picked up a pencil from Bernay's desk and played with it between his fingers.

'The need for what?'

'Unpleasantness.' He snapped the pencil in two and took another drag on the cigarette and his eyes appeared to glaze over as the smoke did its work. 'My colleagues have different ideas.' He waved an arm in an expansive gesture. 'It's so unnecessary.'

Weber shifted closer, and Bernay smelt the cigarettes on his breath. 'Let me tell you this. We Germans, there are four kinds. Those soldiers out there are regular army. They are people who joined up to defend their country and fight out of patriotism. Then there are the thugs, the SS and their like who enjoy inflicting pain. They are sadists and you should never allow yourself to fall into their hands. The Gestapo, they are evil,' and he shook his head at the thought of it. 'They will go to any lengths to manipulate the circumstances to meet their agendas. They have no friends, only enemies. Last, we have people like me who are...' Weber struggled to find the right word, '... facilitators, I suppose. And we combine all three. You love your country and want to do your best for it. Commendable. I'm in the same position. You want to defend what's left and, naturally, I want Germany to win this war, so we can return to a normal life. Who's in charge is of no importance, I'm given a job to do and I'll do it to the best of my ability for my country's sake. I suppose we're both prisoners of our patriotism.'

Weber waved aside his attempted reply and leant over and picked up his glass. 'Ah, beautiful. Irish crystal, perhaps? What's happening in Europe is changing everything – the way we live, the way we think, and to whom we owe our allegiance. Opposition to the Nazis is futile, you know. There is nowhere to hide. We'll take Britain soon. Italy is with us. Spain is sitting on the fence. And we can swat Switzerland and Portugal as if they were flies.'

The German studied him to see if he understood his meaning. 'You probably still think France can be saved. It can't...'

The glass dropped from his hand and shattered on the hardwood floor, spreading out fragments across the room and staining the wood with the Armagnac. 'There's France – the whole of Europe.' He moved some shards of glass with the toe of his shoe. 'Like that crystal it's shattered, and you'll never get your France back in one piece again.'

He lit another cigarette, repeating his ritual.

'So, Philippe, you can see it's better you answer my questions now.' His voice had an edge as if the conversation had ended and it was time to do business.

He waited in silence to hear what Weber wanted to know.

'Platinum?'

He shifted in his chair.

Weber smiled at his unease.

'What do you know of platinum, Philippe?'

'It's the world's most valuable metal.'

'Don't patronise me, monsieur director.' Weber's lips curled into a sneer. 'What have you done with the platinum?'

'I have no idea what you're talking about. I know nothing about platinum.'

'Arnaud Renard.'

It was both a question and a statement, and Weber's eyes narrowed waiting for a reaction.

The director gasped, and Weber watched as the blood drained from the banker's face. The German smiled knowing he'd opened the door to his victim's mind.

'Yes, Renard. He had interesting information.'

'You killed Arnaud?' His voice only a croak.

Like an eagle surveying a lesser species it was ready to eat, the German said nothing although his unblinking eyes never left his face. 'Poor Renard. He pleaded with me to allow him to die. Let's not waste any more time. Tell me about the platinum.'

He shook his head.

'I know about the platinum and Ben Peters.'

'This is all fantasy,' he said, realising his denials were useless.

'Sounds like it. Ingots of precious metal strapped to the chassis of your Bentley.'

Another shake of his head.

Weber ignored the denial and leant across the desk, so close Bernay felt the spray from his mouth. 'Tell me, Philippe, for everyone's sake.'

What had Renard told him?

'He couldn't tell me where the bullion was headed, unfortunately.'

That was a relief, and he watched warily as Weber got to his feet.

'It's pointless to consider lying. Just tell me what you planned.'

'I've nothing to tell you,' he stressed.

Weber sighed with a look of disappointment as if dealing with a recalcitrant child.

'I can call in my colleagues now,' he gestured to the door, 'and they'll take great pleasure in beating the truth out of you...'

Weber picked up the photograph of Bernay's family and walked behind him causing him to turn in his seat to follow him. Weber studied it for several seconds and Bernay thought he saw his features soften. 'Sweet,' he muttered, 'as I said, let's be civilised. We're both family men.'

Somewhere inside his head, he heard alarm bells ringing.

'There's always a way to get things done. You know the old story about the sun and the wind?'

The director looked puzzled.

'At school, they taught me this tale about the wind and the sun looking down on an old man trudging along a road wearing a heavy overcoat. The wind wagered the sun that it could get the man to take off the coat. The sun replied that he wouldn't, but that he could. The harder the wind blew the more the old man clung to his coat and wrapped it around himself. When the wind was blown out, the sun smiled on the old man, illuminating the road with his rays. And the man was so hot he removed his coat.'

Weber waited for him to understand. 'So, look at me as the sun. I believe it's better to encourage people to talk.'

He dreaded what Weber was going to say.

'Your wife and two daughters are enjoying their holiday, are they not?'

He felt a numbness spreading through him and a desire to be sick.

'They went for a walk this morning along the Promenade des Anglais in Nice. They didn't return for lunch. Perhaps it's time you talked to your wife.'

# 33

THE MOUNTAIN AIR SHARPENED THEIR APPETITES AND ALENA RUSTLED UP hot coffee and bread and cheese supplemented by the scraps from the car, and they devoured them. The mysterious man had left, and Ben had no idea when or if he might return. Or where their next meal was coming from. When food is scarce, the need to eat is always greater, and they were hungry. And cold. As the afternoon settled, the temperature dropped and up in the mountains it was much colder than on the coast.

While Alena and Freddie explored the grounds of the inn, he scouted farther afield, climbing the slope behind the building hoping to discover a route over the mountain. To his disappointment, he saw nothing resembling a trail. The climb was hard, and the slopes thick with trees. It might be possible to make it on foot, although difficult with Freddie, but to drive would be impossible. Yet he convinced himself there had to be a way over the mountains. Thousands of refugees fled along the whole range of the Pyrenees and cross-border smuggling was the main industry in the area. He was sure that even if they had to ditch the Bentley they could escape.

The higher he climbed the easier it became to get his bearings. He looked over the treetops and down to the Basque coast stretching from

San Sebastian in Spain in the South to the beaches of France's Biarritz in the North and the sun glinted on the white Atlantic breakers. On the slopes, herds of pottok, the solid little horses that live wild on the mountains, roamed and redheaded manech ewes grazed and, high above, the fauve vultures circled in their endless quest for food.

Oceans and mountains spiritually influenced him, and the silence was so absolute it was as if time had halted and they existed in a parallel world untouched by what was happening on the coast. The feeling passed as swiftly as the shadows of clouds rippling across the mountain. He was fooling himself if he didn't think they'd soon be back there facing the same problems. No longer did he blame Bernay for having put him in this situation. He was beyond that. His priority was to get Alena and Freddie to safety even if it meant leaving the Bentley and the platinum. He wondered what Bernay would have done if he were in his shoes, and it was a decision he preferred to delay until the last moment.

At times like these, he wished he could speak to his father who always provided wise counsel. When confronting a problem, his father laid out the facts before him and investigated the possibilities before making a judgement. But, he supposed, not everyone had that unique mind although he wasn't sure his decisions were always right. Just to speak to him, to listen to him talking through the possibilities. He'd always sought his father's company because he loved him and liked him, too. Maybe that was the reason he fished with him even though he hated sitting on the banks of a river with the damp eating into his bones and nothing happening for hours. When he first went at the age of eight, his father asked as they were packing away their gear 'What did you think of it?'

'Great,' he lied, 'but we caught nothing.'

'No!' His father stopped what he was doing and smiled at him as if ready to impart a mystical truth. 'That's what makes it a great day's fishing. To sit here all day and not catch a thing.'

He shook his head as if he believed it to be the greatest experience a man could have and hesitated when he saw Ben's questioning look. 'It's perfect,' he explained, 'you don't feel any guilt about killing a living creature. The day I catch fish, I'll give up fishing.'

Ben returned the next week and the next and on until the pressures of teenage years diverted him from doing anything other than that which provided basic pleasures.

Freddie was shrieking with laughter and Alena calling after him as they played hide and seek in the woods. And he smiled to hear them having fun because things would get much harder.

Inside, the inn had a brooding presence as if haunted by terrible secrets. He looked around for proof that the man still lived there which would mean there was a chance of his returning and not just pocketing their money and disappearing. The stairs creaked under his weight and cobwebs wrapped around his face and stuck to his hair. No one lived up here. Years of undisturbed dust lay inches thick on the wooden floorboards and most of the rooms were empty save for the odd chair or cabinet. In one, a hand mirror and hairbrush, still with dark hair in it, lay on the window ledge as if someone had been interrupted while brushing their hair. And in another, a broken doll and old newspapers yellowed with age. Echoes of another life. It was as he feared. The man had taken their money and disappeared with no intention of returning. The decision he needed to make approached him like a gigantic wave.

By the time Alena and Freddie returned, he'd gathered enough wood to light a fire so that the room glowed with warmth. Flushed by their exercise, they entered the room stamping their feet on the stone-flagged floor against the biting chill. She looked at him for news and the confidence drained from her face when he didn't reply.

'He's not coming back, is he?' she asked.

'Don't know.'

'The bastard,' she swore, and tears welled up in her eyes. 'What'll we do now?'

Freddie looked up at him with expectant eyes.

'We'll stay here for the night. At least we'll be warm.'

'Yes,' shouted Freddie and punched the air with a fist, pleased the adventure was continuing.

'It would be crazy to drive down the hill now.' He needed time to work out their next move. 'If he hasn't returned by the morning, we'll retrace our steps and take it from there. Who knows, the Spanish border might be open by then,' he added not believing it.

## 34

THERE COMES A TIME WHEN A PERSON KNOWS THEY ARE BEATEN AND THERE are no means of escape. They may not admit it or show it, yet deep within the realisation they cannot win suffuses their being. This was the case for Bernay when he heard his wife's frightened voice on the telephone and his daughters crying in the background.

'Philippe, what's happening?' she asked, her voice breaking.

He mustered his strength to sound as calm as possible. 'It's a misunderstanding, *ma chérie.*'

'But I'm scared – the girls are terrified.'

She babbled on telling him that while out walking Nazi agents had stopped them and bundled them into a car. They had driven them to a house on the outskirts of Nice where they were being held under armed guard.

'Don't worry,' he tried his best to reassure her. 'I'll get them to return you to your hotel –'

Weber stepped in and took the telephone from him, placing it on the desk between them keeping the line open, and Bernay slumped forward with his head in his hands.

'Now you understand why it is imperative you tell me everything,' demanded Weber.

He shook his head with a weakening defiance.

Weber tutted. 'A fine display of bravado, however stupid in the circumstances.'

He glared at him.

'I understand what you're going through. You're cornered. You've nowhere to turn. We have your family. You're helpless.'

He hoped his face showed no emotion.

'Very well, let's not play games.' Weber shook his head. 'I'll give you several options and it'll be up to you what happens.'

He dropped his gaze to the desk and waited for what was coming.

'Refuse to tell me and it will be your choice and one you must live with.'

He stared at him wondering what he meant.

'You must choose now which of your daughters is to survive.' Weber waited for him to react. 'We will shoot one girl now and if you want your other daughter and your wife to live, you must talk. If you don't, then both your remaining daughter and your wife will be killed.'

The director glared at him with all the hate he could muster and shook his head.

'If you refuse to choose, both girls will be executed. It's up to you.'

He gasped, wanting to run at Weber and hit him although he had lost the power of his legs and arms.

'Choose now which of your two daughters you want to live. Do it now.'

Weber checked the time as if working to a deadline.

In times of danger, the brain is supposed to speed up and make instant decisions. All Bernay experienced was a kaleidoscopic jumble of emotions.

Weber reached over and picked up the receiver. 'Okay, Otto, kill them both now.'

He could hear agonised screams coming down the line from Nice.

'No, no, no.' He jumped up and grabbed Weber by the lapels of his coat.

Weber removed his hands and pushed him back into the chair and picked up the telephone again. 'Otto, hold your fire,' he ordered. 'There could be another solution, Philippe. If you stop playing this futile game and tell me everything, I will set free your wife and daughters.'

He snorted in disbelief.

'I'm a man of honour. I keep my word.'

'You're a Nazi.'

'No, I'm a German. Nazis are members of a political party, and I don't agree with them.'

'How can I tell you'll keep your word?'

'If you don't help me...' Weber raised his arms.

'How can I tell?' he insisted.

'You can't. From where I stand, your only choice is to tell us everything.'

He shook his head and rubbed his eyes and looked beyond Weber and out through the now open shutters at the streetlights switching on and tried to calculate his options. If he'd gone to Nice with his family, this wouldn't be happening.

Lighting another cigarette, Weber waited, a finger tapping on his gold cigarette case. He had to speed things up. Every minute lost was vital and an obstacle to the success of his mission.

'Tell me again about my family?'

The German picked up the phone and waved it at him. 'The line is open and your family intact for the moment. Once you tell me what I need, I'll instruct my men to take them back to their hotel and release them unharmed. You have my word.'

'Okay,' he sighed, accepting he'd no choice. 'What do you want from me?'

'Where's the platinum going?'

'Out of France.'

'Yes, but which route?' Weber showed irritation.

The hands on the clock on the wall were crawling now.

'By now the car should've crossed the Spanish border and be out of your reach.'

Weber made a clicking noise with his tongue and stubbed out his cigarette. 'Not necessarily, Franco has closed his borders and any French refugees in the country are being rounded up and are being held in camps before being sent back.'

Could they have made it to Spain, he wondered. He looked at his watch again and tried to work out the distance and the hours, but his mind didn't respond.

'Spain is not the destination, is it Philippe?' Weber persisted.

'Mmm....'

'Let me see, if they managed to make it into Spain, the next friendly country? Portugal?'

He glared at Bernay and saw by the resigned slump of his shoulders he was right.

'Yes, that makes good sense.' Weber paced the room. 'Estoril?'

He didn't answer.

'ESTORIL,' shouted Weber.

'Yes, yes.' He felt a deep pain in his chest and a tributary of sweat ran down his cheek knowing he'd betrayed Ben.

'You're trying to ship the platinum to England, aren't you?' Weber rounded on Bernay.

He didn't answer, and he knew he was right.

'So, who's arranging it for you, I wonder?'

'No one, I...'

'With respect, Philippe, a banker such as you doesn't have the contacts to arrange this.'

'I did...'

'It must have been British Intelligence at the embassy,' mused Weber.

He just stared at him.

'To be picked up by an RAF flying boat, probably.'

Feeling guilt at having given away everything without a fight, he exhaled.

'Thank you, you've been very helpful.'

He again picked up the telephone and waved it at the banker to remind him his family were still under a death sentence.

'Give me the name of the woman?'

The question caught him unawares although he recovered enough composure to appear confused. 'Woman? What woman?'

'Come on,' Weber chastised him.

He shook his head.

'The woman's name,' said Weber, sitting on the edge of the desk. 'Renard told me.'

'You're mistaken.'

'Remember, your family will be freed only if you tell me everything, and it has to be everything.'

'Perhaps it was his girlfriend, I...'

'Don't take me for a fool.' Weber raised his voice again. 'Let me tell you what happened – you sought the help of the British to transport the platinum and in exchange they demanded you help the woman escape...'

Weber was going after the car, so it didn't matter whether the woman was aboard. 'I wasn't given her name. I thought she was a wife, a mistress, a girlfriend of someone important at the embassy.'

Weber looked thoughtful as if he could believe it. 'And she's going to England as well?'

'Yes, although I know nothing about her and the child.'

'Aha!' He sparked into life and shoved his face into Bernay's.

For the first time, the director realised the German was more interested in the woman and child than the platinum.

'Well done, my friend, well done,' said Weber in triumph. 'The woman and the boy are very important to us. I'd swap all the platinum for them. Hitler has a particular interest in this and when they are returned to Germany, I shall be free.'

He interrupted Weber's gloating. 'My family, what will happen to them?'

Weber snatched up the telephone then paused. 'Where were they planning to cross the border into Spain?'

'Hendaye.'

The German played with the phone in his hand. If the Bentley couldn't get through the border point what might Peters do? He almost chuckled. It was a crazy idea, but one he'd attempt if necessary. He had to move quickly, and he gave a curt order before replacing the receiver. 'Your family will be released.'

Bernay slumped back in his chair and let out a massive gasp of relief.

'There's only one problem now,' said Weber. 'I must report what you've told me about stealing the platinum which is our property. My colleagues on the other side of the door won't be pleased. Although I won't tell them about your family, they'll get it out of you and we won't be able to protect them.'

Bernay put his head in his hands and groaned.

Weber took a Walther PPK out of his coat pocket and slid it across the desk towards him.

The pistol lay before him and he looked up into Weber's cold grey eyes and back at the gun wondering what the German intended. Could he snatch it up and shoot Weber? But the guards would burst in and kill him.

Weber's gaze narrowed, gauging his reaction. 'In the pistol is one round, and it's up to you. Yes, you can shoot me. However, if you do, your family won't be freed, and they'll be placed in a work camp where I understand the survival rate is low. Or to protect them...'

Bernay understood. Weber didn't need to finish. The German shook his hand and to his surprise he reciprocated.

'Thank you, my friend, it's been good talking to you. Today we may have saved two families.'

Weber walked to the double doors and hesitated with his back to Bernay presenting him with a large target, and he almost wished the banker would shoot.

As he was closing the doors behind him, the officer made to return to the room, but he took his arm.

'Walk with me, I need your help.'

They went downstairs and out into the lobby before Weber stopped and turned to the soldier.

'I need a plane and six of your best men in plain-clothes. Have them at the airport as soon as possible. We must leave within the hour.'

The officer snapped out a salute and, as he turned, the noise of a single shot echoed around the building. There followed a silence and then a scrambling of soldiers' boots as they ran to the origin of the sound.

Weber smiled. If Bernay had lived, it would have caused problems. It was imperative no one knew the details of his mission.

# 35

IT COULD HAVE CHANGED EVERYTHING.

Their spirits were low and there was little Ben could do to raise them. Freddie was oblivious to everything around him and found pieces of wood from which he attempted to build a castle. Alena retreated within herself and became engrossed in arranging changes of clothes for her and Freddie from a case she'd brought in from the car. And she avoided speaking to him.

With nothing better to do, he found a broken mirror and took a candle and a bowl of cold water and shaved the stubble that made his face appear dirty. He never spent much time looking at his reflected image, not liking what he saw. But this time it was worse – the haggard face looking back at him with bloodshot eyes was narrowed with worry.

By arranging two armchairs together so they formed a secure cot, she made a bed for the boy, and he was excited at this new adventure. She covered him with jackets and when she leant over to kiss him goodnight he wrapped his arms around her neck and kept kissing her.

'Ben, Ben,' the boy called, and he went to see what he wanted.

He stood on the other side of the makeshift bed from her, and

Freddie put up his arms. 'Now Ben must kiss me goodnight,' the boy demanded.

Alena continued to tuck in the jackets around him as he leaned over, and Freddie grabbed him around the neck and he kissed him on the forehead.

'Goodnight, Freddie. Tomorrow we'll have more fun.'

As he pulled back, Freddie laughed. 'Now you must kiss teddy.'

As he lowered his face, Alena did the same to finish tucking in her son. The closeness of her and her scent made his head spin. He looked up and her face was inches from his and her defenceless green eyes glinted in the firelight. Her lips were open and moist and in touching distance and their fullness pulled him in like a magnetic force. She stared back and hesitated before she met his kiss with equal hunger. And her lips were soft and warm.

'Look, look,' Freddie cried, laughter shaking his tiny frame. '*Maman's* kissing Ben. *Maman's* kissing Ben.'

Horrified, she pulled back and raised a hand to her lips as if stung. 'Go to sleep, Freddie.' She turned away as her cheeks coloured.

Kicking off her shoes, she went to the far end of the sofa in front of the fire and sat, tucking her legs under her. He followed her over, and a coldness grew between them.

'Shouldn't have happened.' She shook her head. 'It was a mistake.'

'I'm sorry, it was my fault.' And she didn't deny it.

He retrieved a bottle with the remains of the wine and poured two glasses and shoved one into her hand.

'Thanks,' she muttered, not looking at him. 'Why?'

'Why what?'

'Why do you have to do this crazy thing?'

He looked down at his drink and didn't know how to answer her.

Her voice rose. 'Even if he doesn't come back, on our own we could probably find a path through to Spain although not with that car.' She almost spat out the words. 'I'd rather chance it on the mountain than go back to face the Nazis.'

'I have to take the car.'

'Nonsense,' she shouted. 'What's so special about it? Is metal more important than flesh and blood?'

'A lot depends on it getting through.'

'What does that mean? If you can't get the car through, you'll stay with it?'

'No, I –'

'We still have a chance to get out of France, Bernay would understand.'

'I have to get it to Estoril.'

Alena now knelt on the couch, facing him with her fists clenched. 'I just want Freddie to enjoy a life,' she cried. 'We'll die if we don't get out of France. There's no safe place here for people like us. You've no idea what I've done.'

'I'll do everything I can to help you...'

She pushed her hair off her forehead.

'You're so selfish.' And she turned away from him, ending the conversation.

'Let's see if he returns with help first.' He wondered if the man was now spending their money in a local hostelry. 'He could still come good.'

'It makes no difference,' she shouted. 'It's obvious that you don't care for us. Tomorrow, Freddie and I will cross the mountain whether or not you come with us.'

The old oak door rattling on its rusty hinges halted his protest in mid breath as it swung open letting in a blast of the freezing night air.

# 36

WITHIN FIFTY MINUTES, THEY WERE ABOARD A TWIN-ENGINED SIEBEL SI 204 and Weber held his breath all along the runway as crosswinds buffeted the plane and it seemed to struggle to free itself from the ground. Beads of sweat stood out on his forehead and upper lip and he daren't look out at the lights below. Instead, he stared straight ahead. He sat behind the two pilots and in front of his six men, looking even more like soldiers in their civvies. And they couldn't see his discomfort. It wasn't wise to show any sign of weakness.

He hated flying and always tried to find an alternative route, going by road or by boat. Anything other than by plane. Although he didn't have the time on this occasion. A small plane magnified his discomfort. The claustrophobia of the smaller cabin and the continual swaying as it rode the air currents contributed to his deep-seated fear and an over-whelming feeling of nausea. Once it levelled out he wanted to relax, but as they climbed, he listened for a change in the engine note warning of mechanical problems that might send them plummeting back to earth.

Weber moved in the small seat to extricate a cigarette and lit up oblivious to the clouds of smoke drifting towards the back of the plane. At last, events were fitting into place. Before his meeting with

Bernay, he'd no idea of the woman's whereabouts. Now he knew her route. Germany had eyes everywhere, and the Spanish refused to let anyone through their borders. He doubted that Ben and the woman would return to France. They had to stay with the Bentley and in the car they couldn't hide. Going over the old smuggling trails might be the way out. But it was nigh on impossible with the car. For Weber, the car wasn't important. No one else knew about the platinum. That was a bonus. His mission was to bring back the woman and child – or as a last resort the child and eliminate the woman – and the safety of those he loved depended on his success.

He and his men were heading for a military airfield in Bilbao just over the border in Spain. Surrounded by mountains and with the wind coming off the Bay of Biscay, they faced a difficult landing and he tried to bury the thought at the back of his mind.

They would be waiting for them if Ben and the woman made it over the Pyrenees. Although he'd considered going straight to Estoril, the earlier he caught them, the better. The woman's secret must not get out, and they needed to kill the American if she'd confided in him.

He settled back in his seat and the low voices from behind and the drone of the plane almost lulled him into sleep. He wondered what his family were doing and was glad they'd no idea of what might happen to them should he fail. Too many people – even good Germans – disappeared without trace in Germany. The word was they were sent to work camps. Anyone who showed any disaffection or voiced their protests was regarded as a danger to the state and taken away never to be seen again. Find the woman and the boy. That was the key to his family's survival because he didn't question Himmler's threat. Bernay had done likewise; he'd sacrificed himself for the safety of his family. He respected him. As for this woman, she was an enemy of the Fatherland and had to pay.

## 37

A SMALL MAN STOOD IN THE DOORWAY. HIS SKIN WAS SO BROWN IT WAS almost black, its texture resembling a walnut, and when he smiled his teeth were a white beacon. He could make a gargoyle look attractive with large flapping ears and a hooked nose and he'd combed his black hair forward to hide a receding hairline. Although he had a slight stoop, Ben realised he was younger than he looked and walked on the balls of his feet like a cat.

The man studied them before speaking with a thick accent they found hard to understand.

'My name's Sebastian, so you want to go to Spain?' He said it as if they were contemplating a routine tourist ramble.

Alena sprang to her feet, a big smile spreading across her face, and Sebastian put up a hand to stop her from rushing up to him and lifting him off his feet.

'It'll be very difficult.' Sebastian paused as if counting the obstacles in his mind. 'I can lead you over the mountains. No problem. It's whether you're fit enough.'

'We can do it,' Ben said.

'Are you with child?' Sebastian peered at her.

'Yes… I mean no,' she said flustered, glancing at the sleeping Fred-

die. 'No, I'm not pregnant.' She laughed and shook her head to emphasise it. 'I can climb as well as anyone.'

Sebastian followed her gaze. 'Ah, we've a problem. A big problem.'

'What do you mean?' Concern crept into her voice.

'We can't take a child there.' Sebastian gestured with his head.
'Impossible!' He waved away her pleas.

'I can carry him,' Ben interjected.

Sebastian rubbed his chin. 'I don't think so.'

'He'll be riding in the car for most of the time.'

Alena shot him an angry glance.

Sebastian pulled out a chair and flopped down with a sigh. 'You
said a car,' he chuckled.

'I did, we have to take it with us.'

Sebastian snorted in disbelief. 'What are you going to do, carry it on
your back?' He laughed, a high-pitched whinny like a nervous horse.
As if to add weight to what he had to say, he got to his feet. 'The car
has to stay here. Without it, you have a chance of Spain and freedom.
Although the mountains may look beautiful from a distance, they can
be dangerous places. There are brown bears up here. Funny things can
happen and if we attempted to take a car, it would be suicide.'

'If I can't, I must find another way,' he said. 'I've no other choice.'

Sebastian started to worry about his money.

'Perhaps they could go on without you?'

Alena glanced at Ben.

Sebastian edged towards the door and touched his forehead in a
salute. 'So, I will bid you goodnight.' He kept moving trying not to
show his haste, hoping he could make it before they asked for their
money back.

'No, wait,' she said.

Sebastian was on the threshold ready to leave. Once outside in the
dark, they'd never find him.

'The car's vital to us.'

Sebastian shook his head and edged out. Another step and he
would disappear.

'What about this?' She walked over to him pulling something off
her hand.

'A ruby ring?' Sebastian said, peering at it.

'No, it's much more valuable, it's a red diamond ring. It's worth more than the car itself. Would you accept it as payment?' She flashed Ben a determined look. 'But you'd have to agree to take the car.'

Sebastian inspected it, holding it up to the light from the fire before relaxing and smiling again. 'Let me see this car,' he said and led the way outside.

He walked around the Bentley several times muttering and giving it a slap on a wing with the palm of his hand and nodded as if agreeing with his own argument before returning to the inn.

'I'll do it.' Sebastian slipped the ring onto the little finger of his left hand. 'But we must go now.'

A pleased Sebastian left them to prepare for the journey. He'd decided before he arrived at the inn to lead them and the car over the old cattle trail. A good night's work, the red diamond a welcome bonus besides the money he'd pocketed less the commission paid to the innkeeper. The car, the woman and the boy were too valuable to let go.

# 38

In the intermittent moonlight, Sebastian worked hard in an area of what appeared to be impenetrable foliage about fifty yards from the inn. He'd placed a lantern on the ground by his feet and used ropes he'd fastened around branches to pull them to one side. Refusing Ben's offer of help, Sebastian carried on working in a way that suggested he'd done it many times. Eventually, he created an opening big enough for the Bentley.

'*Voila*!' Sebastian turned to them pointing towards the opening. 'The road to Spain.'

Freddie jumped up and down clapping and shouting without knowing what he was celebrating, and Alena calmed him and put him in the back of the car.

'We must be quick, are you ready to go?' Sebastian picked up the lantern and looked up at the mountain.

'We're ready,' Ben replied, and she returned a hesitant smile.

'Understand this,' Sebastian said. 'You must do what I tell you at all times. The ground will have crumbled away in places. It's very danger-ous. You must not use your headlamps, they could be seen from far away. Near here is a village where the men are gendarmes or smugglers.'

He pointed into the darkness.

'Often brothers in the same family are on opposing sides. If the gendarmes hear of us, we're in trouble and if the smugglers discover what we're up to, you'll lose the car and much more. Our only light will be my lantern and –' he gestured towards the skies '– what there is of the moonlight. I'll walk on ahead and you must follow me. If I swing my lamp to the right –' he demonstrated '– you must move to your right. Understand?'

They both nodded.

'In some places,' Sebastian continued, 'we'll be travelling along a track with big drops on the side. You must stay in the car because take a wrong step and you could fall hundreds of metres. One thing, never look down.'

They bundled into the Bentley and in his haste to find reverse he crunched the gears making a horrendous metallic scraping noise.

Sebastian wasted no time in setting off and they saw the lantern swinging as he climbed away from the inn. Without the headlamps, he found it difficult to pick out a path, and it was almost driving blind. He had to put his trust in Sebastian and concentrate on keeping the Bentley's flying 'B' mascot aligned with the lantern as they drove at walking pace. The moon again slipped behind the clouds. And in the dark only the sound of the engine indicated the steepness of the gradient ahead. Alena sat forward in her seat with her face pressed up against the windscreen and for a time all they saw was the swing of the lantern. Sometimes it appeared to be moving away from them and he squeezed the accelerator and as the car speeded up, it bucked and shuddered over the rough terrain.

Such was Ben's concentration, he didn't blink in case he missed a signal from the lantern as his eyes strained to pierce the darkness. Every so often, the clouds parted, and the welcome moonlight lit up the path ahead, and they both gasped in amazement. They were driving along a route that from below appeared impassable. And just as quickly night plunged them back into darkness.

He could tell by the straining of the engine the climb was becoming much steeper, and he worried the effect the extra weight of the bullion was putting on the car. Ahead, Sebastian's lantern signalled to move to the right, and he turned the wheel not aware of what lay ahead. The light swung even more, and he pulled harder on the wheel and the back of the car swung out. The wheels spun in the mud and for several seconds it seemed as if they were stuck and not going anywhere, then the car found traction and it lurched forward and upwards.

For several hours, they drove in silence, the only noise being the heavy breathing of the sleeping Freddie and the comforting drone of the car's engine. They followed Sebastian, adjusting to the swings of his lantern, and his eyes felt as if scraped by sandpaper. When the moonlight peeked out from behind its curtain of cloud, it highlighted the towering grandeur of the Pyrenees investing them with a mysterious glow yet far below the valleys were still dark.

The terrain changed, and it sounded like gravel beneath the wheels. He could see nothing to his right, just black, and he realised they were moving along the side of the mountain. To his left and through the clouds was the dark blue of the night sky.

Sebastian stopped and put down the lantern on the ground and walked back towards them. He pushed his head through Alena's window. 'There's danger ahead,' he reported. 'Part of the track has gone. I don't know if we can get through.'

He stroked his chin, weighing up their options. 'I'd suggest we turn back, for your safety you understand.'

They both spoke as one. 'We must go on.'

'Very well, but you must realise, m'sieu, you and the car are most at risk.'

'I have to, I've no other option.'

'Then Madame you must walk with me and carry the child,' Sebastian ordered. 'If you stay by my side, you'll be safer.'

Alena sighed and woke up a grumbling Freddie, coaxing him out of his warm bed on the back seat.

'M'sieu, you must take the next stage slowly. You understand?' Sebastian waited for his agreement.

'You must keep your wheels straight on my line. Don't let the wheels spin. If you do, it could erode what remains of the track – and you'll fall a long way.'

# 39

For many, Estoril was the centre of their new universe. Emperors and empresses, kings and queens, dukes and duchesses, counts and countesses, deposed presidents and tyrants, conmen and courtesans, and spies, they congregated here for different reasons. And some came for the natural spas where the healing waters bubbled out of the ground at a temperature of thirty-two degrees Celsius and were said to heal broken bones. As royalty regarded it a suitable place to exile, it became known as the Coast of Kings. The Jews and refugees fleeing Nazism saw it as the gateway to America, the jumping off point to freedom, and soon the town's population doubled.

Every night they partied and partied hard as if it were to be their last, and for a brief time they felt untouched by a war ravaging the rest of Europe. Yet fear lurked behind the mask of gaiety.

They stayed at the hotels clustered around the park that was dominated by the casino, and the Palácio was the best. Some took villas or palaces in the hills behind the town. And at night they came out to play. In and around this panoply the spies and intelligence services thrived like industrious cockroaches.

Rafe Cooper loved the cooling wind sweeping off the ocean at night. It took on a magical glow in the moonlight as the phosphorescence of the breakers spread along the coastline. And there was the smell. He couldn't describe it, did it emanate from the billions of microscopic life coming out to play at night? At home, he'd lie awake in bed with the windows open and listen to the constant swishing, as secure as being in the womb. Mankind evolved from water and at various stages in our lives we're drawn back to it. Whatever it was, he'd prefer to live his days by the sea. Although he loved the climate, he liked the ocean when it became angry, turning from a benevolent blue to an angry grey with white-topped breakers queuing to storm the beach. The wind picking up and chasing clouds, now grey and black, across a bleak sky and the capricious wind hissing through the fronds of the green and yellow palm trees. It always amazed him how the sea changed moods in an instant. Just like a woman, he thought.

Dressed in a white linen suit, he felt as smart as he ever did. His old school tie loose around his neck, he whistled as he wandered along the promenade inspecting its profusion of well-lit bars and restaurants stretching all the way to the red roofs of the old town of Cascais. And every so often he paused to fill his lungs with the sea air. He'd struck lucky with this posting and he knew it. He'd done nothing to upset his bosses back in London and tried to keep it that way. Do a good job here and maybe they'd let him stay. He looked at the moonlight spreading across the sands. Estoril was the place to be, a world away from the madness.

He headed for the casino. He'd checked in with his contact and told him his plans and what he'd arranged for the woman and child, the platinum, and the American. It was a backup in case anything happened to him, yet what could happen here? The safest place in the world.

Most nights he made the same journey. First, a visit to the casino, a martini and people watch. See who was there and what was happening. He didn't gamble. He never gambled. That would be a risk. He never took risks. Afterwards, he'd stroll to the Hotel Palácio for a nightcap or two in the piano bar.

The casino's uniformed flunkey touched his forehead in recognition as he ran up the steps of the casino. Inside, the hatcheck girl gave him her most welcoming open-mouthed smile.

'Good evening, Rafe, Fritz is on the tables and gambling big.'

Rafe thanked her although he still couldn't remember her name. One night, or rather an early morning, they'd shared a drink and one thing led to another. Now every time he saw her he knew she was waiting for a repeat invitation, but he couldn't, not with a girl whose name he didn't know. He had standards after all.

Entering the large room, he soon saw the two Germans sitting at the *chemin de fer* table each with a large stack of chips in front of him. The official line was they were German businessmen forging trade links with the Portuguese authorities although everyone knew they were spies. They gambled big often winning and at times losing even more. He marvelled at their expense accounts. He could imagine telling London he'd lost a packet on the tables and he'd be recalled and posted to a godforsaken outpost or worse still somewhere there'd be real danger. He watched them for a while from the bar where he sat sipping his martini. Often when they gambled big something was about to happen and they were gambling big.

Soon after, he left for the Hotel Palácio, which was where the agents gathered to drink. The Germans stayed at the Park Hotel next door, but it was the Palácio they visited to exchange information. He remembered when first posted here he was told to go to the Palácio where the allies' agents were billeted. When he asked how he should dress so his people could recognise him, he was told to wear an Irish tweed jacket. So he did. On entering the piano bar for the first time, he realised everyone was wearing an Irish tweed jacket, even the Germans.

At the Palácio, you only had to ask the concierge to find out the state of the war. The bar was a barometer of the conflict. Every night, spies crowded in and there was no doubt who they were. It was if they were attending a trade conference with each country having a little flag on its table. There were no flags, yet it was just as obvious, and on the fringes, journalists hovered picking up any scraps that fell their way.

It was simple. Whoever bought champagne had something to celebrate. A telephone call to the concierge was enough to learn who was popping the corks. The press agencies called it the champagne news.

Rafe left the casino, skirted the fountains and walked through the geometrically laid-out park under the palms and cedar trees and cut over to the left and up the steps of the Palácio. From inside came the tinkling notes of the piano and a woman's shrill voice cutting through the night air.

He never understood why Jorge, the concierge, saluted as he entered the lobby. Maybe he thought he was an officer and a gentleman. 'Good evening, Mr Cooper, welcome as ever.'

Rafe smiled back his acknowledgement.

'The Germans are celebrating tonight, they invaded Paris this morning.'

So that was it. He felt a twinge of fear – where would the Germans stop?

# 40

Ben watched as Sebastian led Alena and Freddie along the track occasionally glimpsing their worried faces reflected in the lantern's light. The guide headed for a safe place a hundred yards away, a shelf in the rock face, and made them sit there before coming back for him.

'M'sieu.' Sebastian pushed his head through the open window. 'Are you sure you want to do this? One mistake and puff.' He exaggerated the word with a flick of his fingers. 'You'll be gone.'

The determination in Ben's face gave Sebastian his answer.

'Okay, follow my lead and imagine I'm the mascot on the bonnet. If I move a centimetre right or left, you steer that much.'

With the lantern held in his right hand high above his head, Sebastian rested his left hand on the bonnet of the Bentley as though steering the car.

It was slow progress.

He knew he shouldn't take his eyes off Sebastian. But he couldn't stop snatching glances to where Alena and Freddie sat although now it was difficult to make out anything other than dark shapes huddled together.

After twenty yards Sebastian slammed his hand hard on the bonnet – the signal for him to stop – and disappeared into the night to test the track. He got on his knees, peering at the earth, and returned shaking his head and muttering something incomprehensible. Again, they set off moving forward inch by inch. It was so slow he wanted to put his foot down, believing their impetus would carry them through although he realised it could lead to disaster.

The frustration and strain were telling. His head and eyes hurt as if someone had taken an axe to his skull. A lapse in concentration, and he wandered a fraction off Sebastian's route and received a warning shout. Now the car wasn't responding to the wheel and whichever way he turned nothing happened. Thinking he needed to speed up, he stamped on the accelerator. The car shuddered, wheels spinning and scoring a deep groove in the gravel. And with a throaty roar it took off, showering stones in its wake and launching myriad sparks like tiny stars into the night sky.

'Stop, for Christ's sake, stop.' Sebastian slammed a hand on the bonnet as he hung on for dear life.

Alena and Freddie's screams and an angry grating noise assailed his senses. They were slipping sideways and the earth beneath them appeared to be disintegrating. Again, he turned the wheel and pulled on the handbrake, but nothing stopped the Bentley's inexorable slide towards the drop.

Almost as soon as they'd started, it came to a juddering halt. The car was tilting at a precarious angle, and he feared they'd slipped off the edge of the track and between them and the ground far below was only air.

His face now white, Sebastian lay flat out on the bonnet and peered at Ben through the windscreen. 'Don't move a muscle,' he shouted. 'Stay still.'

He did as he was told, and Sebastian slipped off the bonnet and examined the damage. For what felt like an eternity, he sat not daring to blink, and with every shift and groan and creak of the chassis his level of panic rose. Now he didn't care a damn about the Bentley and whether it spun off into the valley, taking the platinum with it, as long as he wasn't aboard. He'd tried, he'd given his best and Bernay could not reproach him. The desire to get out of the car as soon as possible was increasing, but any movement could dislodge it and it kept him clinging to the wheel.

The guide reappeared on the passenger's side of the car with a grim smile. 'You can get out now. On this side. Slow now.'

He took his hands off the wheel and waited. No movement. He levered himself out from behind the wheel and moved into the passenger seat. The car shifted with a squeal of protest. Not daring to breathe, he froze and sweat streamed down his face and across his back making him itch. After what seemed forever, he plucked up courage and swung his legs out onto firm ground. There was no further movement. He held out his arms and Sebastian pulled him clear.

'The good news,' said Sebastian, 'is it won't slide down the mountain. It's wedged on a large boulder and as long as it holds, the car is okay. But on our own we can't move it.'

'What can we do?'

'I'll go back for help.'

Although they were relatively safe for the moment, the deadline in Estoril was fast approaching.

Sebastian turned to go, and he caught his arm. 'You'll come back?' he asked and wished he hadn't.

As if it were an insult, Sebastian grunted and spat in the dirt. 'You have my word.'

As Sebastian made his way down the track, the lantern swinging with the rolling gait of his walk, Ben watched until the light grew smaller and for a time was just a pinprick then nothing.

## 41

THE LANDING AT BILBAO WAS SMOOTHER THAN WEBER BELIEVED POSSIBLE and he alighted from the plane and extricated his cigarette case and lit up another smoke in relief. A visiting committee of two officers and a civilian awaited him. The officers, standing to attention as if their lives depended on their posture, greeted him with the respect his mission demanded. They saluted, and the civilian shook his hand and ushered him into a Nissen hut in which there were couches and tables and hot coffee was served. Outside, a car, its engine running, waited for him, and his six soldiers and their armoury were shepherded onto a covered truck.

Although the civilian looked Spanish, he spoke perfect German with a Berlin accent and Weber noticed the man didn't offer a name and neither did he ask him for one.

'What have you for me?' Weber took a swig of the strong aromatic liquid. He loved their coffee. The one good thing that could come out of this war would be if they assimilated the best cuisines of occupied countries into the German diet. If it were true that an army marched on its stomach, then the Fatherland's cause was lost.

'I've been to the border near Hendaye,' the civilian said, joining him with a coffee. 'French refugees were stopped at the border and turned back. There was a long queue of traffic and some refused to disperse. The gendarmes went down the line ordering people to leave and a car pulled out and instead of turning around headed up a lane for the foothills of the mountains.'

'The car?'

'Resembled your description although it was hard to tell the colour because it was covered in mud and appeared to be damaged. They said it could have been a Bentley.'

'Aha!' He doubted the border guards could tell a Bentley from a horse and cart. 'Perhaps we're getting somewhere.'

'But...'

'What?' he snapped.

'It got away. The gendarmes didn't follow the van; the lane was too narrow.'

'Weren't they ordered to track it down?'

The civilian spread his hands in apology. 'We can't order them... yet. They said it wasn't their business if someone wanted to drive into the mountains.'

He looked angered by this incompetence yet in reality he was relieved. If they'd taken them into custody and asked too many questions, it might have delayed the outcome of his mission. And if they'd discovered the platinum, it would have been difficult to get to the woman and her son.

'So, is there a route over the mountains?'

'Yes, smugglers used them for centuries.'

'Ah, so...'

'However, it's be impossible to get a car through.' The civilian shook his head to emphasise it. 'Impossible!'

Weber didn't care about the car or its bullion. The woman and her child were his targets, and he had to be careful what he told the civilian and the soldiers. They believed he was after an American driving a Bentley, and Peters, who had important information, was to be seized at all costs. Weber wondered what decision they'd made. They might ditch the car and attempt to make their way into Spain on foot. *That makes them much harder to find.*

He tried to quell his impatience. 'What if he's found a route for the car?'

The civilian flashed a look of annoyance.

'Humour me,' he snapped.

'Then whoever is helping him must be in the pay of Juan Callas Garza.'

He stared at him, his cold eyes demanding more information.

'He's a local bandit who reckons he's the Count of Pamplona. Controls everything around there.'

'So!' He sighed, foreseeing complications. 'The American with or without the car gets over the mountains, but he's in the hands of this Garza. Will Garza help him escape to Portugal?'

'Possibly. Garza only does things for money or for more power. The American needs to have money to get his help.'

'Oh, I believe he has.'

'Okay.'

'Can we strike a deal with this man?'

'That's what he exists for,' said the civilian.

'So we offer him money and, if we have influence with Franco, perhaps his claims to the area could be legitimised.'

The civilian nodded, thinking through the possibilities.

Weber clapped, signalling it was time to move. 'Good, Garza can hand over the American and the car –' he raised an arm to acknowledge it was doubtful the car would make it '– and the Count gets what he wants. Everyone wins.'

'Apart from the American,' the civilian said and wished he hadn't as Weber glared at him.

# 42

Ice spread through her brain and froze all impulses. Alena was cold and only a wetness from beneath provided any warmth. She couldn't move and yet there was no pain. A metronomic drip of water from above nagged at her consciousness and the cold whispered at her to surrender. She had to choose although the decision was made for her in the end

A faint rustling of the wind whispered along the grooves in the rock on which she lay before dying away. Seconds later, another noise, growing louder and louder. A scraping and scrambling as hundreds of tiny feet struggled for purchase on the slimy walls. She peered into the darkness and thought she saw their sharp button-like eyes marking her out for the kill. Still the squeaking, almost a hungry screeching like metal being dragged across metal, grew louder, and she tried to block it out.

Out of the gloom, the advance guard darted. It ran halfway up the rock face and stopped, watching her, its head cocked to one side and its nose and whiskers twitching as it identified the alien scent of a human. With a whisk of its tail, it disappeared back into the blackness, shrilling its report to the host that responded with excited eagerness. Another scuttled out, bigger and with a black sheen to its short round body, its pink tail curled high above as though it were an antenna. Then another, and another, growing bolder. One lost its grip and fell into the water with a splash and swam towards her. The water was now up to her neck, trapping her arms. The rat made good headway and kept on coming straight at her face. Dirty water lapped into her mouth and she spat it out in disgust. She fixed her stare on the swimming rodent and didn't notice the two that had crawled along the other side of the rocks. They jumped onto her bare shoulders, claws digging into her flesh as they struggled for purchase. All she saw was the rat's eyes. Behind it came others, and behind them even more...

Ben shook Alena awake.

Sweat soaked her clothes as she came to, her eyes blank at first as she took in her surroundings followed by a smile of recognition and relief.

'You were crying out in your sleep...'

'Sorry.' She reached out for his hand and squeezed it. She'd learned to live with this nightmare visiting her often during her captivity, perhaps only when she was free and safe would it disappear forever.

The moon slipped behind a bank of interminable cloud and it was dark and still on the mountain as they waited for Sebastian to return. Freddie slept, covered by jackets on the rock ledge, and they sat with their backs to the cliff wall, their closeness generating the welcome warmth of intimacy.

He realised she was watching him and turned to look at her. At first, she offered a little smile, the corners of her mouth barely lifting, and her unblinking stare devoured his face. 'Are you okay?' he whispered, and the smile widened, and her eyes joined in before she blinked and averted her head as if to break the spell.

Then she glanced back, welcoming. 'Thought we were losing you,' she said, touching his cheek with the back of her hand.

He put an arm around her and she rested her head on his shoulder.

'Do you think we'll ever get out of France?' Her voice on the verge of breaking.

'We will,' he reassured her. 'I promised Bernay.'

'What if Sebastian and his helpers can't move the car, what will you do?'

He was in no doubt now. 'If we can't get the car moving, I'll leave it.'

She made to speak, but he stopped her.

'We'll go on foot if we have to. It's important to get you and Freddie to Estoril and then on to England.'

'After what you've been through, are you sure?'

'It's a simple choice – you and Freddie or the car.' He shrugged. 'No contest.'

'You'd do that for us,' she said, reaching up to put her arms around his neck.

He didn't get the chance to answer as she peppered his face with kisses. And she found his mouth and kissed deep and hard and it felt good and as it should be. And as her tears flowed down his cheek, he held her close.

'What's so special about the car, anyway?' She broke away, dabbing her eyes dry with a lace handkerchief.

'What you don't know can't hurt you. The Nazis would love to get their hands on it. Maybe it would be best if it stayed up here in the mountains. They might never find it.'

She nodded as if she understood and traced a pattern on the gravel with her boot.

'What will happen to our world now?' she asked. 'I love my country, but the France I knew has gone forever. I'll never be able to return and for the rest of my days wherever I am there will be something missing, and I won't ever be able to replace it.'

'You and Freddie could come with me to America.' It was the wrong thing to say.

Her face hardened, and she pulled her hair away from her eyes.

'I don't want to be a refugee – someone just living in a country because they have nowhere else. I want to feel I belong where I'm living.'

'Did you have a sense of belonging in Germany?'

'Never. Well, a bit at first.'

'You lived well there?'

She shook her head and turned to look at him as if she couldn't expect him to understand. 'We did, although I wasn't allowed to leave. I was a prisoner in a castle.'

'What were you doing in Germany?'

She looked at the ground, her head nodding, debating whether to tell him. 'I went there to work at the French embassy years before the war. I was excellent at languages. French, naturally –' she chuckled '– English, Russian, my grandparents were Russian, and especially German.'

She swept her hair back and found a cigarette, taking a long time to light up as she planned what to tell him next.

'We didn't know what we know now. We'd lots of contact with the Germans as you'd expect – some were polite and quite charming – and they were impressed by my linguistic skills. They asked for me to act as the liaison between the embassy and the Nazi party headquarters. At first, it seemed harmless. Then I had more to do, and it became dangerous. In the end, the Nazis aimed to kill me.'

She raised a hand as she caught her breath.

'How did you escape?'

'In Germany, there is an underground movement against the Nazis. Many ordinary Germans are against what is happening in their country. They were alerted about my position and it was in their interests to get me out of Germany. Almost didn't work out.'

'How?'

'We were hidden under sacks in this farmer's old van and the guards stopped us at the castle's gate. A soldier searched the back of the van and he'd a bayonet on his rifle and stabbed into the sacks. Some fell away, and he froze when he saw us. He was one of the soldiers who'd played football with Freddie in the gardens and he told me Freddie reminded him of his son, who'd died of meningitis around the same age. His corporal asked him if there was anything there and he just stared hard at me and shouted all clear and slammed the doors shut.'

'So you made it, yet you're still running?'

'Yes, because of what I've done, I cannot stay in France. We may be safe in England, but who knows.'

She lay back on the rock and exhaled, sending out clouds of smoke into the air as if excising the remnants of those memories, and he wondered where Freddie came in her story. There was something she wasn't telling him.

## 43

SEBASTIAN'S DISAPPEARANCE OVER THE EDGE ALMOST MADE BEN VOMIT. IT was a sheer drop, and nothing could prevent his fall apart from a few shrub-like trees growing out of the cliff-face several hundred feet below. The Bentley rested on a large rock and the guide leapt onto it as if stepping onto a boulder in a stream.

Their guide had returned after first light and even a pristine dawn did little to lift their flagging spirits. Accompanied by the innkeeper who was leading two Pottok ponies, he fixed ropes to the car's front axle and attached them to the horses' harnesses.

The rear of the car's chassis was grounded on the rock with one wheel hanging out into space and the other just touching the track. Kneeling on the stone, Sebastian attempted to insert the end of a long iron bar as a lever underneath the car.

Ben held his breath hoping the guide didn't discover the bags of platinum fixed to the chassis rails. He couldn't imagine what would happen then and wondered if they'd die on the mountain.

After much swearing in a combination of French, Spanish and Basque, Sebastian was satisfied with his work and climbed back up onto the track and flashed a confident smile at Alena and Freddie.

'Can you handle horses?' Sebastian asked.

Ben nodded; he'd try anything.

'I need you to hold their heads and lead them away from the car when I give the word. My friend will use his strength to lever the bar under the back and try to raise the car. I will push from the rear. You must keep the horses moving, if they stop we'll fall backwards.'

The horses were roped up and he took hold of their harnesses in each hand. They grinned at him with broken yellow teeth and their breath smelled foul and they shook their heads as if they believed it was crazy to even try it.

'Right, now,' shouted Sebastian, and Ben tugged on the horses' halters trying to pull them towards him.

They didn't budge.

Sebastian picked up a long stick and threw it to him.

'Just hold the lead horse's halter, this one. Give him a sharp whack on the rump and pull him at the same time. When he walks, the other will follow.'

They tried again, and he hit the horse hard on its hindquarters and thought he heard bones rattle. The pony stumbled forward bringing the other one with it and in the background he saw the innkeeper's immense biceps bulging as he used all his strength to force the iron bar down. The Bentley lifted a fraction, and he redoubled his efforts with the animals and they shuffled forward, and he felt the strain. Behind them, the car groaned like an old ship going under followed by a scraping of metal on stone.

It moved. Perhaps only an inch and Freddie cheered.

'Come on, you buggers, pull,' he shouted at the horses, who didn't seem to grasp the importance of their task. And he gave them a reminder, and they lurched forward, and again there was a grinding noise and the car moved a fraction more.

It may have been for only a split second, but he relaxed his grip on the horses and they stopped and with a sigh the car settled back to where it had come from.

Sebastian threw up his arms in exasperation. 'When you feel it move you must keep going, don't stop or we'll never get it out,' he shouted. 'Right, let's go again.'

He now realised there was a rhythm to it. Once the horses had momentum, it was easier. They kept going, and they pulled hard, and he encouraged them, not allowing them to stop, and when they looked as if they might, he gave them another reminder.

It was gradual at first and the car began moving until one of the rear wheels had traction and Sebastian jumped on the back of the car to push it down on the track. Now his colleague also put his shoulder to it and the car lifted clear. Like a prehistoric monster getting to its feet after a long sleep, it lurched forward and with a final loud bang all four wheels landed back on the track.

Sebastian whooped, and the big man slumped to the ground, his breathing laboured and his torso covered in a sheen of sweat.

Alena and Freddie ran towards them shouting. Much to Sebastian's surprise, she kissed him and the big man before she found Ben with a long lingering kiss on the lips that promised more.

Sebastian halted the celebrations. 'We must go now. There is little time. If we delay, we will run into patrols.'

They thanked the innkeeper who had a heated conversation with Sebastian before turning to head back down the mountain.

'Stop,' Alena shouted and ran to the trunk of the car and found two loaves of bread they'd taken from the inn. She went over to the ponies, feeding each of them their reward.

# 44

THE BROODING MOUNTAIN LOOKED DOWN ON THEM AS IF MOCKING THEIR attempts to scale it and for now they went around instead of over it. The pock-marked and rutted track made the ride rough and jolting. His teeth rattled, and he worried the platinum might be shaken free. Alena and Freddie now rode with him in the car, following Sebastian's unbroken stride mile after mile. The sharp morning sunlight glanced off the brown granite of the mountains making them sparkle like precious stones. And in the unspoilt air he almost believed their troubles were behind them. But it was a passing thought soon supplanted by the trepidation of what awaited them in Spain.

As they turned a bluff, the track sloped downhill, and they came upon a wide ravine with sheer walls. The only way across was over a narrow wooden bridge. He thought it might support pedestrians but not a Bentley laden with bullion. Even without anyone on it, the bridge swayed and walking across would take nerve. Up here, they were wrapped in an eerie stillness. Not even birds moved in the air as if nothing living should be allowed. Like the silence of an audience anticipating an act of either great daring or stupendous foolishness. He brought the Bentley to a gradual stop and let out a frustrated sigh.

Ahead, Sebastian walked up to the bridge for a closer look and returned shaking his head. 'Not good, not good at all.' The guide didn't want to catch his eye. 'It's unstable. The supports underneath are rotting away. I doubt it'll take even our weight.'

Sebastian glanced at him but knew the answer without asking, and his shoulders dropped in resignation. 'I'm going across to see if we can make it.' He turned away shaking his head and cursing himself for being so stupid to even attempt it.

As he picked his way across the bridge, moving forward and back with the balance of a ballroom dancer, it lurched, and he grasped the side to steady himself. Every couple of yards, he stopped, unsure whether to risk it. At last, he made it to the other side and waved.

'Come on.' Alena gathered up Freddie. 'Let's go.'

He put a restraining hand on her arm. 'Wait until he comes back, and we hear what he has to say.'

Sebastian returned with as much care as before, and his face was grim. 'It's dangerous, very dangerous. I'd advise against it.' He waited for a reaction but getting none continued. 'I'll have to lead the woman and child over. Some planks are splintered and could fall at any time.'

Worry etched Alena's face as she convinced herself they had no choice but to continue. 'What about Ben?' she asked.

'I'll get you across first,' replied Sebastian. 'Then we'll see if it's still standing.'

As though saying farewell for the last time, Freddie and Alena embraced Ben before Sebastian led them away. Alena clutched Freddie's hand and warned him not to glance down. Like crossing a river using stepping-stones, Sebastian first tested a section of the bridge before calling them on.

The bridge moved alarmingly with their weight and a creaking noise sounded as if the joints and supports were about to give way under the stress.

It was agonising to watch Alena walking hunched, fearing every step could be her last. Beside her, Freddie chattered constantly and treated it as if it were a game, now and then trying to pull his hand away for which he received stern rebukes.

Even a puff of air would be enough to send them and the bridge crashing hundreds of feet to the black ribbon of a river. The farther they progressed, the more the bridge yawed from side to side and the groaning increased.

Freddie stumbled. As he attempted to regain his balance, a plank dislodged and tipped up and slipped through a hole in the bridge. Sebastian and Alena were unable to move for fear of starting a chain of events they couldn't stop. Freddie wobbled. And he was gone, following the plank through the hole.

Still hanging onto his little hand, Alena dropped to her knees, and he was screaming '*Maman*, save me. *Maman*, save me.'

## 45

THE REDHEAD LAY SPREADEAGLED AND BLINDFOLDED AND NAKED ON THE black silk sheets, and silk scarves secured her wrists and ankles to the corners of the large four-poster bed.

She saw nothing, but she heard the door opening and the man enter the room. He walked around the bed and into the adjoining bathroom. He unscrewed the top of a bottle and there was a slapping sound as he patted himself with scent. The mattress depressed as he climbed onto the bottom of the bed, but he didn't speak and nor she to him.

A hand on each ankle caressing the ties not intended to cause pain, and his rough hands moved up the inside of her legs, stroking them. Heavy breathing, the bed moving as he gathered himself on his knees.

A pause.

He'd removed his hands.

She waited.

*What next?*

Her orders were to keep quiet, not to speak to him, and she noted her breathing was faster and more irregular the deeper the silence and the longer the wait.

It seemed like minutes and then he moved between her legs, his head burrowing into her and his tongue seeking the softness of her womanhood. She moaned and writhed as she'd done so many times. Almost at once his body was on hers and she felt the oiliness of his skin, the sweet smell of scent and the girth of his belly pressing down.

She gasped as he took her, and his teeth nibbled at her breasts and then her ears. After several violent thrusts, he grunted and collapsed. Kissing her on the mouth, he forced his tongue between her teeth before climbing off and padding away into the bathroom. The toilet flushed, and she sensed he was dressing. He walked out and around the bed and she heard the door open and close behind him.

She was alone. She could speak.

'Hey, what about me?' she shouted.

No one came.

## 46

'BEN, BEN, I CAN'T HOLD HIM,' ALENA SHOUTED AS SHE SCRAMBLED FOR purchase to prevent herself from following her son through the hole growing wider in front of them.

He stepped onto the bridge, but Sebastian screamed at him. 'Don't move an inch.'

He took another step forward. 'For Christ's sake,' Sebastian shouted. 'Your extra weight will bring it down.'

He hesitated.

'Stay there, I'll get them.' Sebastian dropped to his hands and knees and crawled towards Alena like an exotic crab.

'Help us,' she cried. 'Help.'

Freddie was struggling, trying to get back up, and his hand was slipping through fingers wet with sweat.

'I can't hold him much longer,' she sobbed and stretched out flat on the bridge flinging her other hand through the gap and grasping his shirt which came away in her hand.

'Hold on.' Sebastian inched his way forward, sweat pouring from his face and dripping off the end of his nose.

'Please, oh God, please, he's going.'

Both Sebastian and Ben shouted as one. 'Hold on.'

'I'm losing him,' she shrieked in desperation.

Over the last few feet, Sebastian speeded up and leapt forward thrusting his right arm into the gap to clutch the boy's arm in a vice-like grip. Together, they pulled him up screaming and wriggling like a landed fish onto the bridge that was shaking as if it might collapse at any moment.

'Okay, okay, I have him.' Sebastian raised an arm in triumph. 'Wait there until I get them to the other side.'

Relief shining out of her eyes, Alena hugged her screaming son, who couldn't be consoled. She smothered him with kisses and held onto him as if she'd never let go of him again.

A tap on the shoulder brought her out of her trance. 'Come on,' Sebastian whispered. 'We're almost there; let's get off this bridge.'

She rose to her feet clutching Freddie and, watching every footstep, they made it to the other side and she waved, but still she clung to the boy.

Sebastian made the return journey in quicker time, realising the bridge couldn't last much longer. 'You can see how it is,' he said, wiping the sweat from his face. 'We might just get across ourselves.'

Ben stared at the bridge wondering what damage time and weather had done. To drive onto it would be the biggest gamble of his life. Under the weight of two adults and a child, there had been considerable movement. He doubted it could take the Bentley plus the bullion. The other way was to leave it behind and go on foot because he was determined not to let Alena out of his sight.

He didn't realise he'd spoken. 'I must get the car across.'

Sebastian shook his head and his shoulders slumped.

'You must be crazy, man. That's suicide.'

Now Alena and Freddie were at least safe on the other side and almost in Spain, he'd give it one last go. He couldn't fail Bernay now. He had to try.

'I must,' he insisted.

'Okay, okay, it's your life.' Sebastian put both hands in the air in an act of surrender. 'Let me get halfway across and I'll guide you. Take it slow, if you go more than a snail's pace, it'll collapse.'

Holding his breath and in synch with every turn of the Bentley's engine, he edged the car onto the wooden structure and sensed it pitch with the weight of the vehicle. Having watched Alena cross, he had identified the danger points and, although the bridge was narrow, he believed it possible to manoeuvre past them.

Ahead, Sebastian waved and shouted instructions, but behind Ben planking in the centre of the bridge slipped through a hole growing larger by the second. The natural inclination was to speed up although that would be disastrous. He must grit his teeth and be patient, taking it inch by inch.

Where Freddie had disappeared, he saw the damage and pulled to the left hoping the wood was strong enough to support him. It meant driving hard up against the wooden railing which gouged a deep groove in the side of the Bentley, ripping off its door handles, and the friction caused the bridge to shudder.

Sebastian reached land on the other side and gesticulated for him to keep moving. But the bridge gave a terminal groan and with a loud bang pulled clear of its mountings behind him and swung right and then left and toppled backwards. With a domino effect, wood crashed into the ravine and the bridge tipped upwards so that the nose of the Bentley rose pointing towards the sky.

# 47

DRESSED IN A LONG CHINESE SILK DRESSING-GOWN, THE SELF-STYLED Count of Pamplona, Conde Juan Callas Garza, padded across the marble floors of his sumptuous residence. He took the steps to a terrace where a table set for breakfast stood by the side of his swimming pool. On sighting him, his manservant poured a cup of black coffee and prepared juice from oranges picked from Garza's own orchard and squeezed minutes earlier.

The scent of the woman still lingered, so he loosened his dressing-gown, letting it fall to the ground, and dived into the cool waters of the pool. A lazy freestyle took him to the far end of the pool via a refreshing detour under the fountain imported from Italy before returning to his starting point. Bathrobe in hand, a servant, placed it over his master's shoulders and, as the count tightened the cord, produced a long black cheroot and lit it for him.

The woman was a good start to the day. He might keep her and when he tired of her, he could always sell her to his customers in Africa. They liked white women, and the redhead was almost alabaster.

From his poolside seat, he looked towards the distant Pyrenees and peered closer as if seeing movement. The Germans weren't coming yet although nothing was certain. The Pyrenees had always been good to him and with so many French escaping over the border it was a lucrative business. Juan Callas Garza controlled everything from Pamplona to the top of the mountains and east and west of where he sat – cross-border smuggling, drugs, illicit liquor, women, the slave trade. Whatever turned a buck. Even Franco's people valued the support of powerful men in the regions. Garza didn't support Franco. He'd met the general, and he didn't trust him and worried what he might agree with Hitler. Rumoured that the two were meeting at Hendaye later in the month, he wondered whose ego would prevail. Would Franco join with Hitler or might he upset the Führer who could decide Spain was his next conquest? He could handle Franco, but the Germans on his patch would be bad for business.

Transporting escaping French refugees was a profitable business. Desperate to evade the Nazis, they paid good money to cross the mountains. Some he let go, others he handed over to the authorities, who returned them to France. Only the men. The young, attractive women and children were separated from their men folk and taken to Cadiz and shipped over to Africa. There, they paid top dollar for white skins. He loved the expression. In fact, he loved everything American.

# 48

As the bridge fell back on itself, he felt the Bentley sliding on the wooden planks being torn up as if split apart by an earthquake. He didn't have time for choices. A second's delay would mean the car toppling into the ravine and him with it. He hung on to the wheel and with all his strength stamped on the accelerator pedal.

The car coughed and coughed again. 'Oh, God, not now,' Ben shouted.

The Bentley seemed to hesitate, and he kept his foot down hard, standing on it until a throaty rumbling rippled along its length. Wheels spinning, it fought for grip sending up a cloud of black smoke and an overpowering smell of burning rubber. Finding traction, the car jolted forward launching into the air so that it shot up the remains of the bridge and almost flew to the safety of land.

It missed Sebastian by inches. And if he hadn't braked hard, the car would have careered on and over another rise and into even greater trouble. It shuddered to a halt in a cloud of dust while the last of the bridge collapsed into the ravine behind him, the noise of falling debris crashing onto the slopes below continuing for several minutes. He staggered out of the car giving it an affectionate slap. And, as his knees buckled, Alena and Freddie leapt on him and the three of them hugged in a mixture of shock and elation.

'We're over the worst,' said Sebastian with a smile as wide as the vista and Alena hugged him, too. '*Voila!*' The guide opened his arms as if presenting them with Spain's Pamplona Basin stretching out inviting and free in the morning sunlight.

From here, the track ran downhill, and Sebastian no longer had to walk and sat on the bonnet, holding onto the roof. They bounced down the slopes towards Spain although Ben had to brake hard to stop the Bentley from running away.

Near the bottom, as they approached a copse, Sebastian knocked on the windscreen and indicated they should pull in under the trees. 'This is as far as I go,' he said climbing off the bonnet. 'Someone will be with you soon and they'll make sure you have safe passage.'

He nodded and shook Sebastian's hand. Whatever they'd paid him it was worth it.

'*Bonne chance,*' said Sebastian, touching his head. He waved and was gone without a backward glance, and they watched him climb until he disappeared out of sight. They didn't have long to wait for a putt-putt of motorbikes within minutes heralded the arrival of two unsmiling men, with heavy beards and carbines across their backs. They rode under the trees and brought their machines to an extravagant stop, showering them with sand. One dismounted and appeared to inspect them, walking around the Bentley and coming up to the car to peer at its passengers.

'Come.' He gestured to them to follow in the car.

'How are you?' He asked Alena as they followed the bikes along winding tracks and past ploughed fields.

'I don't know.' She leant her head on the leather seat. 'We're out of France, but there's still a long way to go before we're safe.'

'It's downhill from here,' he tried to reassure her and they both laughed at his joke.

# 49

Trees stripped bare, mutilated by shells and explosions. Yet in a moonlight bringing everything into sharp focus, they took on a stark beauty as if living again. The whiteness of the light froze everything in its beam. The rutted ground pockmarked with shell holes. Puddles of slimy green water icing over and reflecting the pale light. Nothing moved in the moonscape that was No Man's Land. It was the most horrendous sight he'd ever seen or one of the most perverse beauty. No gunfire. An end to the constant whining of shells overhead. A stillness as before a storm.

Except for birds chirping.

Weber rubbed his eyes, realising the birds weren't part of his dream. He needed a smoke, and he reached for his cigarette case and found he wasn't wearing his coat but instead something flimsy. He glanced down. It was a white gown. Puzzled, his eyes swept around him. It was almost ethereal – a white room with bare walls except for a wooden crucifix halfway up and from somewhere came the sound of muted music and voices raised in song. He attempted to turn his head to the left, finding it painful, and looked out of a small window onto a court-yard of trees full of those damned birds.

A dull ache throbbed in his head and he put up a hand to touch its source and a sharper excruciating pain shot through him making him shake.

He heard footsteps in the corridor outside the room and he called out. 'Hello, hello, *kommen hier.*'

No one came.

Pulling himself up onto his side with difficulty because the pain increased with movement, he manoeuvred his legs out of the bed. Putting his feet on the cold stone floor, he pushed himself up. He staggered forward and to stay upright had to sway backwards and was forced to sit back on the bed. How did he get here? He tried to remember. All he recalled was sitting in the car on the way from Bilbao airport to meet the gangster in Pamplona.

Although it hurt, he couldn't just lie there. 'Where am I?' he shouted at the top of his voice. 'Where the fuck am I?'

Still no one came. As he attempted another sortie out of the bed, he heard scuffling footsteps outside his room and voices and the door opened and a nun in a white habit peeked in. Seeing him awake, she gave an acid smile and hurried away again shutting the door behind her.

'Come back,' Weber shouted after her. 'For Christ's sake, come back.'

Then more footsteps, and he was pleased to see the civilian entering followed by the nun.

'What the hell happened to you?' he said, seeing the civilian's two black eyes making him look like he was wearing goggles. 'I need a smoke where are my cigarettes?'

The civilian fished out his cigarette case from a bedside locker and offered him one and lit it for him as the nun tut-tutted in the background

He sucked in the smoke and lay back and the dull throbbing in his head seemed to recede.

'Don't you remember?' asked the civilian.

'If I knew, I wouldn't be asking.'

The civilian cleared his throat not wanting to remember.

'We were in a car crash.'

'Car crash?' Weber screwed up his face. He still couldn't remember anything.

'We were driving to Pamplona –'

'Yes, yes.'

'– you were sitting in the front with the driver and I was in the back. You were asking the driver a question about Pamplona. There was a long sweeping right-hand bend, and the car drifted across the road and a truck coming the other way hit us a glancing blow. The driver lost control. Although he struggled with the wheel, we skidded off the road and somersaulted down an embankment hitting some trees.'

He took a sharp intake of breath.

'When?'

The civilian looked puzzled.

'When did it happen?' he asked, wanting to determine how long he'd been in this room.

'Last night.'

He thought for a minute.

'Why didn't we go on to Pamplona? We still had the truck.'

The civilian looked at his feet.

'The driver was killed outright.'

'So?'

'Your head went through the windscreen and there was blood everywhere.'

He felt the top of his head and winced.

'You were also unconscious.'

'Jesus Christ,' he shouted, and the nun gave a nervous smile and coughed in embarrassment. 'We could've lost them.'

He looked at his watch and tried to figure out the timescale but couldn't.

'Your men were worried you might bleed to death, so we took you back to the hospital here in Bilbao.'

He thought if he'd lost the woman and child it might have been better if he had bled to death.

'You were in a bad way,' the civilian continued. 'You almost sliced off the top of your head. Here.' And with sadistic pleasure passed him a hand-mirror.

He gasped. It wasn't a pretty sight. His face had turned yellow with the bruising around his eyes and myriad cuts dotted his face. A large white bandage wrapped around the top of his head as if he were wearing a turban.

'Jesus Christ,' he growled and again the nun coughed and made to smooth out his blankets.

'Go away,' he shouted at her. 'Get my clothes; we've got to get to Pamplona as fast as we can.'

The civilian hesitated as if that wasn't the best option, but he insisted. 'Now.'

'I've a car outside,' said the civilian, 'and your men are ready.'

With help from the nun who tried to avert her eyes as he pulled off his gown, he climbed into his clothes.

'How long will it take?'

'About two hours.'

'Right, let's go.' He stepped forward and fell flat on his face.

# 50

THEY KEPT UP WITH THE TWO BIKES EVEN THOUGH THE RIDERS WENT HARD for it and made no concessions. Now and then the men glanced back ensuring they still followed. Meanwhile, Alena sat in the front holding Freddie tight, determined that no one would take him from her.

Sebastian said these men would take them to the most powerful person in the region who lived outside the white-walled town of Pamplona in the hills of Navarre. Sebastian stressed they'd need help in Spain if they were to escape and Ben presumed this was part of the service. He expected them to suggest the best route through Spain and how to avoid the dreaded state police, the Guardia Civil.

As the countryside became more populated and the dense pine forests made way for fields with animals grazing and the odd house and finca, the riders slowed and rode with more care. Eventually, they came upon a long, white-painted stone wall lined inside by tall trees making it impossible to see what lay beyond. The wall ran for a mile before the riders almost came to a halt, one of them flapping his arm ordering him to slow. Around a corner, more men, wearing the blue berets of the region and with carbines over their shoulders, guarded an open gate. They looked bored as if no one dared pass and they glowered at them and waved them through. The long drive ran past more fields and then manicured ornamental gardens in which an army of gardeners worked, cutting grass, weeding and watering plants. They rounded another bend and came upon a large white house.

Passing a cluster of barns housing a collection of exotic cars, they drove under an arch and into a cobbled courtyard. The riders jumped off their bikes and wandered off without a backward glance while a man wearing a white tunic and black trousers with black patent leather shoes ran down the steps of the house to greet them.

'Please,' he said as they climbed out of the Bentley. 'The Count is waiting to meet you.'

Alena and Ben surveyed their surroundings with uncertainty as he ushered them up the steps and into a large reception area opening onto a swimming pool complete with fountains and marble statues reminiscent of a Cecil B. DeMille movie set. A table was set poolside and his stomach reminded him it was hungry.

On the other side of the pool, a young redheaded woman sunbathed nude, and she grabbed a towel and covered herself when they entered.

The servant left them standing and disappeared without a sound. As they took in the opulence, Freddie scampered around, shouting '*Maman*, can I swim, please?'

'He can.' The voice came from behind and they wheeled in surprise.

A small man walked towards them with a pecking step and rolled from side to side like a penguin. A pencil moustache was the only hair on his head and his tanned body shone as if oiled. He wore gold chains around his neck and wrist and he held a black cheroot. His paunch obscured the briefest of red and grey striped silk briefs. His dark eyes showed no emotion, but an interested smile played around his mouth like a prospective buyer inspecting a purchase he knew he could afford.

'Xabi,' he called, and the servant reappeared. 'See to it the boy has some swimming trunks... and Madame?' He turned to Alena.

She shook her head.

'A pity, maybe later,' he said with the hint of a smile. 'My name is Conde Juan Callas Garza. I control everything in this area.' He proffered a hand. 'And you are?'

'Ben Peters and this is my, um, wife, Alena, and son Freddie.'

'Ah, an American, I adore America. You're a very lucky man.'

He didn't know whether Garza was referring to his being an American or being related to Alena and Freddie or both.

'You must be tired and hungry after your night on the mountain.' He led them over to the dining table by the pool. 'Please, eat and drink.' And he opened his hands in a welcoming gesture.

By this time, Freddie had jumped in the pool and a young maid threw a ball to him and kept watch as he splashed around whooping with excitement.

They were ravenous. Garza's manservant brought orange juice and steaming coffee. And, while Alena restricted herself to sliced fruits of every variety, he brought Ben a large tortilla and slices of Bayonne ham, an inch thick with sauteed potatoes.

As they ate and drank, Garza explained his role in the region and how it was his responsibility to look after his people and help get them jobs. Then when they lost jobs, he helped them to pay their bills and feed them. He sounded more a saint and several times he took a surreptitious glance at the redhead on the other side of the pool and wondered what he did for her. It was a one-way conversation because Garza expected no interruptions when he spoke, and they were content to concentrate on eating. Although several times Alena called Freddie to come and eat, he was enjoying himself too much in the pool.

When he finished his plateful and had taken another swig of coffee and orange juice to wash it down, Ben felt ready to talk. 'Your people must love you.'

Garza gave a mock bow in appreciation.

'Will you help us?'

Garza paused, and his face hardened and it was obvious he was on the point of lying because he could see him formulating an answer. At that moment, the two bikers walked up to the table and laid Ben's yellow notepad and wallet of pencils, the penknife, and Bernay's revolver before Garza.

The Count waved them away, and they retreated to the shade of a pillar.

'What have we here?'

Picking up the revolver, Garza pointed it at him with a laugh 'Bam, bam.' He blew the imaginary smoke from the end of the barrel. 'What were you expecting to do? Take on the German army single-handed?'

'It's an old family heirloom.'

'Perhaps, if you were French. It's loaded, were you expecting trouble?'

'In these times ...' he made an expansive gesture with his hands.

'And what's this?' Garza replaced the revolver on the table, but out of his reach, and pulled the notebook towards him.

Garza flipped it open and peered at some writing on the first page.

'It's no use, I can't read what you've written.'

'Neither can I.'

A smile flitted across Garza's face.

'Tell me, Ben, what do you do?'

'I'm a writer.'

'Ah.' Garza nodded towards the notebook.

'An American writer?' Garza said. 'I met another one here several times although it was years ago. Here every July we have the Festival of San Fermin and every morning we have the *encierro*.'

'What's that?' Alena asked.

'The running of the bulls,' said Ben.

'We've been doing it for hundreds of years even before your country was discovered.' Garza said turning to him.

She still looked puzzled and Garza explained.

'Bulls are released from corrals on the other side of the town and they race through the streets to the bullring where they are killed in the bullfight. Young men from all over Spain and even elsewhere run in front of them, trying not to be gored.'

'That's dreadful for them,' she said.

'They know what they're doing.'

'I meant it's terrible for the bulls.'

Garza laughed.

'Perhaps. At least, it gives them a chance to get their own back. Men die doing this. It's most dangerous when they get to the ring. Because there's so many of them, it's hard to get out of the way and it's difficult to climb over the *barrera*.'

'The bulls must be terrified.'

Again, Garza laughed.

'I think you misplace your concern. These beasts are a ton of muscle. They're vicious and their horns are as sharp as knives. I've done it several times, and I never ever felt sorry for the bulls. Now I leave it to younger men; I no longer need to impress anyone.'

'Is the writer Hemingway?' Ben ventured.

'Yes, yes, you know his work?'

'I do.'

'An amazing man, such presence. A big drinker – wine, vodka. Entertaining friends. There was another writer with him on one occasion, John Dos Passos. Hemingway didn't just spectate. Every morning he'd grapple with the bulls and wrestle them to the ground.'

'Is he a good man?'

'Yes! I liked him as did his friends, especially the senoritas. He had fun in our town. I like everything American,' he laughed and slapped Ben's thigh, 'That's good for you, is it not?'

He mumbled a reply.

'Tell me one thing as a writer? Hemingway said when he'd trouble starting a piece of writing he'd write the truest sentence he knew and from there the rest would follow. I tried it and I still couldn't get a second sentence. What do you do in that situation?'

'I go straight to the third sentence,' he replied deadpan.

Garza thought, digesting the answer behind his black eyes, and threw back his head and roared with a girlish laugh.

From the shadows, his two minders joined in not knowing what they were laughing at and Alena also enjoyed the joke.

'You know here in my house I have a private cinema and I'm sent the latest movies from America. I see them all.' He got to his feet and moved to stand behind Alena's chair. 'There is a big new star in American films, a beautiful blonde lady, Veronica Lake, you know of her?'

He nodded. He'd heard of her although he'd seen none of her movies. His mission to France was to learn more about their culture, not waste time on films from the homeland.

Garza placed his hands on her shoulders and Ben tensed in his chair. She didn't approve and tried to move out of the way, but he held her. 'If I hadn't known better, I'd have thought this was Veronica.' He used his right hand to move the veil of blonde hair away from her eye. He touched her as though handling an object for sale and Ben detected a change in the atmosphere, a drop in the temperature. Now he feared Sebastian's offer of help might have an ulterior motive.

'Will you help us, count?' Ben mustered as much respect as he could manage.

'First, tell me why you were so desperate to get out of France.'

He looked at Alena. 'For the safety of my family, I didn't want them to live under the Nazis.'

'Understandable, I suppose.' The count resumed his seat. 'Then why did you risk your life in taking the car when it would have been easier and safer just to walk over the mountains?'

'We have to get home to America.'

She glanced at him wondering how far he was going with this story.

'I'm broke, I've no money. The book that was to be published has been abandoned because the publisher fled Paris. Through a contact, I found a man in Lisbon to buy the Bentley and so give us enough funds to book our passage to New York and safety.'

'Mmm.' Garza stroked his chin as if not believing him. 'As you can see, I'm a very powerful man. The people who helped you work for me. I understand you paid them well so they're happy. In business, everyone must be satisfied. I wouldn't have been interested had it not been that you had a Derby Bentley, which I want to add to my collection, an amazing woman with film star looks and a child. That was a very impressive package. The car is of particular interest. A three-and-a-half litre engine, six cylinders, 115 horsepower, synchromesh gearbox and in an aluminium body. Do you know they call it the silent sports car because even at speed it's so quiet?'

He laughed. 'No longer, it rattles as much as an old tin can.'

'Perhaps,' said Garza with a faraway look in his eyes.

'The car's not much use to you. I'm afraid it's in a bit of a mess and I suppose the man in Lisbon will lower the price now.'

Garza spread his arms. 'No problem, my friend, I've a collection of fine cars and the people to look after them.'

He saw Garza's eyes flicker over the playing Freddie and settle on Alena, who stared at her hands, and he felt Garza's anticipation as hot as a lover's breath on his skin.

'Let's talk about the woman and the child...'

# 51

ANGER SIMMERED UNDER THE SURFACE AND EVERY SO OFTEN HE AIMED A kick at whatever was in range. This was his operation. He was responsible for the safe departure of the woman and child and, with a bit of luck, the platinum. Rafe Cooper was in charge, or so he thought until he'd taken the call.

The orders were specific. A top agent from the British Embassy in Paris had been dispatched to make sure everything went to plan. This was too important to fail. The agent would arrive in Estoril either late on the Saturday night or early Sunday, the same day he expected the arrival of the Bentley with its valuable cargo. The agent would make contact and he must follow his orders to the letter.

It didn't help that Rafe's head hurt as it had never before. Those Germans knew how to celebrate and while he'd stayed at the Palácio to glean as much information as possible he wasn't averse to a free supply of good champagne. He'd always marvelled how well they got along together. Elsewhere they were shooting each other. Here it was as if they were fans of rival football teams joining in the celebrations of victory or commiserations of defeat.

And he'd sought out the hatcheck girl at the casino as she finished her shift. He'd still not found out her name, but by then he didn't care and now he couldn't remember if she'd told him her name.

Then the phone call. The agent had better not change his arrangements, he thought; he'd paid out enough money, and it was too late to rearrange things. That would put them at risk.

He set off to see Armand, the shopkeeper he'd known since he first arrived and trusted with his life. Armand kept reminding him the alliance between the English and Portuguese was the oldest in the world and it was their duty to continue it. Armand ran a fruit and vegetable shop in a cobblestoned side street just off the Avenida Marginal, Estoril's main road running along the sea front. And Rafe had paid him for a lock-up in a quiet lane close to his shop.

He'd no intention of burdening the shopkeeper with the details. And Armand, not wishing to know, had put up a hand and said: 'In ignorance there's safety.'

He collected the keys from Armand, cracked a few jokes with his teenage son, Christiano, and walked over to the garage and unlocked the door. It was empty apart from wooden crates piled high in a corner as he'd requested, and a malodorous smell of rotting vegetables assailed his senses. Overhead lighting picked out a ramp on which they'd drive the Bentley before relieving it of its bullion cargo.

Perfect! The flying boat would arrive at the beach, Praia da Tamariz, only a hundred or so yards away. And they'd work here extricating the platinum and preparing it for transfer to the plane.

He couldn't see any flaws, and he hoped when he told the incoming agent he wouldn't either.

## 52

'WHAT ARE YOU SAYING?' BEN TRIED TO KEEP HIS VOICE EVEN, FIGHTING against the alarm threatening to engulf him.

'Well let's say I help people to resettle and make new friends,' replied Garza.

'What do you mean?' His voice was growing louder.

Garza smiled. He could be a patient man when it suited him. 'Africa is just across the Mediterranean from Spain and there they have different ideas to us concerning possessions. Like cattle, people can be possessions and they prefer to buy European –'

'You can't.' He jumped to his feet understanding Garza's intentions.

A biker waiting in the shade stepped forward and jammed his carbine into Ben's ribs, and Garza clutched his arm.

'Let's not be hasty or else he'll shoot you dead. Sit down.'

He did as he was told, and the biker slipped back into the shadows still training his carbine on him. 'Please, let us go now.'

'Let me make a suggestion.' Garza poured another orange juice and took a sip before continuing. 'As you're an American writer, I'll help you get back home and perhaps one day you'll mention me in one of your stories and I'll become famous in America. Maybe they'll even make a film about me. However, in exchange for your freedom, you understand, I must keep the Bentley.'

'No, you can't, we need it to travel to Portugal,' he replied although he no longer worried about the car.

'Simple! I'll give you another car – an old Ford, but it'll get you there.'

Fearing there was worse to come, he said nothing.

'And the woman will stay with me.'

'No,' she shouted, horror radiating from her eyes.

'Really?' said Garza in mock amazement. 'Perhaps I can change your mind. Let me tell you a story. I have a wealthy customer in Marrakech. Every so often, he buys a young boy from me. He keeps them for a few years and when they get too old for his needs, he moves them on to a contact, who has a demanding clientele. He'd be interested in your little Freddie. I can let you go to Lisbon, but the boy will be sent to Marrakech. Or you can stay with me and as long as you keep me happy the boy will stay here. It's your choice?'

She glanced at him appealing for help and the tears were welling up in her eyes. Eventually, she mumbled a reply.

'I'm sorry, I didn't quite hear what you said,' insisted Garza. 'Louder!'

'I'll stay with you,' she forced the words out and her eyes blazed with a defiance making her look all the more beautiful.

'You see.' Garza smiled and turned to him as if they'd completed a satisfactory business deal. 'I knew she'd agree.'

'You can't do this.' He got to his feet. 'We will leave now, and you'd better not stop us.' And he reached over and grabbed Alena's arm.

Garza nodded, and the two men again emerged from the shadows, their carbines pointing at him.

'This is tiresome,' said Garza. 'My offer was generous. Your freedom for theirs. No one refuses Conde Juan Callas Garza. I make an offer only once. You've dishonoured me.'

Garza thought it would have been pleasurable to break him as he'd done with so many. Reduce him to a whimpering wreck. Emasculate him so he'd nothing left. No dignity. No pride. Play with him and discard him as you would a broken toy. Then he'd beg for death. But he wanted to concentrate on the car and the woman. He loved having the power of life and death; it made him feel like a god. Often, he wished he could bring them back to do it all over again to see how they reacted to different methods. The trouble with death is it is so final.

With a yawn, Garza turned to his men. 'Do it, now.'

One stepped forward, eyes narrowing as his finger tightened on the trigger. Ben heard Alena begging and saw visions of his parents standing in front of their upstate New York home smiling and beckoning to him.

The shot was as clear as a cough in a library.

# 53

THE SNIPER WATCHED HIS BULLET ALL THE WAY TO THE TARGET THROUGH the telescopic sight of his Russian Mosin-Nagant rifle modified for this purpose. With satisfaction, he observed the surprise on the victim's face a fraction of a second before the top of his head disintegrated. He adjusted his aim and squeezed the trigger sending another bullet speeding from the hill on which he hid.

The location had been reconnoitred earlier, and he found it perfect for what he planned. He could rest his arm on a large rock and the surrounding bushes gave him cover so that he couldn't be spotted from the hacienda. His jacket and spectacles rested on top of another rock. He didn't need them. He had perfect long sight and only used spectacles for reading. The layout of the house was ideal for this task, and he had a clear view of all the targets. And with this rifle he could hit the head of a matchstick give an inch or two from around five hundred yards.

The second guard, frozen in shock, had no time to raise his carbine before the bullet hit him foursquare in the forehead throwing him backwards over a chair.

Garza dived under the table, but not knowing where the fire came from it didn't provide complete cover. The sniper squeezed off another missile, shattering the count's spine, and as the Spaniard rolled free from the table, he put another into his head.

Garza's men ignored Ben and Alena as they scrambled for protection behind pillars and tables believing they were under attack. Perhaps the Germans had invaded. The guards from the gate joined them and fanned out around the pool and fired up at the hill although they were aiming at the wrong target as the sniper monitored the spectacle unfolding beneath him.

In the ensuing chaos, Ben and Alena, carrying Freddie, inched towards the door and passed out of sight of the watcher on the hill.

The sniper stood up, dusted himself off and put on his jacket and spectacles. He dismantled the rifle and packed it away before walking down the other side of the hill to a car waiting in the shade of a copse of trees fifty yards away.

# 54

Instinct told Ben to stand still because he realised they weren't the targets. Movement would put them at greater risk. As the chaos unfolded around them as if in slow motion, men died with fear in their eyes. Only when there was a pause in the firing did he grab a shocked Alena and Freddie, who were white-faced and frozen with fear, and propel them out of the house towards the car.

Garza's followers had flooded into the house and were no longer interested in them and they took up positions and fired indiscriminately at where they believed the invaders to be.

'We've got to get away, we've got to get away,' she kept repeating as he bundled them into the Bentley. He gunned the accelerator willing it to respond and with a leap it shot out of the courtyard and onto the drive.

The Bentley stopped.

'For Christ's sake what's wrong?' she shouted and tried to turn the wheel as if that might keep it moving. 'We must get out of here.'

'Hold on.' He got out and ran into a barn housing Garza's automobile collection. It didn't take him long to find what he was looking for and he half-ran back to the Bentley carrying two jerrycans of fuel and forced them into the back of the car.

'We need gas,' he told her jumping in and releasing the handbrake. 'I don't know if we'll be able to get any up ahead.'

Still the intermittent crack of carbines continued as they drove away from the hacienda.

Freddie spotted them first. 'A car's coming,' he warned.

Without looking, Ben pulled hard on the wheel and they lurched off the drive, down a slope into a field and bounced to a stop behind a hedge. He switched off the engine, and they sat in silence not daring to breathe as two vehicles swept up the drive. A saloon car, which had one passenger sitting up front who appeared to be wearing a large white turban, was followed by a covered truck with two men up front and more in the back.

'Nazis,' said Alena without hesitation.

He took her word for it; she knew her Germans better than he. It terrified him. Until now, their pursuers had been a possibility. Now they were right on their tail.

As soon as the Nazis disappeared out of sight, he fired the ignition and drove back to the drive and picked up speed. He'd decided they would not stop for anything and the increasing sound of gunfire reinforced the feeling. There was one guard on the gate and he lay in a pool of blood still clutching his carbine. All Ben could do now was put as many miles as possible between them and their pursuers and hope the Germans would be delayed at the hacienda.

Gradually, the purring of the Bentley's six cylinders replaced the sound of gunfire. Now they were out on the open road he put the Bentley through its paces for the first time and the car responded like an animal escaping captivity.

The maps Bernay had left for them were still in the car and Alena poured over them tracing a route through the middle of Spain with a finger.

'It looks as if it's a straight run,' she said turning to him and brushing her hair out of her eyes. 'We head for Valladolid.' She prodded the map. 'Salamanca and then it's not far to the Portuguese border.'

'How far?' He turned towards her with a smile. Again, she studied the map and tried to judge the distances between her thumb and forefinger.

'Around six hundred miles to Estoril.'

'To the border?'

'Maybe three hundred.'

She glanced again at the map. 'Or two fifty.' She shrugged, irritated she couldn't be more exact.

He tried to calculate when they might arrive in Estoril if they had no further setbacks. The road ahead was quiet and if they could average fifty miles per hour, they'd reach their destination late that night. They'd have all of Sunday to extricate the platinum and prepare for the flying boat's arrival on Monday.

In normal circumstances, the Bentley could outrun the Nazis' car and truck. But he couldn't be sure if it had sustained serious damage and by how much the extra weight of the bullion would slow it. And he realised he might yet be forced to do what Alena had asked of him when they first met. Kill them both.

It was then he realised in his haste to escape the hacienda he'd left the revolver on the dining table and for the first time he wished he still had it in his possession.

He swore under his breath, fearing more her reaction if she found out he'd left it behind, and he pressed all the harder on the accelerator pedal.

# 55

THEY MADE GOOD TIME, AND HE KEPT HIS FOOT FLAT TO THE BOARDS AS they swept through the Spanish countryside with the heat shimmering on the road ahead. At every opportunity, Alena glanced back, expecting to find the Nazis roaring up behind them. Although he said he was keeping watch in his mirror, it didn't reassure her. Seeing the pursuers in the flesh brought back all her fears. Only now, they were magnified.

Fatigue overcame her, and she fell into a deep sleep with her head resting on his shoulder. In the back, Freddie had also fallen asleep, clutching his teddy bear, and so it went mile after mile.

He continued to check the fuel gauge as the needle crept closer to empty and he wondered if a stray bullet had punctured the fuel tank. He didn't want to risk refuelling yet as he was determined to build a lead on their pursuers, and he didn't want to awaken Alena and Freddie. What he couldn't figure out was whether the car running low on gas might damage the engine and prevent it restarting.

He ran over in his mind what awaited them in Estoril. Bernay had told him to check in at the Hotel Palácio and wait for the British agent Rafe Cooper to contact them, and he'd make the arrangements. As Portugal enjoyed neutral status, the Germans didn't have jurisdiction, but he wondered if they'd be safe. If the Portuguese allowed them to enter the country, they'd also let in the Nazis.

It seemed a lifetime ago they'd left Paris and the longer the journey was taking, the more his questions mounted. What did the Germans want? The platinum or Alena and Freddie? Or both? Who'd killed Garza? A local rival or was someone else after them? What made Alena so valuable? He wanted to wake her up and demand an answer. But seeing her in a deep sleep, he took another glance in his mirror and returned his concentration to the road ahead.

WEBER STOOD by the pool and lit a cigarette as he surveyed the detritus of battle scattered around him. For a moment as he inhaled, the smoke masked the smell of cordite causing him to sneeze. Although a short gun battle, it increased the pain in his head and he wanted a quiet and darkened room and the opportunity to lie down.

Garza's followers lay around him. Most were dead. Those who survived were dispatched with a bullet to the brain. While Garza's men had taken positions against what they thought were attackers on the hill, Weber and his men walked in and wiped them out before they had time to retaliate. Although they'd been tough men, they were no match for his professionals.

A small brown man in briefs lay by the side of a table with a hole in his back and another in his head. And he guessed it was Garza by the amount of gold around his neck and wrist.

Weber kneeled to inspect the body and its wounds and nodded as he regained his feet. A sniper.

*Efficient!*

He looked up at the hill to to pinpoint the sniper's position, realising he'd be long gone.

A flickering movement on the periphery of his vision diverted his attention. Here amidst the corrupted air and the chaos, fluttered a beautiful and fragile creature unaware of the surrounding dangers. He put out a hand and held it open, palm up, and smiled as the butterfly landed and its light touch tickled his skin. Admiring the red of its wings, he stroked its back and closed his hand on the flickering of its trapped wings. He smiled to himself as he placed it gently on a nearby flower.

They found a frightened man hiding in a cupboard and dragged him out to the poolside so that he was aware what awaited him if he didn't talk.

The civilian conducted a smooth and painless interrogation in Spanish and the manservant couldn't stop talking, nodding after every sentence ensuring the civilian understood what he'd said.

Three people had come over the mountain. An American with a woman and a boy. They drove a Bentley. The American argued with the Count. Then the Count and two of his men were shot. By whom? He shrugged, he didn't know. But he pointed up towards the hill.

Weber followed his hand, and his brow furrowed. Who was the gunman? He didn't need added complications. It would have been simpler had it been a local rival intent on settling an old score, but this operator was a professional. Yet a wave of optimism helped deaden the pain in his head. He was close to the woman and child. It would be only a matter of time. She'd get little help in Spain and the authorities would offer any assistance needed. It might be more troublesome if they crossed into Portugal. Like a hunter moving in for the kill, he smelled blood.

Had Garza known what a treasure he'd had in his grasp. Probably not. He would have preferred if he had known and then for it to have been taken away.

'*Schnell*, we must head south,' he ordered his men and turned and swept out to the courtyard.

The civilian made to follow but doubled back. Still on his knees, the servant clasped his hands in prayer with his eyes closed. He walked up to him and tapped him on the shoulder and as the servant turned in surprise, the civilian shot him through an eye.

# 56

BEN DIDN'T SEE THEM COMING. THEY'D SKIRTED THE TOWNS OF Valladolid and Salamanca when the Bentley started coughing and spluttering and a weakening panic spread through him. They were on the open road and with no shelter they'd be defenceless if the Nazis caught up with them. The fuel gauge was showing empty and at the first opportunity he pulled over onto the grass verge awakening Alena.

'What's wrong?' she asked, sitting upright and rubbing the sleep from her eyes. 'Where are we?

'I've got to put in more gas,' he said.

He'd no idea how close behind the Nazis were, but he had to refuel. He pulled a jerrycan out of the back of the Bentley and dragged it to the fuel cap. To his relief, the cap on the can unscrewed easily, and the liquid glugged out. He wanted to force it in as fast as possible, but he took care not to waste any of the precious liquid. And he kept glancing back along the road.

It was important to put both jerrycans of fuel into the Bentley at this stop. Fetching the second can, he attempted to open it, but the thread was out of synch and wouldn't budge. He used all his strength yet still he couldn't move it. From under the Bentley's hood he retrieved a large hammer, used for removing the car's wheels, and banged at the cap. On his knees and straining hard to open it, he didn't hear a car pull up in front of the Bentley.

For a fraction of a second, he glimpsed the butt of a rifle before he felt a dull blow to the side of his head. He fell forwards onto the road, scraping the skin from his forehead.

He felt as if he'd been out for an age. In reality, it was only seconds. The side of his head throbbed and was wet to the touch and when he inspected his fingers, he found blood. Shaken by the blow, he rose to his feet to see two officers with their three-pointed patent leather hats and green uniforms – the Guardia Civil, Franco's hated police – with Alena. In Franco's police state, the Guardia relished their main role of seeking spies and agitators against the regime. And he knew he and Alena fitted their description as enemies of the state.

She was arguing with them and Freddie was crying, and he stumbled as one officer came around the side of the car and stuck the barrel of his rifle into his ribs.

'No se mueva,' the policeman said, and he stood still as ordered.

She tried to talk to the other officer in what sounded passable Spanish, but he forced her against the frame of the car door as if he wanted her to sit back in her seat. Although he didn't show a gun, he was big and powerful and growing angrier as she spread her arms to stop being forced back inside.

He said something to her in a low voice, and she spat in his face with a look of distaste. A backhander caught the bottom of her lip, splitting it open, and blood smeared her face. Freddie was screaming, but the officer cowed him into silence and he crouched behind the seat in the back of the car.

The policeman guarding Ben shouted encouragement to his colleague who grunted in reply. As she reeled from the slap and her hand went to the wound on her lip, he grabbed the collar of her blouse and pulled it with such force that her bra came away exposing her breasts. He paused and, encouraged by this show of flesh, put his hands on her legs and forced her skirt up over her knees and kept pushing it up her thighs until he could see the white flesh above her stocking tops.

Again, Ben's captor urged his compatriot on and the policeman moved closer to her, one hand going around her neck and pulling her head closer to him.

# 57

WEBER OPENED THE CAR'S WINDOW AND FLICKED OUT HIS CIGARETTE ASH unperturbed that it blew back into the face of the civilian sitting behind him. The man didn't object. Weber wasn't someone to argue with and after talking to his soldiers the civilian realised his orders came from the very top so whatever he said had to be obeyed. Weber drew long and hard on his cigarette and coughed into his hand. He loved the smell of cigarette smoke in the fresh air. It conjured up many memories, happy memories – attending his first football match with his father where cigarette smoke lay in clouds above the spectators. For the first time, he felt he was making progress. And he could almost smell the woman. They might have a faster car, but the weight of the bullion was a handicap and all it needed was a minor hold-up and they'd be on them.

'Faster,' he shouted at the driver and slapped a hand hard on the dashboard. 'Can't you get more out of this tin box?'

The driver's foot was flat to the floorboards and he shifted in his seat and gripped the steering wheel harder as if that might squeeze more out of it.

It was important to catch up with them before the Portuguese border. While in Spain, the Spanish authorities would help if asked. But with an American passport, Ben Peters should have no problem in crossing over. And, as Portugal was neutral and more inclined to support the allies, he couldn't expect any assistance, making his task harder although not impossible. He'd already put in place arrangements to transport the woman and boy back to Paris. There were still those who'd do anything for a price.

As for the platinum, he hadn't worked out what to do. In an unguarded moment, the fantasy of keeping it presented itself and that appealed to him. Once he'd brought the woman and boy back for his superiors to decide their fate, he would return home to Munich. Perhaps they'd let him return to work as a journalist on the *Munchener Zeitung*, and he'd try to forget the chaos and misery elsewhere in the world.

He didn't see the point of war. Enemies now would be allies in another ten years. What he saw around him he'd already experienced. He'd been one of the lucky ones to survive the Great War campaign unscathed, apart from the memories. Memories he didn't want to remember. Memories that continued to dominate sleepless nights…

Rain ran red like blood down his cheek.

It slanted in at an angle of forty-five degrees and every drop was as sharp as shards of glass, cutting his skin and reducing his visibility to only ten yards. Night was black, yet so was day. The thick grey dirt, which blew into every crook and cranny, lay like a swamp of evil-smelling porridge causing them to sink up to their knees. Choice? There were no choices. Be blown apart by the British or drown in the sludge. They shelled hour after hour. A sentry shouted above the din. 'Minnie up'. Pointless. A red spark traversed the sky like a steam engine as it flew overhead. They fizzed and crackled, and you waited for them to fall. The explosions. Screams. Dismembered bodies.

The constant downpour formed a curtain around the sandbag-reinforced shell hole he shared with Horst. And it wouldn't let him get past the memory.

*Sea and sun all mix and run*
*And the smell of ozone, gulls swooping alone*
*People screaming, kids scaring*

*Old men, trousers furled, white hankies on bald pates*
*And deckchair spread-eagled obscenely mates*
*Ice cream vendor calling his wares above the crash of the sea*
*A spade and a pail and a ship with a sail*
*Wet brown sand that you shape in your hand*
*And candy floss and donkey rides and lemonade*
*Cool, frothing waters tingling your ankles*
*Sand in your sandals, and hand in hand*
*They trailed through halls of wax models grand*
*Soft, sharp light making eyes glint and a faint smell of mint*
*A premonition*
*It makes her cry and gasping for air he smoothes her hair*
*Iced buns and lemonade runs down their glowing cheeks*
*Back to the lodging austere and spare*
*Dodging the landlady and leaking sand on the stair.*

He sent the poem about their short honeymoon at Rugen on the Baltic to his wife in the first week of being in the trenches. Written on a colourful postcard embroidered in lace by local women, it amazed him such finery could exist in a place of pure barbarity. And now he kept repeating it over and over in his head.

Because he couldn't see beyond the curtain of rain, his mind wouldn't move forward. No matter how hard he tried, he came back to his memory as a gramophone needle stuck in a groove. In his tunic pocket, he kept a photograph of her and when he showed it to others, he saw the envy in their eyes. What marked her apart from so many were her sharp features, giving her a timeless beauty, and eyes flashing blue streaks of lightning. A cascade of auburn curls flowed around her high cheekbones past her shoulders to the middle of her back. At night, he watched mesmerised as she sat naked before her mirror combing her long tresses accentuating her slender shoulders and the narrowness of her waist. Her full lips were always parted as if ready to speak and showed perfect mother-of-pearl teeth.

Although he wanted to look on her to blot out the horrors of war, the effort was too great. It meant unbuttoning his sodden greatcoat with fingers frozen rigid so if they were blown off he doubted he'd feel pain. He'd found shelter in the lee of a makeshift wall and, although the rain hit his cap and glanced off, soaking the rest of him, he almost felt comfortable. His rifle dripped with moisture and he wondered if it would fire. He couldn't feel his feet. He and Horst had been standing twenty-four hours a day up to their knees in mud for the last week and he wondered if his toes were rotting. They'd better not because it would be a shooting offence. You coated your feet in whale oil to save your toes from trench foot and your life from the firing squad. The consolation, he convinced himself, was the wet killed off the lice infesting his body and making his skin crawl so that it appeared he'd a constant nervous tic.

The rain enclosed him in the small, unreal world he shared with Horst, the only friend he'd kept in this stinking war. Friends were taken away from him – blown into oblivion, broken up into pieces or carted away to the field hospitals from which they never returned. Horst was constant, still hanging in there. You struck a bond when you shared a shell hole. You both used the same tin to shit in, and it was regular because the only hot drink came in petrol tins. Although they were boiled, the petrol oozed from the creases in the tin giving you the shits.

He wondered how mad Horst was. One morning he announced an end to lice and later that night showed him his instant cure. Stripping off, he lit a cigarette and then stubbed it into the infected parts of his body.

'You're crazy,' said Weber. 'Doesn't it hurt?'

'Well, the lice don't bother me for a time.'

They would not bother him anymore as the back of his head gaped open.

Weber believed something still moved inside there, but he didn't want to give up his place of comfort to check it. Must have happened after they shared their breakfast of a third of a small loaf of bread and a slice of cold, stringy bacon congealed in a brownish fat.

He'd no idea of time. Sleep would have taken him away from it if you didn't mind a court-martial and death. Only losing yourself in memories could make this hell marginally bearable and give you a reason for hoping you might survive the lottery. There again it reminded him how much he had to lose.

Win or lose, he'd no idea how the war was progressing, and any initial enthusiasm had been squeezed out of him. No one ran. Even when they went over the top, they no longer ran. Just walked into the guns, praying it was not to be their day. So few of those he'd started with still survived. He wouldn't have believed how fragile bodies were, how a living reasoning being could disintegrate before your eyes, how soon they'd rot and how obscene the stench of death was.

Will anyone come back? See what we died for. A few yards of fucking muck?

He remembered marching to the railway station being cheered as heroes. Arriving at the barracks and soon realising there was no romance here. Collecting what gear they were given. Beers in the canteen. Lights out at ten o'clock. Sharing for the first time with other men. Swearing, farting, and masturbating under the coarse brown blankets. Brief excitement when the news came they were going into action. Existing like sewer rats in trenches. Marching into enemy fire and dying as fodder. Once when inspected by aristocratic officers he saw by their expressions and their words that they were expendable. Human lives but with no worth. When this war was over, he'd go back but nothing would be the same.

Another shell exploded to his right, the closest for some time, filling his mouth with wet mud and lifting him up and blowing him across the shell hole so he ended up embracing the back of Horst's head.

'Sorry, my old friend,' he giggled as if it were a joke.

And blood ran red like rain down his cheek.

# 58

THE GUARDIA CIVIL POLICEMAN ATTEMPTED TO KISS HER, AND SHE AVERTED her mouth so that the fleshy wetness of his tongue smeared her cheek. 'Come here, pretty lady,' the policeman said in a low and insistent growl. 'Do it proper now.' He punched Alena in the stomach forcing the air out of her diaphragm and she folded into him with her head on his shoulder like two lovers meeting.

The wind whipped up, and the sky turned the colour of lead, a premonition of something terrible about to happen, even though far away across the fields the sun still sparkled and brought everything into sharp relief.

She wanted to scream but fear paralysed her vocal chords and all she managed was a croak and she glanced over at Ben appealing for his help, knowing there was nothing he could do.

The fleshy folds of the guard's stomach pressed against her and, with his left hand, he pinched her face so tight her lips puckered. And he kissed her again sending a stream of saliva into her mouth. His right hand moved over her body, kneading it, feeling the weight of her breasts in his hand as if he were buying fruit, seeking her nipples and squeezing them. Down over the swell of her buttocks and between the cleft of her cheeks and around probing for an opening. Her body was rigid, petrified and unable to move – frozen in the glare of his malevolent eyes as she waited for the attack.

His stubby, calloused fingers bruised her as he hooked a thumb into the waistband of her panties and pulled them down. He switched, tracing the inside of a leg hole and with a grunt ripped it with such force the silk came away altogether in his hand. Pushing the cloth into her face, he glared at her, a gleam of triumph in his rheumy eyes.

The officer guarding Ben was so intent on watching what his colleague was doing he didn't notice her right hand reaching behind her for her handbag lying on the car seat. Her fingers scrambled as she sought the opening into the bag.

A flash of silver.

Ben saw her raise her arm to the guard's chest and heard a magnified thud. The guard's eyes changed from a look of lustful triumph to a blankness. They opened even wider at the force of the blow and his face contorted like a rubber mask left too close to the flame as he fell backwards with blood pumping out of his chest.

She dropped her hand holding the silver handgun to her side and collapsed against the frame of the car door.

The other guard wheeled away from Ben in surprise, and he hit him on the back of the head with the hammer.

He ran over to Alena, who had now slumped into the seat and was crying: 'I killed him. Killed him.'

'It's all right.' He put his arms around her pulling her to him feeling the warmth of her body and the tremors flowing through her.

'I'm sorry... I killed him.'

'He's not dead,' he lied. 'You had to shoot him. Did he hurt you?'

'No,' she snapped, defiant again. 'Men can't...' she said between the tears '... can't hurt me.'

Trembling so hard as if it would shake off any vestiges of her encounter with the policeman, she never seemed more helpless and vulnerable as she stared into space. He took off his jacket and wrapped it around her and, picking up her feet, swung her legs around and into the car. He reached over to take the gun from her, but she hung onto it as if it were an extension of her arm.

'We must go now,' she said in a hoarse whisper.

The policeman was dead, and he dragged his body onto the grass verge. The one he'd hit was still breathing although unconscious, and he pulled him over to their patrol car and laid him out across the back seat.

With a backwards glance, he ran back to the Bentley, jumped in and switched on the engine. It started first time, and he swung it out onto the road.

The policemen would soon be found and there would be the possibility of roadblocks ahead, then their escape to freedom would end. The fascist government wouldn't take kindly to foreigners killing their police and would execute them. The British would deny any knowledge of Alena and Freddie and the Spanish would hand them over to the Nazis. More than ever, Ben wished he'd taken the boat to England.

They were approximately an hour's drive from the Portuguese border and now the Bentley would have to show its paces. And he hoped there were few passers-by sympathetic to the Guardia Civil.

Freddie still hid on the back seat, and every time he tried to talk to Alena she gave no sign of hearing as if the trauma of the shooting had blinded and deafened her.

# 59

'*SCHEISSE!*'

The oath from his driver on seeing the road ahead blocked by cars and police vehicles brought Weber out of his reverie.

'Guardia Civil,' groaned the civilian and sat upright in his seat to get a better view.

A couple of policemen guarded a patrol car parked at the side of the road facing them. Another two on their hands and knees inspected the grass verge as if looking for tyre tracks. Others loaded a body, covered by a sheet, into the back of an ambulance. An injured policeman, his head smeared with blood, lay on a stretcher talking animatedly to a man in plainclothes who looked to be in charge of the operation.

As they joined the queue of waiting cars, the civilian jumped out to speak to two more Guardia, who were policing the new arrivals.

Weber wound down his window and lit another cigarette. This was the last thing he needed. There was no sign of the Bentley, so they'd got through before this incident occurred. That would give them valuable time and they would be well on their way to the Portuguese border. His hopes of catching them before they made it to neutral territory were fading.

The civilian, his face flushed, returned to the car, and he looked as if he'd just lost an argument.

'Well?' Weber demanded.

'Not good,' said the civilian slamming the door behind him. 'A guard was shot and his partner attacked.'

'There'd be many who'd do that,' he ventured.

'They are having problems making sense of what the injured man is saying. He has a head wound and is rambling on about a Bentley and a blonde woman who shot his partner. They're taking him away now.'

'Ah, so! No doubt they'll be setting up roadblocks.' It would mean only more problems for them. It would also delay the Bentley, but if they were arrested by the Guardia Civil for killing a policeman, it would be difficult to get the woman back to Germany. And his family's future depended on her being silenced before she talked.

'Maybe, although they think the guard's brains are scrambled.'

'So, what do we do now?'

'Sit tight and wait,' the civilian said nervously.

'*Scheisse*!' He slammed his hand on the dashboard in frustration.

The civilian was deep in thought and, as the two policemen again walked past the car, he got out and called over to them. Through the open window, he heard snatches of conversation and the words '*terrorista*' and 'hospital' in an animated discussion. One policeman spoke to the plainclothes officer and returned. The civilian shook his hand and sprinted back to the car wrenching open the door and jumping aboard. 'Go,' he ordered the driver. 'Go now.'

In his surprise, the driver stalled the car but got it going at the second attempt. The two policemen were now acting as traffic cops and waved them on to overtake the line of traffic.

'Keep driving,' the civilian shouted at the driver who looked back at him for more guidance. 'They're letting us go.'

As they pulled past the scene of the incident, the plainclothes officer turned to look at them and then returned to the job in hand. Weber gave him a wave of acknowledgement. 'For Christ's sake how did you manage it?'

'I've a police ID card from Bilbao,' the civilian said. 'I told them you were an important witness to a major crime affecting national security and if I didn't get you to a hospital, you were in danger of bleeding to death.'

The civilian tapped his own head as a reminder, if he needed one, of his injury.

He turned to look out of the rear window. There was no sign of the truck.

'What about my men?' he demanded.

'You can't have everything,' said the civilian. 'You, I could explain, but six German troopers armed to the teeth would be difficult.'

He exhaled. In one way it could make things more difficult without the backup of muscle; in another it would be to his advantage if he had fewer witnesses.

Back in the queue, a man took off his steel-rimmed spectacles and blew on the lenses and polished them with a large white handkerchief. He replaced them and tapped the top of the steering wheel with his fingers. It was a dilemma. The Guardia Civil were going from car to car checking papers and if they looked in his trunk, they might be surprised to find a sniper's rifle.

He slipped off the safety catch on the pistol in his pocket. This would be tricky. The policemen were too spread out for him to shoot them in one sweep. If he shot the two approaching his car, the others might have time to get him in their sights.

# 60

THE PORTUGUESE GUARDS AT THE BORDER CROSSING SHOWED MORE interest in the Bentley's condition than they did in its passengers. It limped to a halt at the barrier making a loud rattling noise sounding as if it could be terminal. Ben offered his American passport, and a guard thumbed through it in a desultory fashion before ducking to look into the car. He glanced at Freddie in the back and stared at Alena for longer than he should have before going to a cabin to consult a colleague.

The two spoke for several minutes, the other guard leafing through Ben's passport. Eventually, the guard returned with his partner, who also looked into the car and his eyes never strayed from Alena. He withdrew chuckling and said something they couldn't understand to his colleague and Alena averted her face with a look of thunder. With an outsize grin, the first guard returned the passport and waved them through.

'Welcome to Portugal, Americans.' He gave a mock salute.

Some way down the road, she raised her arms and gave out a muted yelp of celebration and Freddie, catching the mood, joined in jumping up and down on the back seat.

'Are we safe?' The tone of her voice indicated she didn't believe it. 'Can we really be free?'

He put a hand on her arm.

'Not yet.' But he didn't want to dampen her mood. 'Don't forget the Germans have the same rights as us in Portugal and if they want you as much as you say they'll be right on our tail all the way to Estoril. You won't be safe until you step on English soil.'

Even then, he wondered, how safe would they be there? How long would it be before Hitler and his Nazis spanned the English Channel and invaded?

Her mood seemed to have lightened, and he realised it was part of an act for Freddie's sake. Although it appeared as if she'd shut out the memory of the incident with the Guardia, she still clutched the pistol with an increasing intensity.

'Please give me the gun?' he asked not wanting to spark any unwelcome memories.

She stared at him, debating what to do.

'When I escaped from the castle, I was given this so if the Nazis caught us I could take our own lives.' She pushed hair from her face. 'So you can understand why I have to keep it.'

He couldn't imagine her killing her own child. 'Surely you wouldn't?'

She glanced out of the window and back at him and there was a fierceness about her stare. 'You don't know what I'm capable of, I will if necessary.'

She said it with such determination he knew she would.

'What I did to the policeman I did out of hatred and revenge. I wasn't in control. I wanted to kill him, make him suffer for what he was doing to me. If the Germans catch us, it will be different. I'll shoot Freddie and it will be an act of love. Escape to a better place, you understand.'

Changing the subject, she turned to him with an enquiring smile 'So you're a writer?'

She made it sound more of an accusation than a question.

He nodded, wondering what was coming next.

'What have you published?'

'Nothing yet, I'm still working on things, so I guess I'm not a writer until I've been published.'

'Not necessarily.' She stretched her arms above her head. 'They say a writer is a person who writes.'

'Well, I do.'

'My grandfather told me that.' She went silent, remembering. 'He was so sweet. Back in Russia where he came from he knew many writers.'

'Did he write?'

'Yes, although he was a doctor of medicine. He liked to quote the line of Chekhov's.'

Ben turned and looked at her.

'You must know the one "Medicine is my lawful wife and literature is my mistress".'

She chuckled.

'You've read them?'

'What?'

'You've read all the major Russian writers?'

'Well, not exactly.'

He glanced at her again.

'It was my grandfather who got me into them when I was a young girl. I wasn't so keen on reading then. I used to visit him after school each day and I'd go to his study and he would read to me. While some books were daunting in print, his readings made them come alive and there in his study I could see the characters playing out their lives before me. It was magical.'

'Which ones?'

'Oh, all of them, all the greats as I suppose you'd call them.'

He nodded in appreciation.

'I had favourites. Tolstoy's *Anna Karenina*. I made him read it to me several times. Pushkin's *Eugene Onegin* because it was in verse, I suppose. Dostoyevsky and Chekhov's short stories.'

She lapsed into silence as she retreated into her memories.

Bernay hoped the platinum would help France's fight against occupation although now he was believing Alena's importance to the British war effort might be even more important than the millions in bullion. And it made him all the more determined to get her to reveal the truth before they reached England. He deserved it at least. First, they had to outrun the Nazis to Estoril, and once there they wouldn't be any safer than in France.

He glanced back at her and she just stared straight ahead immersed in her own secret world, and he took another look in his rear mirror and gunned the car on its way to Estoril.

---

THE TWO GUARDIA didn't know what hit them. Making their inspections of the cars in the queue, they'd sauntered up to a Citroen with French number plates, which appeared empty. It was only when they drew level with the car that the driver sat up and fired just two rounds, one in each of their heads.

People shouted, and some were screaming and several of the drivers got out of their cars to help. Two more Guardia ran towards the sound of the shots, but they were cut down before they'd time to determine what was happening.

The plainclothes officer and the two other policemen, who'd been guarding the original patrol car, stood rooted to the spot bemusement spreading across their faces as a car sped towards them.

A guard lifted a rifle to his shoulder and took aim. The plainclothes officer tugged at his pistol as the driver pulled out the pin of a grenade with his teeth and lobbed the missile between the three policemen. The thud of an explosion cut short the men's shouts of fear. And it reverberated along the line of cars making them shake and rattle as the bodies of the policemen flew into the air ending up on the roof of the wreckage of their patrol car.

# 61

THE HOTEL PALÁCIO HAD THE HIGHEST STANDARDS. IT WAS THE PLACE TO stay in Estoril. Emperors, kings and queens resided at the hotel and the world's most influential and sophisticated people were regular visitors. One didn't expect just anyone to arrive.

Although late, residents still roamed about, some strolling along the promenade or gambling at the casino. Others returning, perhaps to join the revellers in the piano bar until the last drinker passed out.

This should not be happening.

The commissionaire's moustache bristled. He first noticed the car when it turned in off the Avenue Clotilde and the entrance gate's lamps caught it in their light. It limped up the drive and he couldn't understand what he was seeing. As it came closer, it was as he feared. A large car covered in mud and dust. As it moved, part of it trailed along the ground making a scraping and grinding sound, and he believed he saw sparks. Only one headlamp worked. The number plate hung from the front and what looked like bullet holes peppered the bonnet. A crack zigzagged down the middle of the windscreen and deep grooves ran the length of its sides. Part of the hood was detached and flapped in the breeze like an injured gull's wings. The driver must be mistaken; he should be looking for a breaker's yard.

Looking around, the commissionaire in his grey uniform with red flashes hoped there were no witnesses and drew himself to his full height, adjusted his peaked cap and prepared to order the driver to take his heap of junk elsewhere.

The car stopped short of the main entrance as if it had expired and as he marched towards it a blonde woman alighted from the passenger door, her clothes soiled and torn. She wore a man's jacket draped over her shoulders, and mud and blood streaked her face, but her classic beauty shone through, causing him to hesitate. He'd seen many elegant women arrive at the hotel in their finery and it wasn't only their dress but the way they carried themselves, their poise and confidence, that marked them apart. She was different and the most striking woman he'd ever seen.

Before he gathered his wits, she disarmed him with her smile. 'I believe we're expected.'

'Yes ma'am,' he replied, a trifle flustered. 'I'll arrange for someone to take your bags.'

Carrying Freddie, Ben followed Alena in through the doors of the hotel. And he was blinded by the brightness of the grand lobby with the light from crystal chandeliers reflecting off mirrored ceilings, marble pillars and floors, and glass doors. This felt a million miles from what they'd endured out on the road and the prospect of a bath, clean clothes and food and drink made him dizzy with expectation.

The sense of relief was short-lived when he scanned the lobby, seeing a Nazi behind every pot plant and pillar. If the Germans had gotten to Bernay, they'd expect them here. The place bustled with men who could be agents. And he knew they couldn't afford to be off guard for a minute.

He went up to reception and the looks on the faces of the staff behind the counter amused him.

'Yes, can I help?' a receptionist smiled at him, clearing her throat in surprise.

'You've a reservation for us,' he said, and in a hoarse whisper added 'Ben Peters.' And he glanced over his shoulder wondering if his name aroused any interest.

She stared at him for several seconds before clearing her throat again and glanced at paperwork in front of her. She wasn't sure how to react to the man who had a livid cut on his head and congealed blood on the side of his face. And his partner wasn't in any better shape looking as if she'd slept in a field and with blood leaking from a cut on her lip.

A man in a sharp suit interrupted her doubts.

'Of course, Mr Peters,' he said, unfazed by their appearance. He'd come to accept the eccentricities of the rich and famous. 'Welcome to the Hotel Palácio. We've been expecting you and your wife and son. Your reservation was made by Rafe Cooper, and he left this note for you.'

The man handed Ben an envelope which he slipped into a pocket.

'We've arranged one of our best rooms with a view of the ocean, and we hope you'll have a pleasant stay.'

Alena went weak at the knees and stumbled as if in a faint and he caught her elbow.

'Water, please, for my wife,' he asked the woman at reception. 'We've had a long and challenging journey.'

The spacious room would have been perfect if they'd time to enjoy it with a king-size double bed and in the far corner a couch and coffee table and a small writing desk. Double doors opened out onto a balcony overlooking the park and with a view of the ocean. A door led to a smaller room with a single bed and he dropped his bag there. 'This will be perfect for me,' he said and hoped she'd hear the disappointment in his voice.

She returned an apologetic smile. 'I must have a bath, I feel filthy,' she apologised, 'and I must get Freddie to bed, he's so tired he'll sleep forever.'

He changed his shirt and jacket, gave his face a hand wash and flattened his hair. 'I'll go downstairs and scout around, it'll give you time to freshen up. Keep the door locked and whatever you do, don't open it to anyone. Good night, Freddie.'

He took the stairs so that he could check out possible exit routes if they'd to make a run for it and, as he descended, he heard the tinkling of a piano and a murmur of voices. He stopped on the mezzanine floor, which afforded a view of the lobby, and scanned the faces of those waiting there, but he wasn't sure for whom he was looking.

As he descended to the lobby, someone behind him cleared his throat.

'Mr Peters, if I may, Mr Peters?'

He started and wheeled in fright at the mention of his name.

The commissionaire opened his arms apologetically. 'I'm sorry to bother you with this,' he said. 'It's your car...'

'What about it?'

'It's still outside the entrance and it's, it's...' His voice trailed off unsure how to put it.

Ben laughed. 'I understand, don't worry I'll move it.'

The commissionaire looked relieved and smiled.

'It's a valuable car so it must be safe.'

'Don't worry, sir,' the commissionaire replied. 'We can put it somewhere no one will see it and I'll personally make sure it's secure.'

He crossed the lobby, drawn to the piano bar by the sound of music, and as soon as he entered he felt the room's eyes on him. It was long and narrow with tables and chairs along both sides and an aisle in the middle leading to the carved wooden bar stretching the width of the room. A man in a tuxedo picked out notes on a grand piano while a tall blonde in a long dress and glass in hand leant over him. In the main, the clientele was male, and conspiracy crackled in the air with cliques sitting together and talking in hushed voices. There had been raucous laughter, yet as soon as he entered it fell silent and he knew they were watching as he made his way to the bar. He ordered a Scottish malt and the barman, taking pity on his dishevelled appearance, poured an extra large one and served up a glass jug of water with a small bowl of ice.

'What's happening here?' he asked the barman.

'Just the Germans celebrating again,' he grimaced and shrugged. 'Yesterday it was champagne because they'd invaded Paris. Today they've driven British and Canadian troops out of Cherbourg, Brest and St Malo.'

The barman shrugged again, giving the impression he would have spat on the counter if he could get away with it.

He found an unoccupied table in a corner beside the bar and by now the others weren't interested in him anymore and from where he sat he could view the whole room and anyone entering. The Scotch was an Ardbeg, one of the peaty malts from the Isle of Islay and one of the strongest, retaining the maximum flavour. He added a touch of water to open it up and help it breathe, releasing the taste and aroma, before raising it to his lips. The first sip caught the back of his throat making him cough and it burned all the way down and from then on it was liquid gold.

He remembered Cooper's note and fished it out of his pocket. In an extravagant scrawl, Cooper welcomed them to Portugal suggesting they meet at 10 am tomorrow in the lobby.

Under his breath, he cursed Bernay for getting him involved in his madcap scheme. Before this, his life had been straightforward. Do his job at the bank and in his own time explore the delights of Paris and write in his yellow notebooks. Now he was lurking around hotel lobbies playing spies and facing danger at every turn. There again, it wasn't all bad, he raised his glass in a silent toast. Bernay had introduced him to Alena, and he was determined to get her and Freddie to England. Yet he understood escaping Portugal could be the most dangerous part of this affair.

## 62

ALENA OPENED THE DOOR TO THE HOTEL ROOM AFTER SEVERAL MINUTES OF his soft, but insistent, tapping. She wore a white towelling robe and a broad, confident smile. A towel was wrapped around her head and her skin glowed.

'I won't be long,' she whispered and returned to the bathroom closing the door behind her with a click.

He wandered over to the window and opened the double doors and stepped out onto the balcony. All he needed was a long and sound sleep without dreams. Although he felt more tired than he'd ever been, the night air and the aroma of the ocean invigorated him. The more he filled his lungs, the higher it lifted him. From the balcony, he could see the lights of the casino sparkling in the park's fountains and several miles away the fishing harbour of Cascais. To his left, a lone light twinkled and bobbed on the black of the ocean. The sounds of traffic on the Avenida Marginal and the occasional honking of horns drifted up on the warm breeze and voices and laughter and music echoed far away.

On returning to the bedroom, the bathroom door remained shut, so he decided to go to his room, collapse on the bed and welcome oblivion. As he put his hand on the doorknob, Alena came back into the bedroom and walked towards him smiling, her eyes glinting jade green in the diffused light. The towel had been dispensed with and her damp hair looked darker and was tousled around her face.

'Freddie's in there, please don't disturb him,' she said, her smile growing wider, 'he needs his sleep.'

He looked around wondering where he'd sleep.

'Anyway, it would seem strange to the chambermaid in the morning if a husband and wife slept in different rooms.'

Those eyes mesmerised him, and he couldn't move. She loosened the robe, letting it slip to the ground. Stepping out of the garment, she walked over to him, her hands reaching around his neck and pulling him close so that he felt her softness and smelled a hint of Chanel. He traced the outline of those high cheekbones and the dimple like a perfect scar with his thumbs.

'Thank you, Ben,' she said, her voice as smooth as warm honey, 'for everything you've done for us.'

Her lips appeared swollen and were parted and he put an arm around her waist and with the other pulled aside her hair. Kissing the silk of her neck, he let her relax into his arms as if this was the first time she could give herself completely for an age. And she lifted her head until those green eyes were inches from his and her mouth reeled him in. This was what he'd wanted from the moment they'd first met in Bernay's office.

She reached up, pulling him closer, but he stopped her and pushed her away and held her at arm's length. He didn't want it to be like this. For her to be beholden to him, believing she owed a debt that needed to be repaid. 'You don't have to do this, Alena.'

'Oh, I know,' she chuckled and flung her arms around his neck, pulling his mouth to hers. The force of her passion pushed him against the wall and she pinned him there, kissing and nibbling at his mouth and his ears with surprising intensity. Her eyes were glazed, and a kink of blonde hair hung enticingly over an eye like a half-open curtain inviting him to explore what lay behind. With a whimper, she again forced her mouth on his, her scent filling his head and his mind drifted as in a dream. Fumbling with the buttons of his shirt, she pulled at them until she stripped him of it. Her mouth moved on over his chin and the vulnerable softness of his neck to his bare chest, teasing his nipples with her teeth. Her nails dug into his skin as his hands ran over her curves, down over her waist and the ripeness of her buttocks and he pulled her into him so that her pelvis felt his hardness.

She pushed back against his body and, unbalanced and giggling, they toppled onto the bed.

# 63

THE GIRL KEPT FALLING AGAINST HIM, LEANING OVER ON HER RIDICULOUSLY high heels and losing her balance. Rafe Cooper had been attracted by her luxuriant black hair stretching halfway down her backless dress and an ample cleavage escaping from the sides of her halter-top so that she was perpetually rearranging herself.

It was hard enough to insert his key in the lock of his apartment when drink hadn't been taken, but it had, and copious amounts, and many varieties. Tomorrow he would dedicate himself to his work. The woman and her son would be safe with him. His motto was to never refuse a drink or sex and tonight was no exception. Life was too short for anything else.

'Stand still,' he ordered the girl in Portuguese because she spoke no English, 'for God's sake.'

The girl giggled and swayed, giving him a sloppy wet kiss. At the third attempt, he inserted the key and heard the click and the door swung open and they both fell over the threshold. He reached for the light switch and nothing happened.

'Oh, no, not another bloody power cut,' he said, and the girl just giggled and he added in Portuguese. 'Watch your step in the dark.'

He saw the yellow flash before a popping sound and the girl flew backwards against a wall and slid into a sitting position with one arm above her head and a ragged hole in her forehead.

He screwed up his eyes to accustom them to the dark and made out someone sitting in his favourite armchair facing the door.

'Hello?' he asked with surprising coolness. 'Who are you?'

The intruder made no response.

'What do you want?'

The man lit a candle and the flickering light glinted off his steel-rimmed spectacles. He sat legs crossed with the pistol in his lap and pointing straight at him.

'I'm your contact from head office and you're rather late,' the intruder said with the disappointment of an unhappy parent.

'Oh, good, pleased to meet you.' Rafe now remembered the Northern accent on the telephone before looking again at the girl to convince himself it had really happened. 'Why did you do that?'

'This operation's on a need-to-know basis. The fewer who know, the better.'

'For God's sake man, she knows nothing. I met her only tonight.'

'Can't be too careful.' The intruder lifted a glass taking a sip of his favourite vodka. 'There are more German spies here than fleas on a badger's arse.'

Rafe blustered. 'I've got everything under control. Tomorrow we'll transfer the platinum from the Bentley and take it to the waterfront on Monday in time to meet the plane.'

'Good, sounds as though you've thought of everything.'

Rafe believed so, too, and was pleased with his planning.

'Well, almost...'

'Oh?'

He made to step closer to the man, but the pistol moved in his hand, and he thought better of it.

'Your German pals in cosy Estoril may be easy to handle, but the problem is we'll have to deal with another Kraut, who's an altogether different kettle of fish.'

'Who?'

'Ludwig Weber, and he's a right mean bastard. They say he's working on orders from the very top. They want this woman and kid badly. Don't know whether he plans to kill them or take them back to Germany, but she has a secret they don't want to get out.'

'So, when's he due?' He tried to work out how it might alter his plans.

'He's here with a sidekick, and they'll stop at nothing to get them.'

Rafe felt a loosening of his bowels.

'Peters and the woman are at the Palácio. I left a note saying I'd see them in the lobby at ten tomorrow.'

'Oh dear,' said the man. 'That's a shame. The Krauts are planning right now to pick them up.'

He gave out a groan and his knees weakened.

'Where's the car?'

'What?'

'The car, man, with the platinum?'

'Don't know, suppose it's in the hotel car park.'

The man exhaled noisily as if it wasn't the answer he expected. 'Let's hope for your sake we haven't lost everything.'

He hadn't known about the other German, and he could see his plans unravelling.

'Keys?'

He made to throw his apartment keys to the man.

'No, not these. The lock-up where we're switching the platinum. Let me have those.'

He reached into his pocket and then hesitated.

'Why? This is my shout, I'm in charge.'

'You are, I was thinking I could go on ahead and set it up while you're picking up Peters and the car.'

'Oh, I see,' said Rafe and threw him the keys, which the man caught with his left hand.

'Always was a good slip fielder,' he said.

Rafe sparked into action and turned, opening the door to the apartment.

'I'd better get over to the hotel and tell them they're in danger,' he said stepping out into the stairwell.

The man was surprised and sprang to his feet. 'Wait for me,' he shouted and followed him out of the door. 'I'll come with you.'

Rafe didn't realise how close the man was. Then a hand on his shoulder and a push. Suddenly, he was flying forward down the long flight of stone steps and he clawed at the air with his hands in an effort to arrest his fall. He landed with a sickening thump at the bottom, his head twisted in an obscene fashion, and the man ran down the steps and knelt beside him to check he was dead and walked away whistling.

# 64

---

GROUPS OF GUESTS AND COUPLES MILLED AROUND THE HOTEL LOBBY, SOME eager to be seen, others desperate not to be. And on the fringes several individuals lurked, any one of whom might be Rafe Cooper.

After a good night's sleep and the luxury of having breakfast served in their room, he was ready to face the day with renewed optimism. Alena was determined to get Freddie to eat his meal, but he was more interested in the *pasteis de nata*, the local delicacy of small custard tarts. And he kept asking when he might play on the beach.

Although anxious to get things moving, Ben couldn't approach anyone and ask them if they were a British agent. He bided his time surveying the scene from the mezzanine before summoning up courage to go down to the lobby. Standing by a pillar that protected his back, he had a good view enabling him to size up anyone approaching him. At the back of the lobby, a man in an ordinary grey suit polished his steel-rimmed spectacles as if it were the most important thing he had to do. When he finished, he replaced them and glanced up and on seeing Ben gave him a half wave of recognition and walked over.

'Mr Peters? Ben,' the man greeted him and pumped his hand. 'Jolly glad you made it. And the lady and the boy?'

'Yes, all in one piece,' he said. 'You must be Rafe Cooper?'

'Sorry to disappoint you,' said the man. 'My name's Herbert Brown, a colleague. Rafe asked me to take it from here.'

Neither of them made eye contact so intent were they on scanning the lobby for possible dangers although no one gave any sign of being interested in them.

'And the plat – ahem – car?' Brown blurted out not bothered who might overhear their conversation.

He laughed. 'Battered, but it's still standing, more or less.'

Brown nodded with a twisted grin, understanding his meaning. 'Marvellous. Now we must move fast. The Nazis have been tracking you from Paris and they are here in Estoril. I don't know where although they may well be in the lobby right now. Where's the car?'

The commissionaire had been true to his word. Embarrassed at having the Bentley on display, he'd driven it around to the back entrance and parked it out of sight behind a hedge.

'Did you lose any of the platinum on route?' Brown asked as they climbed into the car.

'Not to my knowledge.'

'Perfect, that's perfect.'

He started up the engine and as they moved out of the car park, the rattling and banging and myriad other noises seemed worse than ever.

'Which way?' he asked.

Brown hesitated. 'Just a minute, let me get my bearings.'

It was only a short drive to the garage that was perfect for their requirements, set in a secluded lane and not overlooked. It was deserted as they drove up and Brown got the double doors open after much fumbling with his keys and Ben manoeuvred the car in and up onto the ramp.

Before he'd got his door open, Brown raised the ramp and bent under the car inspecting its underside, whistling in appreciation at what he saw. 'Marvellous, marvellous. They did a good job. Looks as if it's all here.'

The tone of Brown's voice disturbed him. 'Tell me,' he asked, 'I understand why you want the bullion, but why are you and the Jerries fighting over Alena and Freddie?'

Brown didn't respond. He'd opened one bag and extricated an ingot of pure platinum and stared at it with an intensity that suggested nothing else mattered.

He repeated the question and Brown's eyes narrowed as he considered whether to share the secret with him. 'Sorry, can't tell you because I don't know. My orders were to get the platinum and you three on board the plane. Our business is on a need-to-know only basis. Sorry, old boy.'

He found it difficult to believe him as Brown went back to attempting to unfasten another bag of platinum. Looking around the garage, he noticed two carts stacked with wooden cases in the far corner. 'What's the plan?'

Brown stripped off his jacket and pointed to the carts. 'We'll pack the platinum into those cases. Tomorrow morning Armand, the shopkeeper, will cover them with crates of fruit and vegetable and take them to the quay as he does every morning. No one will suspect a thing. When the plane comes in, we can load the bullion and scram.'

He clapped his hands. 'Now, let's get to work.'

They toiled in silence removing the platinum from the car, and he thought Bernay, wherever he was, would be pleased that they had survived the journey. And they stacked them into the crates and loaded them onto the carts and covered them with empty boxes.

They left the Bentley at the garage and before leaving checked to make sure the lane outside was clear.

Where were the Germans?

# 65

THEY RETURNED TO THE HOTEL TO FIND ALENA WANDERING DISCONSOLATE and lost in the grounds and, at first, she didn't appear to recognise Ben as he ran up to her followed by Brown. Putting an arm around her shoulders, he asked 'What's wrong, where's Freddie?' And feared the worst.

Grief aged her face as she appraised him with haunted eyes. Tears tumbled down her cheeks and her shoulders heaved with her sobbing and she collapsed into him burying her head in his chest.

'Where's Freddie?' he asked again, his voice rising with concern.

'Gone.'

'Where?'

'Gone.'

'What happened?'

'I shouldn't have done it,' she said. 'I only wanted to make him happy after what he's been through. It's my fault.'

He pulled her head away from him and pushed back her hair. 'Tell me what happened.'

'It was so quick.'

He kissed her forehead and stroked her hair. 'It's no one's fault just tell me.'

'He's been taken?' she said in a quiet voice and her sobbing had now stopped and she appeared calm.

'Taken by whom?'

She glared at him as if he shouldn't have needed to ask.

'The Nazis.' She started crying again. 'He just disappeared, and I let it happen.'

'Tell me everything,' he insisted and over her shoulder Brown scanned the park with a hand on the pistol in his pocket.

'It would be safer if we went into the hotel,' said Brown, gesturing for them to follow him.

Back in the room, Ben poured her a stiff brandy and sat beside her on the bed. The opportunity to unburden her guilt launched a waterfall of words. Freddie was bored, stuck in the room, and pleaded to go to the beach. She'd given in and they were walking through a tunnel that ran under the railway line leading to the beach when a man bumped into her. She dropped her handbag, spilling its contents, and she bent to retrieve it. Freddie was shrieking with excitement on seeing the sea and she shouted at him to stay with her. Getting back to her feet she looked around and panicked. There was no sign of him and when she turned back, the man had gone. At first, she called out expecting Freddie to reappear, but he didn't, and she searched everywhere at the beach without finding him.

She didn't report it to the hotel. And, as she didn't know where Ben had gone, she continued to patrol the park and the grounds of the hotel, hoping he would come running back to her with his big mischievous smile.

'We should go to the police,' Ben suggested to Brown.

'No, it wouldn't do any good,' Brown said, polishing his spectacles and holding them up to the light. 'If the police get involved, it will make everything so complicated.'

'We've got to do something, Freddie's life could be at risk,' he interrupted Brown.

'Ludwig Weber, one of Hitler's top investigators, is pursuing you. If the Portuguese authorities got involved, we'd be stuck here for ages and might not get another opportunity to escape to England. Weber must have the boy and he needs Alena. It may be that he has to bring both back alive, or at least the boy alive and...'

'And what?' Ben demanded.

'... kill Alena.' Brown glanced away.

Her face turned white, and Ben exhaled in frustration. 'Does Weber know about the platinum?'

She flashed him a questioning look.

'He may not,' said Brown with the trace of a smile.

'So, his priority is Freddie and Alena?'

Deep in thought, Brown nodded.

'We can't just sit here and wait,' she cried. 'There must be something we can do to get Freddie back?'

Brown shook his head. 'There's nothing, nothing we can do. Nothing at all. For the time being, we are in Weber's hands.'

'What do you mean?'

'I appreciate this is painful for you, Alena,' said Brown. 'Weber needs you both, you more than anyone knows why.'

Ben glanced at Alena as she sat still wringing her hands and wondered about her secret.

'I don't believe he'll harm your son yet. You'll have to stay in this room until he contacts us.'

'No, I want Freddie back?' The tears came again.

Brown shrugged, and Ben got up and paced the room, an impotent anger burning inside him.

'He needs you,' Brown continued, 'so he'll use Freddie as bait guaranteeing he won't harm Freddie if you go with him.'

She jumped to her feet.

'Of course, I'll go with him.'

'I know, but it wouldn't be the best option for you and certainly not for us.'

'What do you mean?'

'I can't let you go to him.'

'You'd stop me?'

'I don't think it'll come to that, but yes if I have to.'

She glanced at Ben for support and flopped on the bed shaking her head. 'Just whose side are you on?'

'My country's.' Brown looked at his watch. 'Let me see if I can find out anything. Stay here and on no account answer the telephone.'

'What if Weber calls?' Ben asked.

'I'm sure he won't just yet.'

Brown left the hotel and walked to the garage holding the Bentley and platinum. Opening the doors, he glanced around checking nothing was disturbed. He went over to a crate and removed an ingot of platinum and breathed on it and polished it with the sleeve of his jacket. He chuckled at his reflection in the shiny metal and kissed the ingot, realising it was too heavy to put in his pocket.

Before stepping out into the lane, Brown edged the door open and glanced around. All clear. He locked up but didn't see a figure standing in the shadows of a nearby doorway and the cloud of smoke the man exhaled.

While Brown was away, the telephone rang twice and each time he struggled with Alena to stop her snatching the phone off the hook. She couldn't understand why he was stopping her from speaking to the man who'd kidnapped Freddie, and she shouted at him in anger before dissolving into tears.

'What did you mean when you mentioned platinum?' she demanded and there was a determination in her glare.

He tried to deflect the question with a shrug.

'Tell me, Ben, you must be honest with me.'

They had come so far together and through so much and now her son was in danger he could no longer hide it from her.

'The Bentley's carrying platinum from the Banque de France.'

Her eyes opened wide in amazement followed by bewilderment. 'Where?'

'Strapped to the chassis, it's worth millions.'

He saw an ugly distrust spreading across her face.

'So, that's why you were determined to take the car across the Pyrenees?'

He nodded.

'Nothing to do with our safety?' She turned away from him, engulfed in disappointment. 'You're no different from the others.'

He stepped forward to comfort her, but she waved him away. 'Don't come near me.'

'No, no, can't you see?' he implored. 'I don't care about the platinum now although it might help us if we're able to exchange the platinum for Freddie.'

She flashed Ben a cynical half-smile. He didn't know the real reason Weber was pursuing them, and she doubted the German would be satisfied with just the bullion.

The phone rang again soon after Brown returned to the room and it was obvious the Germans had been watching them. Brown indicated with a nod he should pick up the receiver.

The German voice on the other end asked: 'Who's this?'

'Ben Peters,' he replied, watching her imploring eyes.

'My name's Ludwig Weber.' A polite voice. 'Please let me speak to Alena.'

He handed over the telephone and she snatched it from him. 'Where's Freddie? Tell me he's all right. Where is he?'

Whatever Weber said appeared to pacify her, and she handed the telephone back to him. 'He wants to speak to you.'

'Ben, let's be civilised,' said Weber. 'There's a resolution to every problem. I'm sure we can come to an arrangement. We need to meet.'

He put a hand over the mouthpiece and passed on the request to Brown, who shook his head. 'No way. It's too dangerous for Alena, we can't afford to let her go.'

She sprang to her feet and leapt at Ben trying to wrestle the phone from him 'We must meet him,' she shouted. 'Freddie's all that matters. If we've a chance of getting him back, we must take it. You can't stop me.'

'Impossible,' snorted Brown.

'There's no way I'll go to England without Freddie.' She stated in defiance. 'And I'll refuse to give you what you want.'

He squared up to Brown. 'Alena's not going anywhere without Freddie and neither's the platinum. Either we get the boy back or...'

Brown studied them both, his eyes switching from one to the other. He must get her and the platinum aboard the plane. 'Okay, okay,' he agreed with a sigh, surrendering to the inevitable. 'But it will be dangerous.'

'Okay,' Ben returned to his call with Weber. 'What do you have in mind?'

'Now you're being sensible,' said Weber. 'We'll meet tomorrow – a night without Freddie might focus Alena's thoughts – and I'll come alone.'

'No, you must bring Freddie with you so that we can see he's okay,' Ben insisted.

'So be it, *bis zum morgen.*'

'What did he say to you?' he asked her as soon as he'd replaced the receiver.

She answered in a whisper and the sentence trailed away. 'If we didn't agree to his demands, he'd take Freddie away, and I'd never see him again...'

## 66

IT WAS A RELIEF WHEN BROWN LEFT THEM TO RETURN TO HIS ROOM AND they were alone again. Alena appeared to relax accepting while Freddie was still alive there might be hope of a reunion in the morning. She went out onto the balcony to smoke and paced up and down as if trying to work out a course of action.

'Pour me a drink.' She came back in, closing the glass doors to the balcony and shutting out the noise of the night traffic. 'Make it a strong one.'

Ben insisted on ordering food from room service and waited in silence until the waiter brought it in on a trolley, and while he ate she picked at her food still deep in thought. Once they'd cleared away the food, she climbed onto the bed, kicked off her shoes and stretched out. 'Ben, come here.'

She smiled. 'Please.'

As he lay beside her, she wriggled up close, and he cradled her head with an arm and she turned burying her face in his chest.

'Haven't been honest, Ben.' Her voice muffled. And she couldn't trust herself to make eye contact. 'Kept things from you, but I want you to know because without your help we'd never have made it this far. You deserve the truth.'

She moved closer to get more comfortable, and he stroked her hair wondering what she'd say next.

'I always wanted to become a diplomat. I was very ambitious, perhaps too ambitious. Because I spoke several languages, they singled me out for advancement in the public service in Paris. Even then, there was uncertainty and with Hitler's rise to power we wondered what might happen. French Intelligence recruited me without my knowing it. They told me if I did this or that it would give me an entrée to the diplomatic service. Looks helped, I guess. At first, I did the round of embassy parties and events and the brief was to listen and observe and report back. Just that, no more. Most of what I learned meant little, but some of it must have been important. I was promoted.'

She sat up, reaching over to the bedside table, and extricated a cigarette and lit it. Lying back on the bed with an arm behind her head, she inhaled and expelled the smoke, following its path as it drifted up to the ceiling.

'They sent me to England to be trained by British Intelligence.' She sat up. 'I was stationed somewhere near Manchester and taught how to parachute out of a plane, coming in at under 400 feet, to beat the radar. Hated it. Even though the jump lasted a little over ten seconds. The pilot cut the engines to slow the plane, and you were free falling until the static line yanked you up and the parachute opened. Did the main part of my training in the New Forest at Lord Montague's estate in Beaulieu, and you can't imagine what they taught me there. I returned to a junior title in the diplomatic service although I did little in the way of diplomatic work. After a couple of months, I went to Berlin. But this time it was more intensive and dangerous. I'd been given a wireless radio transmitter to file regular reports and had a contact in Berlin who occasionally gave me orders as to whom I should target for information. He appeared to be German although I don't think he was. I became our liaison to the Nazi party, encouraged to support their odious policies and make myself popular with high-ranking officials. Made me unpopular with colleagues at the French Embassy although it helped.'

She glanced quickly at him and then away and blushed as if he might judge her.

'It wasn't difficult. Berlin was fun. Loved it. Lots of parties, and we enjoyed ourselves. Met many top Nazis and German army officers impressive in their uniforms and their manners were always impeccable. We didn't know then what we know now,' she added almost as an excuse.

'My orders were to forge relationships with them to become friends.' She placed a particular emphasis on the word. 'And elicit whatever information I could in whichever way necessary. They encouraged me to use my charms to keep them interested. In their eagerness to impress, various Nazis said much more than they should have. One even proposed marriage, but I fended him off,' she laughed. 'Though one in particular became interested, and my contact ordered me to do anything to get his trust.'

She looked him straight in the eyes and spat it out. 'In other words, become a whore for my country.'

A pause and a sigh as she remembered things she'd hoped to forget.

'I'd just about hung on to my self-respect when one evening I attended a reception for French and German officials. As usual, we wore our party dresses and had drinks and the Germans were smart and attentive. After a while, they invited us to join them at a local restaurant and we saw no harm because some senior embassy staff also went and had promised to escort us back. Somehow, there was a different mood about that evening. All I can remember was that there was a lot of drink, and I rarely drank because I had to stay in control. We moved onto somewhere else, a private house. I wasn't sure who else had gone although my best friend at the embassy was still with me.'

She stopped, dredging up an inner strength as she tried to remember. 'I don't … don't remember much.'

'It's okay, you don't have to tell me,' he said, realising it caused her pain.

'No, I must, you at least deserve honesty.'

She held her head in her hands as if hiding the images from her eyes. And the words came in a rush. 'All a blur. One minute the man I was targeting was talking to me, the next I woke up in a strange bed alone. It was obvious someone had been with me.'

'What happened?' He put a hand on her arm, not wanting an answer if it caused more grief.

She pulled away so that he couldn't stop her. 'My friend was still in the house, and we shared a taxi back to the lodgings. It was a Saturday; we'd the weekend to recover. My friend was more, um, more experienced in these matters, and she didn't seem to be worried. I was sick with worry though. When I said I wanted to leave Berlin, my contact ordered me to stay and keep seeing the man until Paris decided otherwise.'

She paused to see if he'd understood. 'For the first time, I felt used by our own people. But I carried on doing what they expected. And the Nazis appeared to treat me with more respect. Then I found out I was pregnant.'

'Freddie?'

She smiled.

'One day, my friend took me to a doctor in a horrible back street. I'd no idea. In my ignorance, I thought it was a check-up until I realised they performed abortions. I escaped. Ran as hard as I could. Stayed in my room for several days not talking to anyone least of all the so-called friend. The first morning I felt able to go out again as I walked along the street a car drew up alongside. The passenger door swung open blocking my path and a man I recognised from the party offered me a lift.'

She shook her head, remembering. 'They kidnapped me,' she shouted in disbelief. 'They took me to a castle just outside Munich. The embassy told the rest of the staff I'd returned to Paris, and London and my contact were delighted. What I didn't know was the contact had orchestrated the whole evening and the embassy staff had been ordered to leave me alone with the Nazis. I had another contact who worked as a gardener at the castle, and I had to leave information under a rock in the gardens for him. Although Freddie's father repulsed me, they forced me to continue sleeping with him in the hope he would reveal things in our pillow talk.'

'Were you harmed?'

'Not in the way you're thinking. As long as I did as I was told I was okay. I didn't want for much. I had servants. When Freddie came, there were two doctors and a team of nurses attending the birth. I had everything except my freedom. The father even gave me the red diamond ring I gave to Sebastian.'

'He must have been important.'

She didn't answer, just looked at him in a strange way.

'After a while, his visits became fewer and fewer, and I wasn't able to glean as much information as before.'

'But still you couldn't leave?'

'No, there were soldiers everywhere, some nice, others evil, and it became clear I'd never leave. Then I heard a young Gestapo officer had been too diligent in his work and after arresting my contact in Berlin found out about me. London knew I had to get away or be killed. And I couldn't bear to think what they'd do to Freddie.'

'How did you escape?'

'London organised everything with help from my contact at the castle. Not every German supports the Nazis and a local branch of the resistance did the groundwork to get us out.'

Alena lit another cigarette and sighed as if she'd told him everything, but it convinced Ben she was holding something back – the secret, the reason for British Intelligence's interest in her.

'It's amazing they'd go to this trouble to save one agent,' he said.

Alena scowled at his cynicism and looked as if she'd said too much. 'I have something they want.'

He stared at her, trying to fathom out what that could be, but she didn't elaborate.

'Wars are not just fought with bullets and bombs, psychology can be more important,' she said.

'There's a brave woman agent operating in Germany who set up a mythical "League of Lonely War Women" or VEK in German. The idea was to demoralise German troops. They are fed information suggesting any soldier on leave can go to a house displaying the VEK symbol and get a girlfriend. And many soldiers are deserting to make sure their wives or girlfriends are not involved. It's called black propaganda, and it works.'

# 67

BEN HADN'T BEEN ABLE TO SLEEP ALL NIGHT. THE ROOM WAS EMPTY without Freddie. And he kept turning over in his mind how the meeting with Weber would develop. Just when he thought he'd worked out a strategy, he scrutinised it again and saw gaping holes in his reasoning. Whatever they were doing, they were playing with Freddie's life and he would have offered himself in exchange for the boy but knew Weber didn't want that.

Weber rang at nine o'clock, his voice clipped, authoritative. He told them to meet at the lock-up where the Bentley was garaged, and he expected to see Alena, Ben and the 'Englishman'. No one else. He would be watching and if they attempted to change the plan or numbers, they would never see the boy again.

The German held all the cards. They had no option other than to follow his orders. He was relieved he hadn't mentioned the platinum and hoped it might play a role in convincing the German to consider a trade for Alena and Freddie's lives. It was their only hope, short of killing Weber, and he knew the German would have the backup to ensure that couldn't happen.

The garage was as they'd left it and the carts in the corner were piled high with wooden crates. Alena paced around as if she were measuring its confines like a tiger marking its territory, and she rubbed her arms and smoked one cigarette after another. Brown seemed more on edge than before and checked and re-checked his pistol. The longer they waited, the more the tension between them ramped up and several times Ben started to talk but stopped, realising there was nothing useful he could add to the situation.

Right on time, the double doors' hinges creaked ominously, and they froze as the doors swung open.

No one appeared.

He wondered if it was just the wind and relaxed although Brown reached for the pistol in his pocket and moved towards the door. Alena's hands went to her head, uncertain whether she could face what might happen. The sun streamed through the open doorway and they had to shield their eyes from the glare. A tall man holding the hand of a small boy were silhouetted in the door frame so that it was impossible to distinguish their features.

Weber took several seconds to focus his eyes to the dark of the garage. Before he could speak, Freddie shrieked 'Maman, maman' and made to run towards her, but he dragged him back, lifting him off his feet.

'Oh, my baby,' she screamed. 'Please don't hurt him.' And Ben had to wrap his arms around her to hold her back.

Weber walked towards them still keeping a safe distance and his eyes darted around the garage taking in everything. Behind him, there was a metallic click of a gun being primed and the civilian sidled into the garage pointing a sub-machine gun at them and closing the doors behind him.

'Put your gun on the ground,' the civilian instructed Brown, 'and kick it towards me. Slow, now.'

With a snort of disgust, Brown did as ordered.

'You do the same,' the civilian turned his attention to Ben.

'I doubt if he'd have one,' said Weber, 'he wouldn't know what to do with it.'

The civilian frisked him anyway.

Inspecting the garage, Weber still clutched Freddie's hand, and the boy sobbed taking in big gulps of air not understanding why he couldn't go to his mother. He went over to the car and patted it with the flat of his hand, muttering 'Ingenious, very clever.'

He swivelled, his eyes narrowing and, ignoring both Brown and Ben, he addressed Alena. 'So, we meet at last.' He gave a poor version of a bow. 'We've been looking for you since you escaped from Munich. By the way, your collaborators were arrested and executed.'

Alena sucked in her breath, stunned into silence before finding her voice. 'Please, please let my son go. He can't harm you.'

Weber shook his head. 'You know I can't do that.'

'I don't – don't understand why you need him.'

'My orders are to return you and the boy to Germany. More than anyone, you should know these people. If I fail in this, my family...' He didn't have to finish the sentence.

Alena nodded in understanding. 'Let him go, take me instead.'

Swearing under his breath, Weber switched his gaze to Ben. 'You see a young mother pleading for her child's life. You probably think it's touching. She's not what she seems. She's a praying mantis; they always kill their males. Only while you're useful are you safe from her. She's dangerous and a threat to our country's war effort. By taking her back to Germany, her work will end.'

Alena stole a furtive look at Ben and Brown as if now she might reveal her secret, but she swallowed the words. 'Why don't you just pull the trigger and get it over with?' she shouted.

'You'd prefer that, perhaps. Quick and final. The decision is not mine. It's up to my masters and I'm sure they will have many questions to ask you.'

'Can't we do a trade here?' Ben stepped forward, and the henchman waved his gun forcing him back.

'Go on,' said Weber, his eyes crinkling in amusement.

'We were carrying bullion –'

Weber hesitated. 'Oh, yes?'

'It was hidden in the car.'

'Oh, you mean the platinum,' Weber drawled.

His heart sank. 'How –'

'Philippe told me everything before he died.'

'You bastard, you killed him.'

The German looked disappointed. 'On the contrary, he took his own life. I did him a service.'

A great weariness and helplessness swept through him and he felt unsteady on his legs. 'Let Alena and the boy go, and I'll give you the platinum, which is worth more than you could ever dream.' He nodded towards the carts and noticed the civilian's jaw drop as if he were already counting the millions.

Weber laughed. He hadn't called up more men because he wanted no one else knowing about the bullion. He had plans for that and he would deal with the civilian later.

'Is it yours to give away? I'd intended to take the platinum after we killed you.'

Greed shone out of the civilian's face.

The German walked over to the carts still pulling Freddie's hand. He lifted two empty crates off the top, then more before turning on them.

'There's nothing here,' he said in a fury dissipating to a bitter smile. 'You've just lost what you thought was your ace card.'

Ben felt the ground beneath him disappearing and heard Brown suck in air through his teeth.

'The cupboard is bare, my American friend,' said Weber.

'Of course,' he said regaining his composure. 'You don't think I'd leave the platinum there for you to take. Let the boy go now and I'll lead you to it.'

Weber scrutinised him, irritated by this extra complication, and the civilian looked to him for guidance and shifted his feet with impatience.

A roar of pain. He'd relaxed his grip on Freddie and the boy took his opportunity, biting the German's fingers causing blood to spurt from his hand.

The silver Smith & Wesson materialised in Alena's hand and barked twice. In quick succession, the shots hit the henchman in the shoulder spinning him around and catching him in the back of his neck.

'Don't even think about it,' Weber shouted above the boy's crying. Between the shots, he'd pulled out a knife and flicked open the blade holding it hard against the boy's throat causing a faint line of red to spread downwards staining his shirt.

'Don't move. I'll use this if I must. Nothing has changed. I'll return with more men. Little Freddie and I will now walk towards the door. It would be better for him if you stay still.'

'No, no, NO,' she screamed so loud the walls of the garage seemed to shake. 'He's going nowhere.' And she pointed the handgun straight at them.

'Won't do you any good,' said Weber smirking. 'I'll cut his throat before the bullet hits me. Do you want to take the risk?'

She didn't waver and just kept pointing the pistol, and it dawned on Ben she was intent on doing what she'd threatened when they first met.

'No, Alena, no please don't,' he shouted at her.

Weber's eyes moved between them in bewilderment.

'Don't do it, Alena,' he repeated. 'We can still sort this out.'

'This is the only way.' Her eyes didn't leave the target. 'It's all that's left for us now. We can't go back – it would be worse than death. For Freddie it would mean a lifetime of pain. I told you if the Nazis ever caught up with us I'd shoot Freddie and then kill myself.'

Now Brown shouted 'No' and Weber's eyes opened wide in realisation and he feared for his own family.

'Goodbye, my darling, we're going to a better place,' she said in a hoarse whisper. 'Please forgive me.'

Her finger tightened on the trigger.

# 68

High above the Atlantic, Flying Officer Tom Hawkins looked on the ocean that was as inviting and as dangerous as a woman from the wrong side of the tracks. This was his playground where he hunted German U-boats and rescued sailors torpedoed by submarines. He and his co-pilot, Sergeant Jack Drayton, dismissed missions such as today's as taxi runs, flying over to Estoril to pick up people who were most likely agents. Often, they found the so-called secret agents disappointing and even more ordinary than ordinary folk. Only the thought of the hot date awaiting him as soon as he returned to Poole lightened his mood.

The Catalina flying boat of Coastal Command flew out of RAF Hamworthy on the south coast, but they never mentioned Poole. It was always said the flying boats flew from London, part of the disinformation of war. The Catalina was ideal for long-range operations with its twin Pratt and Whitney engines capable of 2,500 miles without refuelling. Although cumbersome and no match for a fighter in a dogfight, it proved a potent weapon in the war against U-boats. At first, their task had been easier. A submarine on detecting them would dive beneath the surface and they swooped to release their depth charges, which yielded good results. Then the German submarine commanders got smart and hunted in wolf packs, becoming bolder in handling aerial attacks. They developed an arsenal of powerful, large bore anti-aircraft guns that allowed them to stay on the surface so that the attacker faced a withering barrage of fire. To be sure of hitting the U-boats with their bombs, the planes sometimes got as low as 50 feet almost flying down the throats of the submarines. Often, they traded a plane for a U-boat.

Hawkins and Drayton loved the hunt although not as much as the rescue missions when they plucked crews of sunken boats from the sea, and on one occasion saved sailors of a U-boat. Their Cat had been adapted for rescue missions. Usually, the way in was through the gun blisters in the waist of the plane. But that wasn't ideal when taking on board seamen suffering from hypothermia after floating in ice-cold water. So a door was inserted in the side of the fuselage. While fighter pilots had their kills stencilled on the fuselages of their planes, Hawkins had the numbers of the sailors they'd saved instead.

Fully operational, the Catalina carried a crew of seven, but with personnel in short supply and needed elsewhere more often there were just the two of them aboard on these runs. Usually, a Cat carried a flight engineer, who sat out of the cockpit in his position within the pylon joining the wing and the hull. On this plane, the flight engineer's controls were moved to the flight deck for pilot operation. It meant there was no one to man the Vickers .303 machine-gun in the bow and the Browning Model 1919 in the waist and when necessary Drayton played three roles – co-pilot, radio operator and gunner.

He didn't mind the flight to the Portuguese coast although the suggestion it was a bit of a jolly made him feel guilty. Estoril was a popular destination because it sometimes gave them the chance to stretch their legs in the sunshine, a welcome diversion from the austerity of wartime England. On this occasion, their orders were to collect three people plus some crates and get out as quickly as possible. The pickups and their cargo could be of interest to the Germans and it was vital they get away without problems.

Estoril intrigued him. Although Germany and Britain were at war, they co-existed in Portugal as if it were a game. They could fly in and pick up agents while a German-owned hotel on the sea front flew a swastika and from its roof flashed messages from powerful lights to the U-boats waiting far out at sea. And this was allowed to happen as long as it didn't upset the Portuguese.

As usual, Hawkins hadn't been informed about the people or the crates. It made little difference. It contributed to the war effort, and he played his part.

The flight to Portugal was uneventful. Sunny, and the brightness had a hardness to it, which meant they could see for miles, an advantage and a disadvantage. They could spot an enemy plane in plenty of time to take evasive action, but the Cat could also be targeted. Maintaining radio silence as they flew south over Estoril and seeing in the distance the sprawling city of Lisbon, they checked the landing area. Unlike runways, it didn't take much, the odd sailing skiff, to abort a landing. The water was so calm it looked like a polished floor. That would make landing smoother although when the water was flat there was the problem of judging the plane's height above the surface. Once below fifty feet, instruments were not of any help.

He loved this plane and understood it, feeling and hearing every squeak and rattle of its fuselage and change of engine note as if it were alive and talking to him. He held her at a steady seventy knots, descending at around 200 feet per minute, and even on a calm sea the landing was noisy with a rat-a-tat-tat as if hitting gravel. And, as the plane slowed in the water, a bow wave engulfed them.

He had to contact the British agent, who would bring the cargo and help to load it. Yet there was no sign of a welcoming party and after they'd taxied to tie up at their buoy, it was a case of just waiting.

---

THE DOORS FLEW open with a clanging noise that reverberated around the confines of the garage and Armand, the shopkeeper, stood in the doorway with a halo of sunlight around his head.

'The flying boat is –' he started then surprise registered on his broad face and he didn't get to finish the sentence. Brown dived forward, scrambling on the dusty floor, a hand fastening onto his discarded pistol. In one flowing movement, he took aim and fired a single round hitting Weber on the left shoulder knocking him off his feet as he dropped his knife and let go of Freddie.

Alena screamed, and Freddie cried, and in the pandemonium Ben heard Armand shouting.

'It's here, the flying boat is here, you must go now. The crates are on the dock waiting to be loaded.'

Without a glance at the spreadeagled body of the German, Brown was galvanised by Armand's words. 'Come on, the plane won't wait forever,' he shouted.

Brown broke into a run and was waiting for no one, and he didn't bother to look back to see if they were following.

---

HAWKINS AND DRAYTON opened the sliding hatch above their heads and climbed out and sat on the wing smoking and enjoying the sun, wondering if they could get a beer anywhere. The pilot promised the next time he'd take his swimming trunks and have a dip. No clouds in the sky and the sun shimmered off the azure waters stretching all the way to the horizon. The temperature must be in the eighties, and he watched with envy the people cavorting on the beach a hundred yards away and youths queuing to jump off the quay into the ocean.

His orders were straightforward. The agent would be waiting for him with the cargo ready to go. Don't hang around. They hadn't said how long he should wait if they weren't there. By the time he'd finished his cigarette if there was no action he'd get the Cat out of there and head back to Poole.

Shielding his eyes against the sunlight, he stared hard in every direction. No one looked like a pickup. A teenage boy sat in a small boat tied up alongside the quay and he showed no interest in them.

He took a last puff and glanced around again before flicking the cigarette end into the water.

'Right, Jack, we've been stood up. Let's get the hell out of here.'

# 69

BROWN SPRINTED ALONG THE COBBLED STREET HOLLERING AT THE TOP OF his voice, clutching his pistol as if he'd shoot anyone who got in his way.

Ben bundled Alena and Freddie into the Bentley and, with Armand standing on the running board shouting directions, he reversed out of the garage taking another glancing blow to the front wing. They soon caught Brown and Ben slowed, yelling 'Jump on, man.'

The Bentley exploded out of the side street and across the Avenida Marginal then drove down a narrow lane, across the railway line to Lisbon without looking, and onto the promenade. Alena stuck her head out the window and her hair flapped like silver wings in the breeze. 'Wait for us,' she shouted.

As they turned onto the quay, Ben realised their escape route was disappearing. The flying boat's engines kicked into life and it drifted away from its buoy and although Brown bellowed, the pilots couldn't hear above the roar of the engines.

On seeing them approach, Armand's son, Christiano, started the boat's engine and without hesitation first Brown and then Ben jumped into the boat almost swamping it.

They were soon alongside, and Ben leapt and clung on to one of the wing struts. He kept shouting and swinging backwards and forwards until he had enough momentum to kick the plane's fuselage, but its engines picked up and it turned away from the beach. Soon he'd have to decide – hang on in the hope they'd see him before taking off or let go now and drop into the water, and he couldn't swim. Redoubling his efforts, he used his body as a pendulum to launch his feet into the side of the plane as Brown fired his pistol in the air.

The flying boat's engine note changed as it throttled back and a side window in the cockpit slid open and the pilot popped his head out. He looked at Ben hanging under the wing without surprise and at Brown and Christiano on the boat and with a boyish grin drawled. 'You must be our blind date. Blimey, mate, you left it late, another few seconds, and we'd have been out of here.'

With the pilots' help, they transferred the platinum onto the plane, stacking up the ingots on two wooden pallets in the middle of the cabin. Ben then instructed Christiano to return to the quay to pick up Alena and Freddie.

When the pilot questioned why there were four instead of the three he'd been ordered to pick up, Brown overruled him. 'Change of plan, old boy, they want me back at head office.'

Belted in, they pushed off and taxied out. As the engines picked up, spray splashed the windows, and they swayed as if aboard a ship.

Suddenly, the plane lurched, dipped and slewed off course.

'For Christ's sake,' the pilot screamed. 'Are you crazy, man, you'll kill us.'

Brown's attention seemed focused on the platinum, but Ben unbuckled his belt and made his way to the cockpit. A speedboat raced across their bows forcing the pilot again to take evasive action and causing the plane to rock in its wake. This was no accident. The speedboat was making a tight turn.

'Jesus, the madman's coming for us again,' shouted the pilot. 'Don't know if I can get the old crate up before he hits us.'

There were two men in the boat. One steered while Weber stood in the bow holding on with one hand as he gripped a sub-machine gun in his right.

'Have you got a gun?' Ben asked.

'In the bow,' replied the pilot, his eyes screwed up in concentration.

Hawkins now had the plane flat out, pushing it up to the 66 knots needed to allow it to take off, but he didn't know if they'd succeed before the speedboat rammed them.

Weber was pumping rounds at them in an attempt to halt them and the bullets whined and pinged around the plane. Even if Weber failed, a ramming would cause enough damage to incapacitate the flying boat.

He pushed past the pilots and squeezed in behind the Vickers machine gun in the bow, taking hold of the two grips and swinging the gun around until the sights locked onto the speedboat. It was closing on them by the second, and he squeezed the trigger with his thumb and the Vickers bucked into life. He kept it down hard and the gun, firing six hundred rounds a minute, swung from side to side spraying the speedboat and the surrounding sea with bullets so that the water appeared to boil. The speed of the riveted ammunition belt rattling through the gun caused it to overheat and the smoke stung his eyes, but he kept firing blindly across the bows of the boat hitting the driver who fell backwards. Weber continued to return fire then, as the Vickers swung around, a volley of rounds slammed into the German's midriff. There was a puff of smoke. An explosion of red. And in slow motion the top half of Weber's torso, still clutching the gun, toppled over the side as the speedboat veered off course and kept going full speed for the beach.

# 70

---

THEY WERE CLIMBING TO THEIR OPERATIONAL CRUISING HEIGHT OF 5,000 feet when Hawkins felt an insistent tap on his shoulder and turned to see Brown mouthing something to him.

'What's up, mate?' he shouted with a friendly smile.

'You need to change course.'

Puzzled, Hawkins shook his head. 'Why?'

'New orders,' said Brown, his eyes obscured by the thick lenses of his spectacles.

'I haven't received new orders.'

Brown was staring, observing him.

'I'm going back to base,' Hawkins insisted.

'There are new orders.'

'From whom?'

'From me.' Brown produced his pistol.

Hawkins shook his head and glanced across at Drayton for support. 'Sorry, no can do.'

Drayton started unbuckling his harness and Brown pointed the gun at his head and fired at close range, spattering flesh, bone fragments and brains over the windscreen.

'Jesus,' Hawkins screamed making a move towards him, forgetting he was buckled in and causing the plane to dip. 'Why did you do it?'

'Now, do what I tell you,' Brown sneered, throwing him a map. 'The route's there. No tricks. I've flown one of these and it'll make no difference if I have to shoot you, too.'

Brown waited until Hawkins made the necessary adjustments and the plane banked to follow its new routing.

'What's happening?' Ben asked Brown when he returned aft. 'We heard a bang. Sounded as if something fell off.'

'Nothing to worry about,' replied Brown.

'Then why are you carrying your pistol?'

Instead of answering, Brown walked over to Alena and gave her a twisted grin before snatching her handbag. She moved to stop him, but he shrugged her off and, opening it, removed her handgun. 'We don't want this going off on a plane? It could be dangerous.'

Ben unbuckled himself and got to his feet. 'What are you up to, Brown?'

'You'll find out soon enough.' Brown waved the pistol at him to warn him not to come any closer.

'There's no need for that. We're all on the same side.'

'I doubt it.'

'Why has the pilot changed course?'

'We're heading for Lake Geneva.'

'Oh, no,' Alena gasped.

'The plane and I are. I'll have to make other arrangements for you.'

'Alena has to get to England.'

Brown shrugged.

'You – British Intelligence are expecting her.'

'Not my problem, old boy.' Brown chuckled.

'Please, Mr Brown,' Alena interrupted, 'think of Freddie.'

'You should've thought of your little bastard before you brought him into this world.'

'What do you mean?'

'Look, I don't give a damn about you and your sordid little secret now I've got the platinum.' And he patted the pile of bullion.

She put a hand to her mouth as if stopping herself from saying something she'd regret.

'You've only got this far because of me.' Brown looked very pleased, smirking in self-congratulation. 'When Bernay came to us in Paris asking for help to get the platinum out of the country, I saw an opportunity as our people were desperate to get you to London. I'd never have got the flying boat if it hadn't been for you. I set up the whole escape and you've done the hard work for me.'

Brown was enjoying the surprise on their faces.

'Who do you think killed the grease ball at the hacienda?'

Both looked at him open mouthed.

'I've been tracking your progress ever since you left Paris.'

'What did you do with Cooper?'

Laughing even louder, Brown said: 'Let's just say he's retired from the service. Now I've got the platinum I don't need any of you, not even the pilot. People are waiting for me at Lake Geneva. London will presume the plane's been shot down over the Atlantic and by the time they find out what happened I'll be long gone. I couldn't have planned it any better even though I say it myself.'

Brown's demeanour hardened, realising he had to get on with business, and he gestured at Ben with the pistol.

'What do you plan to do?'

'Well, Ben, it's time for you to get off.' Brown grinned as he slid back the cargo door, allowing a blast of air into the cabin causing them to catch their breath as the icy cold cut right through them.

He didn't move.

'Come over here.' Brown waved the gun at him again.

He shook his head. 'You must shoot me first.'

'So be it. I just wanted to give you a chance. Who knows you might survive, but if I shoot you, you'll definitely be dead.'

Still, he didn't move.

Brown sighed and turned to Alena. 'I suppose I'm indebted to you for your help in this. So, I'll offer you a deal – if he steps out now, I'll take you to Geneva and release you there. You'll have to take your chances, but at least you'll be alive in a neutral country. If he refuses, I'll shoot all of you.'

Brown motioned again for him to come forward. 'It'll be painless, Ben. I'll even let you wear a life jacket to give you a sporting chance.'

Just standing up was difficult as the in-rushing wind buffeted him and drove him backwards.

'Come on,' shouted Brown. 'Haven't got all day.'

'How do I know you'll keep your word?'

'You don't, you'll have to trust me.'

His mind raced. What were his options? If he refused, he'd be shot, and Alena and Freddie would be killed, too. If he went out the door, it would be unlikely that he would survive the fall, yet there was a chance Brown might spare them.

There was one other possibility.

The blue of the Atlantic thousands of feet below was hypnotic and seemed to call to him, whispering in the wind. 'Go on jump and you'll fly like a bird and be free. Fly now.'

He shuffled towards the open door his eyes darting around looking for an implement that might help him turn the tables on Brown but couldn't find anything.

Brown moved in behind him and he felt a hand on his shoulder and a violent push. In desperation, his hands grabbed the top of the door-frame and he clung to it wedging himself in the opening. Brown kicked his legs away, and he swung out into the violent slipstream which was as sharp as a knife. The shock of the air froze his breathing and with the slipstream tugging at him he knew he wouldn't be able to hold on much longer. Brown hit at his hands with the butt of the gun trying to loosen his grip and he dug his fingers into the frame and the metal cut deep into his flesh.

Suddenly, the plane banked and with a grating noise one of the wooden pallets loaded with platinum shifted and slid towards the opening. Having released her harness unobserved, Alena pushed the stack of platinum with both legs, speeding up its progress across the floor of the plane.

Wheeling around, Brown realised what was happening behind him as the bullion hit the back of his legs pitching him off balance and causing him to fall forwards onto his knees. The loaded pallet swung round catching him in the side and propelling him towards the opening. He was regaining his balance when the plane righted itself causing him to stumble and his hands tore at the floor for something to slow his slide as his eyes burned with fear.

Ben swung his legs back inside the plane and squeezed to the side as Brown slipped towards him, his hands flailing at anything to stop himself. The agent grabbed at his jacket in desperation, catching hold of the fabric, and for a moment hope registered in his eyes. But the fabric ripped away and with a strangled cry he hurtled past him, somersaulting all the way to the ocean.

Alena scrambled to her feet and reached out and, wrapping her arms around him, pulled him to safety. Holding his face between her hands, she whispered 'I almost lost you'. She embraced him and kissed him and, still shaking, he made his way up to the cockpit.

'Where's Brown?' asked Hawkins.

'I'm afraid he had to step out. Reset your course for home.'

'Wilco, boss.' Hawkins' face was white with shock as he glanced at the remains of Drayton's head.

# 71

THE WAR DID NOT PREVENT BOAC MAINTAINING A REGULAR FLYING BOAT service from Poole taking mail and passengers to the rest of the Empire, including Australia and India. Pilots still had to keep a wary eye out for the sole German plane intent on a bit of sport, so Hawkins asked Ben to join him in the cockpit to help look out for any trouble.

Ben had dragged Drayton's body to the back of the plane, out of sight of Alena and Freddie. He had covered him with his Irvin flying jacket and blankets and had cleared his remains from the windscreen.

As they settled for the flight ahead, Hawkins recounted his and Drayton's exploits, once saving twenty-four crewmen from a torpedoed merchant ship. There was no suggestion of glorying in their heroism in his monotone, and he felt it was Hawkins' way of paying tribute to the bravery of his friend and co-pilot.

Amazed someone so young could become inured to the barbarities of war, he listened, but his mind kept wandering, thinking about Alena, who was just as brave in her way, and wondered what she faced. What was her secret and once she'd shared it would she be allowed to live in peace? They'd been through so much over the last few days his head was muddled, and he was finding it impossible to concentrate on any one thing.

When Hawkins finished his story, he lapsed into silence as if there were nothing more to say and Ben went back to check Alena and Freddie, who were lying in each other's arms in a bunk.

The further north they flew the rougher the weather was becoming and now the blue of the Atlantic was turning to a more forbidding grey.

'Getting a bit dicey, mate,' Hawkins said as Ben returned to the cockpit. Again, Ben was struck by how young the pilot was with his wispy blond moustache looking incongruous on such a youthful face. 'Don't want a full-blown storm now. This area can be a bit of a bugger. Had a friend on one of our biggest boats hit by a forty-foot wave and it just took out the windows on the bridge and disabled it.'

The weather was deteriorating fast. The cloud closed in and the wind battered them, causing the plane to pitch and roll as if it were leaping from current to current.

'Don't worry.' Hawkins caught his anxious look. 'At least if we ditch we can float.' And he laughed, unfazed at the prospect of being in a plane floating on gigantic waves.

'Coffee?'

Ben looked around in surprise almost expecting a hostess in a chic uniform to appear. The pilot reached down by his seat and lifted up a leather briefcase. Taking out a Thermos flask, he poured the dark brown steaming liquid into the cup and offered it to him. 'Helps keep me awake on these long trips.'

He drank it, savouring its warmth and taste and it helped to sharpen his concentration. Draining it to the last drop, he handed it back to Hawkins who rubbed it with his elbow before filling it again while keeping control with his knees.

'I suppose you're a secret agent?' Hawkins asked.

The question surprised him.

'Good God, no,' he said, realising banking might sound mundane to a young man who put his life on the line every day. 'I'm a writer, more of a sedate profession.'

'Oh, I don't know,' said Hawkins. 'Sounds pretty dangerous to me. The Nazis burned a whole load of books before the war, even Ernest Hemingway's.'

'Yes, it's bad enough when the critics have a go at you, but when they burn your books, that's serious.'

They both laughed without conviction and fell into an uneasy silence as if all topics of conversation had been exhausted.

Visibility was now only about thirty yards.

It came at them like an angry hornet flashing past so close the whole plane shook and juddered in its slipstream.

'What in hell was that?' he shouted turning to the pilot.

'Just missed us, went straight over the top.'

'One of theirs?'

'Didn't get a proper look; let's hope it was one of ours.'

In a break in the cloud, he saw it banking towards them with the unmistakable Iron Cross on its battleship-grey fuselage and the swastika on its tail. The pilot's face turned towards them as it levelled out and he saw the flashes of its twin cannons mounted in the wings. At first there was a clattering rat-a-tat-tat as if being bombarded by pebbles. The windscreen cracked, and he heard the bullets ploughing into the fuselage and coming straight through the fabric of the plane and ricocheting around the cabin followed by the stench of exploding shells.

Again, it passed close by with another whoosh of air.

Hawkins whooped like a schoolboy plane-spotter. 'Did you see it? What a beauty! Their new Focke-Wulf; the plane the Krauts reckon will win the war for them.'

Hawkins pushed down on the controls. 'No chance of outrunning it. It'll do more than 400 while this crate will just about get to 195. I will drop back into the cloud. It's our only hope. Be careful, those shells will come straight through us.'

As if it were a rollercoaster, the Catalina dipped and banked hard right until the cloud wrapped around them and the ocean appeared so close he felt he could touch it. Visibility was now almost zero and an added danger was a collision. And he peered into the murk and listened for any sound of the attacker. Again, it was upon them in a flash and the chatter of its cannons beat out a tattoo on the body of the plane.

With a gasp, Hawkins gripped his side and made a low, gurgling noise deep in his throat. Falling forward onto the controls, he sent the plane into a steep dive. Ben grabbed his jacket and dragged him back while pulling on the wheel to level out. The pilot's head was lolling on his shoulders and his eyes were in the top of his head.

He thought Hawkins was dead until the pilot spluttered: 'Been hit.'

Hawkins coughed and winced with the pain. 'First aid box. Quick!'

He rooted around and found the box and brought it to the pilot.

'Brandy,' Hawkins ordered nodding at the box and when he opened it he found a bottle and held it to the pilot's lips.

'More,' he insisted, and Ben kept it to his mouth. Hawkins' cough resembled a death rattle, but the alcohol must have helped because he was able to move forward and peer through the windscreen.

'We've lost him.' He gave a thin smile. 'Let's go home.'

A frightened Alena, holding a handkerchief to her nose and mouth to combat the fumes, popped her head into the cockpit. 'Are you both okay?'

He nodded towards Hawkins and she saw the blood staining the side of his flying jacket and together they helped him into the co-pilot's seat aware by his cries the slightest movement was causing him severe pain.

With Hawkins giving him clipped commands, Ben kept the plane steady. 'Steer as if it's a car, mate, turn the steering wheel clockwise or anti-clockwise in coordination with the rudder pedals to turn and stay level.'

Alena took great care as she stripped him of his jacket and tore off his shirt. The sight of the gaping wound caused her to turn away so that the pilot wouldn't see her reaction, but he noticed her hand go to her mouth, and she looked as if she might faint.

'Bad, eh?' Hawkins made a gurgling sound in the back of his throat. 'Don't worry. Got to get home. Hot date.'

They flew on through the ever-darkening day, Ben clutching the controls with a grip, not even a bear could wrestle from him. And Hawkins, now able to feed himself from the bottle, still giving instructions and slipping in and out of consciousness.

## 72

ALENA KEPT MINISTERING TO HAWKINS' NEEDS. SHE'D BANDAGED HIS wound, and it helped stem the flow of blood although not even the brandy could dull his pain. The periods of Hawkins' unconsciousness increased. Yet as soon as the bottle slipped from his grasp, he came to and gripped it all the tighter.

Ben kept asking her for updates on the pilot's condition, not daring to avert his gaze from the flickering dials in front of him, fearing if he did they might lose altitude or wander off course. There was little to do but let Hawkins sleep. He knew he wouldn't be able to land the plane at Poole without the pilot's help and while they didn't want to disturb him, they would have to when the time came.

The cloud was no longer as heavy, just enough to give them cover and they flew on, the monotonous drone and continual rising and falling almost inducing sleep. And he understood why Hawkins carried coffee in his briefcase. Just when he might have lost concentration, a gust of wind threatened to blow them off course and he made an adjustment and kept an eye on the altimeter. His grip on the wheel was so intense his knuckles turned white and the concentration burned his eyes. Although the cold in the cockpit numbed his senses, beads of sweat stood out on Hawkins' face and Alena dampened a cloth to keep his fever at bay. She had wrapped him in a thick blanket and every time she came in contact with him it covered her in more blood. Refusing to let it faze her, she nursed him, and spoke to him softly.

Time was running out for the pilot and they had to get him back as soon as possible if he were to survive. Their escape from Paris had cost too many lives, and he wanted no one else on their consciences.

His eyes flickering open, Hawkins would rasp instructions about height and course before the effort proved too much, and he'd slip back into sleep.

As if programmed, the pilot awoke as they were approaching the south coast of England and knew their position, giving course alterations that appeared to take them away from their destination. Having no alternative, he followed them to the letter and when Hawkins awoke again, he put a hand on Alena's arm 'Enough, thanks, go back and take care of the boy.'

Hawkins' voice sounded as thin as an old man's. 'Going to have to land... on your own... how do you feel?'

'Terrified,' he said and gripped the wheel all the harder. He'd been able to put the landing out of his mind by concentrating on maintaining altitude and course. But now he had to go through with it.

'Not... hard as it looks.'

'I'll take your word for it.'

'Depends on weather... down there.' Hawkins coughed and brought up more blood and wiped it from his lips. 'Don't want it blowing all over the place... got to turn right now... get in position.'

If you'd asked him to repeat what he was told, he wouldn't have remembered a word of it such was his concentration, copying every command like an automaton.

After what seemed an eternity, Hawkins croaked: 'Bloody perfect... straight run from here... hope there's not too much wind.'

Hawkins signalled he wanted to speak to the controllers at RAF Hamworthy, and Ben didn't take in much of it. It all sounded too technical and frightening and he struggled to see where they were going as sweat streamed into his eyes making them sting and he couldn't remove his hands from the wheel to wipe them dry.

'No... wounded... co-pilot dead.' He heard Hawkins tell the ground.

There was more static and a voice sounding as if it were in an echo chamber and Hawkins replied: 'No... never... bloody good job... so far.'

A long pause as Hawkins mustered his strength. 'For Christ's sake... no.'

'Tom,' he shouted not taking his eyes off the way ahead, 'what's wrong?'

'Too dangerous... to land,' the pilot said. 'Wind getting up... wave height, swell... too strong. Another strip... hundred miles away.'

'Surely it's not that bad?'

'Dangerous... if sea rough,' and he winced as another wave of pain hit him. 'If we land bow down... it'll split... we'll sink... bring engines on top of us.'

'Impossible,' he yelled above the noise of the static and the plane's groaning and grumbling as it rode the wind making them rock from side to side. If they didn't get medical help for Hawkins as soon as possible, he'd die. He wouldn't last another hundred miles. This was his only chance.

'Tell them we're coming in whether they want it or not.'

Hawkins shook his head. 'Can't... it's an order.'

'Balls,' he yelled again above the increasing noise. 'I'm an American; I'll do what I want.'

Hawkins slumped in his seat as if he knew his fight was almost finished.

'Tell me what to do, Tom, and I'll get this plane down.'

Hawkins struggled to make a final effort.

'Get on with it... might make the date after all.'

Despite the controller's protests, they were instructed to land on Flying Boat Runway South 2 in the Wych Channel between the mainland and Brownsea Island. And Hawkins pointed out if he made a mess of the landing they were unlikely to do too much damage to anyone but themselves.

He glanced sideways. Hawkins was looking more vulnerable and younger than ever. Following every command from the pilot, he reduced the Catalina's speed and height as his arms ached from the tension. The wind whipped along the sides of the hull and they rode the currents as if every blast of wind was a hurdle to be cleared and each one appeared to be more of a struggle.

'Bloody lucky... not a few months ago,' Hawkins said.

He flashed him a questioning look.

'Tough winter... boats frozen in ice.'

He hoped water would make for a softer landing than ice but as he looked down, he saw the waves being roughed up by the wind and doubted it.

'Increase revs to 2,300,' Hawkins croaked.

The engine note changed as if it were protesting.

'This is the fun part.' Hawkins coughed, and blood spilled down his chin, but this time he just left it. 'Throttle back... glide in at 85 knots. Good, good.'

He daren't blink as he stared through the windscreen trying to ascertain what lay ahead but could see only the black of night.

'Keep nose up... above the horizon.'

The hull should touch first and not the bow, but he didn't know how high they were above the water, and he clenched his teeth to stop himself from crying out.

Hawkins screamed at him.

'For Christ's sake... lift the nose... coming in too fast.'

# 73

THE FLYING BOAT WAS OUT OF CONTROL.

As they approached the surface, they appeared to pick up speed, and he pulled back on the wheel attempting to slow it. As if it had a mind of its own, the plane refused to respond to his commands, and he shouted for everyone to brace for a collision. He glanced sideways at Hawkins hoping even at this late stage he might say or do something that could avert a disaster. But the pilot's head lay on his chest as he gripped the sides of the seat.

With a great roar, the bow of the Catalina pierced the sea, ploughing in deep and for a moment all appeared still before it resurfaced with its propellers whipping up the waters so that the surface foamed. The impact pulled Ben back then threw him forward and the harness cut deep into his jacket drawing blood. Water rushed up, and he screamed 'hold tight, hold tight' and heard other voices although he didn't know whose.

Icy water washed through the cockpit causing him to gasp for breath and bringing him to his senses like a slap to the face. As it rose to his chest, the intensity of the cold numbed him and desensitised the pain. His head slumped forward as another wave surged through the cockpit and he spat out a mouthful of water tasting of gasoline. They were sinking. If they didn't free themselves, they would go down with it. He strained to reach over to protect Hawkins as another wave moved through, pinning him back in his seat.

He wondered if they were already submerged, if so there would be little hope. The impact had smashed part of the windscreen and water was also flooding in through the bow gun-port. And the structure of the plane was so weakened, it was breaking up as it groaned and shuddered in the death throes of a sinking ship.

Fearing they would be dragged to the seabed with the Catalina, he fumbled with frozen and shaking fingers to unbuckle his harness and waded over to help Hawkins.

'Got to get out of here,' he shouted above the racket of the propellers, 'before the whole thing goes under.'

Hawkins' chin still lay on his chest, and he didn't respond and slipped down in his seat until his mouth was just above the level of the water.

'Come on,' he shouted again and shook Hawkins as hard as he dared, releasing a cloud of red that spread out in the water. There was no reaction. No pulse. But Hawkins' eyes stared ahead as if keeping watch.

The water level was rising fast, and he felt a stab of panic not having heard from Alena and Freddie above the noise of the thrashing propellers, the wind, and the terminal creaking and groaning of the hull. He shouted their names and waded back through the plane, the mini currents sapping his strength and several times knocking him over so that he was immersed again in the freezing waters.

Alena and Freddie were still buckled in and staring straight ahead, immobile in shock and oblivious to the danger, and even when he shouted at them they didn't acknowledge him. He pressed his face into hers and screamed at her above the noise. 'Come on, move, we've got to go.' And he pulled at their harnesses until his fingers bled.

Alena's eyes focused as if she'd come out of a trance. 'Tom?' she enquired, and she was rigid with fear.

There was no time for explanations, but she got her answer from the set of his face and her head dropped and when she lifted it, tears streamed uncontrollably. 'Oh, no! Not him, too.'

He shook them both. 'We've got to get out of here, this thing is going under.'

Alena lifted Freddie into her arms and waded after Ben to the cargo door. Their survival depended on whether it was above or beneath the water level. And he put all his force into attempting to roll it open.

It wouldn't move.

The door must be submerged, and the plane was sinking faster than he'd thought. He searched out another escape route, and they struggled through the rising water to the Catalina's two gun-ports on the top of the fuselage in the waist of the plane. It was slow going and strength sapping and several times they stumbled as another wave hit the Cat, each one bringing an assortment of floating equipment and bags and other objects that were added obstacles.

He was now carrying Freddie and had reached the gun-ports when Alena screamed. In a flash of moonlight, he saw a man's hand grabbing her leg, and she was rooted to the spot paralysed by fear. For an instant, he froze too. Holding a hand over the boy's eyes so he wouldn't see, he waded back to Alena and handed him over to her. He bent and disentangled the hand of the co-pilot, who was floating just below the surface. With as much effort as he could muster, he pushed the almost headless body into the recesses of the plane and, with a hand raised, it floated into the dark.

Time was against them and he struggled to find the catch to release the blister's canopy. He redoubled his efforts, bracing himself against the hull and kicked it with both legs until the canopy broke free.

'We've got to get out,' he screamed at her, but in the furore, she couldn't hear. He motioned for her to step out onto the fuselage, but she hung back clutching Freddie to her breast. He snatched the boy away from her and pushed her out, and she stumbled and fell forward.

'Hang on,' he yelled at her.

Lashed by seawater, the fuselage was slippery and with the propellers whipping up a fierce wind every lurch and wave threatened to sweep them off. Immersed in these freezing waters, they'd last only minutes.

'Look,' Alena shrieked, tugging his sleeve and pointing towards land. 'Someone's coming.'

At first, he thought her mistaken. Then in the distance he saw a flashing blue light and a searchlight, one second scanning the water and the next the clouds as it bounced over the channel.

The rending metal reverberated along the length of the flying boat and heralded its demise, but he doubted the rescuers would reach them in time. Its back broken, the plane slipped beneath the waves. First, the front of the Catalina dipped into the sea followed by the back of the plane breaking away and sliding backwards.

The violent separation tore the fuselage from their grip, and they were catapulted face forward into the cauldron. He heard Alena shrieking repeatedly 'Freddie, Freddie,' as the child disappeared.

He lost his sense of being, and his mind raced as feeling left his limbs. The shock forced his mouth open and water flooded his lungs. A growing pain spread throughout his body. He resurfaced, but his head slipped back beneath the waves. And each time he swallowed more water he knew he was drowning. He had no idea what to do. An instinct to survive forced him to thrash in an uncoordinated effort, but the more he struggled, the faster he sank. The weight of the water in his lungs dragged him downwards and his will weakened as his strength ebbed away. He was sinking fast, and now he almost wanted to let go.

He stopped, something had halted his descent. Had he reached the bottom? He forced his eyes open. To his surprise, Freddie's body was lodged under the fuselage beneath him. An overwhelming feeling of relief gave him a new strength. He just wanted to get the boy to Alena, and his lungs screamed with pain as he worked feverishly to free him. After disentangling Freddie, he kicked hard and began to rise.

Breaking the surface and coughing out seawater, he gulped in sweet, fresh air.

Help had arrived and men in a launch scoured the water for survivors.

'Over here,' one of them shouted. 'There's something in the water.'

The boat pulled up alongside. A rescuer shouted: 'Well done, mate, I've got the boy just give him a push.'

At that moment, the front of the plane went under, its propellers spinning and adding to the swell. The rescuers were finding it challenging to keep the launch close to the plane. And they were in danger of being swamped. Such was the strength of the currents, their boat swung around out of control. He felt a bang on his head. A rush of pain coursed through his body and he was overcome by nausea. And Freddie slipped from his grasp.

The water now seemed as warm as a welcoming bath, and he floated backwards into its arms. As the stress of the past few days receded, he relaxed. It felt good, and he let it happen. The water lapped over his face, and he retched as it invaded his lungs. Free at last. He didn't want to fight it anymore.

Everything was black and still. Above him, a light moved away, and the comforting darkness crept in around him. Images flashed through his brain. Alena. Freddie. Bernay. Weber. His parents. The light was just a pinprick. Then blackness. Such welcome nothingness.

# 74

BEN LAY IN A DARKENED ROOM THAT HE SENSED WAS BARE APART FROM AN iron bedstead and although he couldn't see he heard voices.

Two women.

They were fussing around him and he was being moved, his legs lifted and arms rearranged, and soft hands holding his head, raising it from the pillow, and laying it down again.

'Who's this?' One asked in a soft Scottish accent.

'Don't know. Doesn't have a name.'

He shouted his name. *Ben Peters*.

'How did he get here?'

'On a plane that crashed into the sea.'

'Where's he from?'

'No idea. Apparently no ID.'

'Maybe he's a German,' said the Scottish voice.

'Could be from the moon for all I know. Just dropped out of the sky.'

'He only appears to have cuts and bruises.'

'Don't think he will make it, though, been here for weeks.'

'What if he never wakes?'

'Dunno. I suppose he lies here until he dies.'

'Perhaps he's already dead.'
'Better check. We could do with the bed.'
He felt hands on him again.
'No, he's still with us.'
'There's a pulse?'
'Yes, quite a strong one.'
'Not bad looking, I suppose, under those bumps and bruises.'
'I wouldn't kick him out of bed.'
'What's he like?'
'What do you mean?'
'Down there?'
They both giggled.
He sensed a sheet unfolding from his body.
Again, hands on him.
'Oh, not bad, not bad at all.'
'Bit of a waste him lying here, isn't it?'
Their laughter was raucous now.
The sheet covered him again.
Footsteps.
A door closing.
He screamed and screamed.
Still no one heard.

# 75

LIGHT. A RAY OF SUNSHINE AND IN IT PARTICLES OF DUST FLOATING LIKE planets in a distant galaxy. He'd been staring at it for so long he believed he was in this world and it was all around him. Did it exist, or just live in his mind? He kept staring in case he lost it.

Unblinking.

If he averted his eyes, he might return to the dark and he couldn't bear that. He forced himself to keep his eyes open and to focus until he believed he could see every speck of dust in detail.

Had he blinked? Had he lost consciousness? Was he conscious now? Or was his mind playing games? At night in a darkened room with your eyes closed, you could still see flashing images. Was that what he saw now, an image imprinted on his retina?

The ray of sunshine was still there and the dust or was it different dust?

*Look around, get your bearings.*

He couldn't risk it in case he might lose it. He lay still for a time – it may have been hours or even days – still unblinking until his eyelids felt as heavy as granite.

*Have I a voice?*

When he spoke before to the two women, they didn't respond yet he'd shouted. Perhaps he'd imagined it.

He whispered his name. And again. Louder this time.

Nothing happened.

*Where am I? How did I get here?* The questions came as fast and as painful as hailstones in a blizzard although there were no answers.

Changing his focus, he attempted to take in his surroundings – a high-ceilinged room, with walls painted white and an overpowering smell of antiseptic. Was it a hospital?

*Why? Why am I here?* They'd said something about a plane crash, but he had no memory of it.

He returned to his dream about the two women. One had said he was close to death.

*How bad are my injuries?*

He moved his fingers and lifted each hand in front of his eyes. He felt his face with his hands; everything was in place. Could he move his legs? Left and then right.

*Good, okay.*

Now he felt confident enough to move his head away from his fixation on the ray of light.

Little interested him about the room apart from a window, and he rolled over for a better look. Outside, expansive lawns led down to the water and in the distance, an island. Nurses in starched uniforms ministered to men, some in wheelchairs and others sitting on benches in dressing-gowns. Many read newspapers, and some smoked and there was an interchange of banter.

A noise caught his attention, and what looked like a seaplane landed on the water sending up a splash magnified by the sunlight.

Memories should return when prompted although not this time, apart from one. In Paris, he sat in a café, writing in one of his yellow pads and sipping a cognac because the writing was going well. Something made him lift his head from his work, and at a table nearby he saw a woman with a small boy. The woman's blonde hair, cut across her cheek, hid her features, but she appeared to be crying.

'So, the sleeping beauty is awake.' Said with a soft Scottish accent. He hadn't seen the nurse with rosy cheeks and her dark hair in a bun enter the room.

BEN WAS PROBED AND PRODDED, visited by doctors, fed pills, injected, and given bed baths for what seemed an eternity in a place where every day lasted a week. Eventually, they allowed him to be wheeled out to the lawns and parked under a tree for hours at a time.

This was a hospital for aircrew injured whilst operating the planes based in the area. Although he enjoyed watching them landing and taking off, he had no recollection of any involvement with them.

The memory of the blonde woman and the boy – memory, he decided, not a dream – stayed with him. And no amount of questioning of the medical staff elicited information about how he happened to be in this hospital. It was as if they'd been ordered not to say. And he discovered no one had ever come to visit him.

One day when his frustration boiled over, the Scottish nurse left his bedside and returned with a large brown envelope and handed it to him.

'What's this?' he asked.

'I've no idea. It was with your possessions, or should I say your only possession, that'll be returned to you when you're discharged.' She pointed to the envelope.

He turned the soft and bulky package over before tearing it open. After staring at the object inside for several seconds, he recognised it – a child's worn teddy bear.

Without knowing where it came from, he uttered one word 'Freddie' not sure whether that was the name of the bear or the boy in his memory.

When he couldn't bear this incarceration any longer, a doctor with a luxuriant silver beard and a red weather-beaten face gave him the all clear.

'Nothing more we can do for you here, old chap,' he said, a cigarette hanging from the corner of his mouth. 'You can leave tomorrow.' The doctor beamed and clapped him on the shoulder. 'Well done' as if he should be proud of having achieved something.

'Where will I go?'

'Don't worry. Someone's coming for you.'

# 76

BEN SAT IN A RECEPTION AREA WEARING A DEAD MAN'S SUIT AND HOLDING a small brown case carrying a change of underwear, socks and two shirts and toiletries, and the teddy bear. He felt like a puppy waiting to be chosen by new owners at a dog pound. He'd no idea who was coming to meet him although he'd fantasised during a sleepless night that it might be the blonde woman from his memory.

It was the same as any hospital waiting room. A bleak, functional space with polished floors and an overpowering smell of antiseptic, and patients waiting to be collected. One with a bandage over his eyes. Another missing a leg in a wheelchair. Others going home to die. Government propaganda posters plastered the cream walls aimed at lifting spirits and reminding everyone they were in this together. Two were strident with white lettering on red backgrounds.

Your courage
Your cheerfulness
Your resolution
WILL BRING
US VICTORY

and

## KEEP CALM
## and
## CARRY ON

He caught the aroma before he saw him. Pipe smoke preceded a tall, heavyset man wearing an English gentleman's uniform of a tweed suit and sturdy brown brogues. 'Peters, Peters,' the man, who carried his weight well, called from across the room as if he'd known him all his life. 'Good to see you.'

The man extended his hand and pulled him close. 'Name's Pickering,' he said as if it were a secret between the two of them.

'Are you from the hospital?' he asked.

'No, no, London.'

'London?'

'War Office.' Pickering lowered his voice and glanced around to make sure no one else heard. 'Anyway, how are you, old man?'

'Okay, I suppose.' Unsure if he was.

'Ready to go?'

'Where?'

'Time to talk.' Pickering gave him a conspiratorial look.

Not understanding, he shook his head.

'Debriefing.'

'Why?'

Pickering studied him for some time, stroking and probing his beard. His eyes, a watery pale blue, ran over Ben's face and the prominent veins in his red, bulbous nose appeared to pulsate. 'It's okay, you're amongst friends.'

He still looked puzzled.

Pickering pursed his lips. 'Wait here.' He disappeared down a corridor, returning minutes later with a set of keys. 'Follow me,' he said.

The man from the War Office let him into a small office with two chairs and a wooden desk, and they sat either side of it. He ordered tea and biscuits and scrutinised him as if trying to read his mind, drumming his fingers on the table until the tea appeared.

'Must say you did rather a splendid job,' Pickering said. 'Let me, I'll be mother.' He poured it for him and added milk and sugar whether he wanted it. 'Everyone's pleased.' He pointed at the ceiling.

'They are?'

'Commendable, old man. Relax, it's okay to talk to me.'

'Don't remember anything,' he said, a sense of impotence rising within him.

'Nothing at all?' Pickering raised his arms ready to field anything that came his way but, realising it was hopeless, dropped them again.

'Why am I here?'

He recalled the memory of the woman and the boy in Paris. 'That's all I can remember.'

'No recollection of what you did?' Pickering flashed him a dubious look.

Like a schoolboy who'd misbehaved, he shook his head. 'Of what?'

'No memories of your mission?' Pickering looked as if this wasn't part of the script.

He laughed. 'I'm a banker; you make me sound as though I'm a secret agent. You've got the wrong man.'

'I've definitely got the right man.'

Pickering extricated his pipe from his pocket and made to light it. 'Take it you've no objection?'

He shook his head.

Leaning back in his chair causing it to creak under his weight and, with the pipe clenched between his teeth, Pickering steepled his fingers across his stomach.

'If I mentioned Bentley. Mean anything to you?'

'Easy.' He smiled. 'A rather unique motorcar. My boss at the bank in Paris has one.' Something in his subconscious wriggled to get out.

'Ah, great.' Pickering said with a hint of sarcasm. 'So at least you remember that.'

He nodded, wondering what else there was to remember.

Pickering studied the ceiling. 'So, you have no idea how you got from Paris to England?'

His look confirmed that.

'What about the woman in your memory?'

He was relieved that he had acknowledged it was a memory, not a dream.

Pickering wheezed and worked his beard even harder before getting to his feet. 'Perhaps, we're going too fast. Sometimes memory can take time to return if ever. Other times, something happens, a trigger opening the gates. Don't worry. I've booked us rooms in an old country inn near here. Thought you might appreciate some normality before driving to London. A decent meal and a pint or two of real ale, none of that dreadful French plonk, eh?'

Over dinner, Pickering was surprisingly good company and Ben sensed he was prompting him, trying to unravel his memories, although Pickering was careful not to put images into his mind. Whatever he remembered should be his own, not something planted by someone else. The beer was going down well, and he was pleased to find a good malt whisky that helped him to relax although it did nothing to lubricate his memory.

As the evening progressed, Pickering became more agitated and kept glancing at his watch as if he'd a deadline.

He predicted something was about to happen or Pickering was building up to tell him something he didn't want to hear. Eventually, Pickering pushed away from the table.

'Ben, want you to come to my room,' he said. 'Something you must hear. Take your Scotch with you.'

Upstairs, Pickering ushered him into an armchair, switched on a contraption in a corner of the room, fiddled with knobs, and silenced him with a raised hand when he tried to talk.

'You know, old man, modern warfare is propaganda and dirty tricks. Counterespionage, double agents. All sorts of things. Smoke and mirrors. Good propaganda can be worth more than several air strikes; it's great for demoralising the enemy. Jerry is at it. And so are we.'

He had a vague feeling of being told something similar before but by whom and when he couldn't remember.

'Did you know the Nazis tried to deliver a box of Churchill's favourite cigars to him? Only they were exploding cigars. Almost frightened the life out of the Post Office. Make no mistake; it will be propaganda that will win this war for us. Could tell you things that would make your hair curl.' But he didn't intend to and gave a nervous laugh as if the prospect frightened him.

Growing serious, Pickering pointed at the machine in the corner. 'You must listen carefully to this.'

## 77

'THIS IS THE BBC IN LONDON' A VOICE WITH PERFECT DICTION EMANATED from the contraption, announcing it would be broadcast all over Europe and repeated in German.

Pickering leant across to whisper that the content of the broadcast would be printed in leaflets and dropped by RAF planes to German troops and cities. This was a common practice as they often carried out leaflet runs to disguise the fact they were also parachuting in agents behind enemy lines.

Ben wasn't paying attention as the announcer rambled on for what seemed several minutes as he was concentrating more on what Pickering had said to him and what it was he should remember.

A new voice spoke. 'My name is...' The voice sounded tinny and far away and there was an echo, but it was as clear as water in a mountain stream. Time seemed to stand still, and he felt as if he'd been hit by a sledgehammer.

'My name is Alena...'

Pickering perched on the edge of his seat supporting his weight on the balls of his feet as he stared at him.

Everything moved in his mind as if they were blocks being knocked away before a ship slides down the slipway for the first time.

It was unstoppable, and Pickering saw in his eyes the pain of remembering. The memories flooded back in a kaleidoscope of sound and colour each battling for prominence. If he'd been standing such was their power, they could have bowled him over. Instead, he was pushed back in his chair as they played out in vivid flashes of remembrance and he gripped the arms of the chair so hard his knuckles turned white.

'I want to send a message to the German people wherever you are,' she continued.

'Is this going out now?' he asked.

Pickering looked irritated. 'No, this is a recording. It hasn't been decided when it will go out.' And he held a finger to his lips

As though the two halves of his brain were working independently, he listened to her words and yet was seeing something like newsreel footage of their escape from Paris.

'Although I am French, I know Germany well and lived in your country for many years. I worked for *Fonction Publique Française*, the French civil service, in Paris and before the war I went to Berlin to work at the French Embassy. While I was there, I made many German friends. As Germans, you know everywhere you go now you have to carry the *Ahnenpass*, a passport listing up to six previous generations of your family to prove you are pure Aryan. Those who do not meet those requirements disappear as part of Adolf Hitler's campaign to rid Europe of the Jewish people whom he detests as *Untermensch*, and whom he believes to be enemies of the German state. It is now illegal in Germany or German-occupied countries to consort with these so-called sub-humans, and if found guilty, you can be executed or placed in work camps.'

He felt numb and was finding it hard to breathe, and Pickering offered him another drink to help relieve the symptoms of shock.

In a calm and slow voice, Alena was now recounting the story she'd told him earlier about her experience in Berlin and Freddie's birth.

'The man who raped me, a Nazi, kept us out of the public eye by imprisoning us in a castle near Munich where he came to visit his son. He gave me a ring, a priceless ring with a rare red diamond. It was one of the Nazis' spoils of war. As you may know, the Nazi hierarchy keep for their own use the treasures their troops plunder. This was part of my son's father's collection.'

He nodded remembering the ring Alena had given to Sebastian, the mountain guide, to persuade him to take them over the Pyrenees. It was probably worth many thousands, and he wondered if Sebastian realised its value.

'As far as my family back home in France were concerned, I'd vanished, and they presumed I'd died. I haven't been able to let them know I'm still alive because the Nazis would come after them. In your name, the Führer and his armies are imprisoning and killing innocent people because they are mentally or physically handicapped, gypsies or Jews.'

There was a gleam in Pickering's eyes knowing what was coming next.

'My name is Alena and I am French. My family originated from Russia. My grandfather and my grandmother emigrated to France.'

There were now long pauses between words as if she had to rein herself in from blurting everything out in an uncontrolled rush and in the silences he heard the loud ticking of a clock somewhere in the room.

'My grandparents were Jews as are my parents. Therefore, I am Jewish and proud to be so.'

There was an even longer pause as if she were giving the listeners time for this piece of information to sink in.

'Freddie, my little boy, something of beauty born out of a vile act, is Jewish. But he also has Aryan blood from his father, a Nazi. His father, the man who raped me, has broken the laws you must follow. This man is at the centre of the Nazis' campaign to rid the world of Jews. Yet he has a Jewish son who he has had to hide away until now. Why can this be so if it's illegal under punishment of death to have any relations with those of the Jewish faith? My son's father should be answerable to the German people.'

And there was another long pause.

She mumbled something inaudible.

Another even longer pause.

'My son's father is...'

Now the ticking of the clock dominated the pauses. And Pickering twitched with impatience.

'The man who wants to kill Jews has a Jewish son.'

Again, she paused, gathering her strength until she almost shouted it out.

'The father of my Jewish son is –'

Pickering bit hard on the pipe between his teeth and glanced over at Ben, who felt a painful knotting in his stomach.

ADOLF HITLER.

'Freddie is the son of Adolf Hitler.'

# 78

THE LETTERBOX RATTLING MADE BEN FREEZE. ANY UNUSUAL NOISE THESE days made him start and he tensed as though ready to flee. It could be entirely innocent, a postman pushing through a letter. Or the sound of an intruder. The afternoon was deteriorating into a foggy dusk as he loafed on a battered old armchair in his apartment off Kensington High Street reading a manuscript he hoped would be his first published book.

At first, Ben hoped to see Alena again, and every time a letter dropped through the letterbox he quickened his step and picked it up in anticipation. But now he doubted if they'd ever be reunited. She and Freddie had disappeared behind an impenetrable smokescreen set up by British Intelligence. And when he nibbled at Pickering for any titbit of news the man, who professed to be a friend, gave a good impression of being nothing more than a messenger.

'Couldn't tell you even if I knew,' Pickering would say, shrugging his shoulders, looking genuinely apologetic. 'Top secret and all that, old man.' Alive and safe, they were living somewhere in the country with new identities, Pickering revealed before repeating almost without taking breath: 'Don't know where, I'm afraid.'

His mission was deemed a success after Ben confirmed that the platinum was on the plane. Divers retrieved the bullion from the wreck of the Catalina and it was sold to the Americans and the proceeds used to help fund the Free French Forces' fight against the Germans.

It was of secondary importance to him. He wanted to find Alena and was frustrated by Pickering whom he was sure knew where they were being kept. When he pushed for information, Pickering looked weary as though the weight of his lies were too great a burden. Pickering stayed in touch and helped him get a job in a financial institution in the City of London whether out of guilt or friendship he wasn't sure. His Wall Street bank wanted him to return to New York to resume his career, but he had no wish to leave Europe. He felt part of their struggle against the Nazis and wanted to support them in any way he could, and he also knew he couldn't face the mundanity of returning home. Even though life was hard, the British, especially the Londoners, inspired him with an indomitable spirit that would never surrender. Leaving now would be running away when your buddy was being beaten.

He put down the manuscript and rose from the chair. He saw there hadn't been a delivery, but he sensed a presence behind the door and he opened it with trepidation.

Startled, Pickering stepped back, his fist raised ready to knock.

'Thought you were the postman.' He tried not to show his disappointment, and in return received a reproving look from Pickering.

'I suppose I have a delivery of sorts. Car's downstairs. Come on, got something to show you.'

He grabbed his jacket and followed him down to the car.

Pickering kept his hands on the wheel with his teeth clamped tight on his pipe as though struggling with a secret that might escape if he opened his mouth. They turned into a cobbled lane running alongside Waterloo railway station lined by lock-ups built into the arches of the railway bridges.

'Here we are,' Pickering said and halted the car in front of wooden double doors secured by a rusting chain and padlock. It wasn't promising. Weeds poked through the gaps between the cobblestones and most of the lock-ups were neglected with their doors in need of painting. And Pickering appeared agitated and, with his collar turned up, looked as if he were a spiv waiting to complete a black-market deal. 'You can't rely on the buggers,' he shook his head and swore under his breath.

They were alone, and Ben felt vulnerable and the asthmatic gasping of steam engines only added to the mood.

Still muttering, Pickering strode over to the doors and tried the padlock. 'Wait a minute,' he said and returned to his car and, after rummaging in the back, emerged with the car's starting handle. He slipped it through the loops of the chain and pushed down with all of his strength until the chain snapped and fell to the ground.

He wondered what Pickering was so eager to show him as the doors creaked open. They peered into the gloom until their eyes became accustomed to the dark and he could make out the shapes before him. He gasped. It was as if he were being transported back to when Bernay showed him the Bentley for the first time. Then, gleaming, she'd stood proud and magnificent. He'd forgotten the damage and blows she'd endured. War wounds that had ravaged her body. Cracks scoring the windscreen. The front bumper hanging off and trailing on the ground. Shell holes in the bonnet. Cobwebs festooned the mascot and those large headlamps, yet her class shone through the indignity.

He glanced at Pickering as though requiring his permission and Pickering knew what was in his mind and nodded agreement. Trembling with anticipation, he pulled open the driver's door and eased behind the wheel. The smell of leather still lingered, and he reached to switch on the ignition and when it started with some coaxing, they both roared with laughter. As he sat there, the engine made everything around him vibrate with its naked power and above it he heard Alena's voice and Freddie's laughter echoing around the car. His memories played out on the dusty windscreen before him. Leaving the panic of Paris. The drive through the French countryside with Alena by his side and Freddie chirruping in the back seat. The two French children. Escaping the brigands. The perilous journey over the Pyrenees. The Spanish gangster's attempt to steal the car and hold her hostage. A run-in with the Guardia Civil. Intrigue in Estoril. A hair-raising flight on the flying boat, yet it felt empty without her.

He didn't care what Pickering's motive was; he was just grateful to him. Being with the car brought him close to Alena and gave him hope one day they'd meet again. Pickering knew he had promised to return to Estoril once the war was over and reclaim the Bentley, if it was still there, and give it back to Bernay's family. But Pickering had trumped him and arranged for the car to be transported to England on a freighter out of Lisbon. He'd also arranged for some restoration work on the Bentley. Ben was speechless, and he glanced at Pickering with a grin spreading across his face, and Pickering understood.

While it took several weeks for the car to be restored to a semblance of its former glory, he again felt himself slipping into a despond. He realised the longer that time elapsed, the gulf between him and Alena was widening. Not even picking up the Bentley, which still carried some of its duelling scars although it could still turn a few heads, could entirely lift his spirits.

To celebrate his repossession of the car, Pickering suggested Ben drive to Cornwall and join him for the weekend at his country cottage by the sea.

He was happy to get away from the privations of London and it was an opportunity to reacquaint himself with the Bentley and it would benefit from having a long run. He set off on a Saturday morning and headed for the coast with the windows open, and the Bentley purred like a big cat devouring the miles. And he imagined a Stuka bomber swooping out of the azure sky and looked across at the passenger seat convinced Alena was with him.

Although a long drive, he was still relaxed when he reached the outskirts of the village. It comprised one narrow road meandering down the hill to the sea and flanked on either side by white painted cottages, many with thatched roofs. The road gave way to a slipway leading to a small harbour in which several fishing boats bobbed on the tide. Pickering's cottage was the last on the left and closest to the sea. And he parked the Bentley and made the rest of the way on foot.

He pushed open the gate and knocked on the old oak door. After knocking several times, and getting no response, he entered a small sitting-room dominated by an open wood fire and low oak-beamed ceilings.

'Pickering,' he called out. 'Where are you?'

As he didn't get an answer, he searched from room to room on the ground floor. No one appeared to be here. He went through the open French windows to a patio with views of the sea. To the left was a small lawn with a row of trees at the bottom. As he drew closer, he saw an archway of roses between the trees and stone steps leading to another tier of lawn and beyond a stone wall and a drop to the beach and harbour. Halfway down the steps, he came over dizzy and stopped to hold onto a railing as his vision blurred and he rubbed his eyes to try to clear the impediment.

Someone was slumped on the bench and wrapped in a blanket appearing as though they'd been looking out to sea and had grown tired of waiting and fallen asleep. As he approached, his pace quickened, and his mouth became dry and his heart rate increased.

The person on the bench didn't move.

He couldn't hold back and called out.

'Alena.'

Her head came up with a jolt. And she turned to see who had awakened her, yet still he couldn't see her face as it was shielded by the blanket.

She unfolded from the seat and stood up and he saw her eyes still burning green as a flame. She hesitated as if not registering what her eyes were telling her and then she broke into a wide, open-mouthed smile. He didn't know whether they ran to each other or walked, then she was in his arms with her hands cradling his head and her lips nuzzling his face and burying into his chest. And he felt the firmness of her body through the thin stuff of her dress.

'I never thought I'd see you again,' he whispered.

She looked up at him with tears in her eyes.

'I love you,' she said.

He traced her high cheekbones and the enigmatic dimple like a perfect scar with his thumb and her lips moved up searching for his mouth...

'Ah, there you are, old man.' Pickering awakened from his nap on the bench and stared at him, a question forming on his lips.

Blinking hard to refocus, Ben emerged from his reverie to confront a disappointment as heavy as a blow to the chest.

'Did she behave herself?'

'What?'

'Good drive?'

'Oh, yes.' He shook his head, feeling foolish and wondering what he'd just experienced. A hallucination or a premonition?

'Good, good! Got you here for two reasons, old man. Thought the drive would do you the world of good but also wanted to talk to you about something I didn't wish to discuss over the phone.'

'Alena?' His heartbeat increased alarmingly.

Pickering studied him and for the first time his affected speech and airs had deserted him. 'Yes, it's about Alena.'

'Is she here?'

'Afraid not, old man.' Pickering started to set up his pipe then dropped it on the grass as if it were no longer of use to him.

'We believe she's back behind enemy lines...'

He stared at him in disbelief. 'What?' Incredulity shone out of his eyes and he heard the anger in his voice rising. 'How could you?'

'It's complicated...'

'Why in God's name did you send her back there, you know every damned Nazi will be after her?'

'Not my decision, old man.'

He shook his head and slumped on the bench.

'It's very complicated.' Pickering dropped his voice as if he thought someone might be listening. 'I shouldn't be telling you this.'

'But after that broadcast–'

'That's another story –'

'What do you mean?'

'In the world of intelligence, you often have opposing views within the same camp and while we're involved in one project, some are working on many others.'

'Explain yourself, man.'

'Alena's secret is of great propaganda value to us and it's just a case of our picking the right time to broadcast it so it will have the best effect. Within Germany, there are factions opposed to Hitler and we believe some are planning attempts on his life.'

'So?'

'Someone, high up, has the view if the Germans themselves assassinate Hitler the people might have no stomach for fighting on and it would end the war.'

'Who?'

'The very top,' Pickering said and nodded when he saw Ben understood to whom he was referring. 'His view is if Hitler dies his followers will disappear back into their holes like the rats they are. But if they discover Hitler has a son and heir, it might give them a reason to fight on and for generations the faithful would have a figurehead to rally behind even if they lost the war.'

'He's overruling the intelligence services?'

Pickering gave a wry smile as if it were an everyday occurrence.

'Are you telling me the broadcast might not happen?'

Pickering looked at his feet.

'So, people died for nothing?'

'No, not at all. Your mission was a great success. You got the platinum out and the money will help De Gaulle's men in their fight against the Germans, and you saved Alena and Freddie from the Nazis.'

'What's happening to Alena?' He was already dreading Pickering's reply.

He hesitated as if unsure whether to tell him. 'We don't know. We have no information. Nothing. No sightings. We know who the Gestapo are arresting. Been listening in to their radio traffic for some time. No news, she hasn't been mentioned. She's vanished, although she may be lying low somewhere.'

'Or she could be dead.'

Pickering's face was expressionless.

'You promised me she was being looked after and safe.'

'I know.' Pickering's face reddened. 'I lied.' And he was unwilling to make eye contact.

He ran a hand through his hair and exhaled. 'What about Freddie?'

'He's okay,' Pickering broke into a smile. 'He's still at the safe house. But he is guarded day and night. And will be for a very long time. If we survive this war, Freddie will still be the target for any Nazi sympathisers, who would regard him as the second coming of the Messiah. That's why the government are adamant documentation relating to his case is locked away in the archives and not released until a hundred years after the war ends. By then, Freddie will have departed this mortal coil and with a bit of luck people will have forgotten about Hitler.'

'You made me drive all the way here to listen to this?'

'There was a reason.'

'Why couldn't you have told me in London?'

'There are bugs in your apartment. MI5 are listening to your telephone calls. Agents are on your doorstep watching who visits you.'

'Why?' He jumped to his feet and paced back and forth on the lawn. 'Why me? What have I done?'

'It's not you, necessarily.'

His eyes narrowed with suspicion.

'They think Alena might try to contact you.'

'Hopefully. Why should it be a problem?'

Pickering didn't answer and looked as if he wished he hadn't started this conversation.

'After all, your people sent her back behind enemy lines.'

Pickering shook his head and strode over to face Ben. 'That's just it, we didn't.'

Ben ran a hand through his hair and looked out to sea. 'I don't understand.'

'Just a minute.' Pickering raised an arm and did a lap of the gardens before he disappeared into the house. He returned with a smile and looked more relaxed. 'I think the coast's clear.'

'What do you mean?'

'I told them you were coming to spend the weekend with me and I'd keep an eye on you. I still expected them to have someone following you, just in case.'

Exhaling, he put his head in his hands.

'I shouldn't be telling you any of this, Ben,' Pickering continued. 'I could get locked up – or worse.'

'So you're saying Alena escaped from her safe house and left Freddie?'

Pickering nodded. 'Perhaps not escaped, but she's gone missing.'

He found it hard to believe. All the time they'd been fleeing the

Nazis, she had been a protective mother never letting Freddie out of her sight. Now she'd gone off, leaving the boy behind, and travelled beyond enemy lines. It didn't stack up.

'So, she's gone back to war. Why?'

'Bit of a mystery, old man.' Pickering glanced away.

'I presume she's working for British Intelligence or one of your agencies?'

'Not that simple, I'm afraid. We don't share secrets. There's no way of telling. The people who believe they ran her didn't send her anywhere.'

He sat heavily on the bench. What had made her run off and desert Freddie?

'There's more.' Pickering came over and sat beside him. 'Alena may not be quite who we thought she was.'

'Go on.'

'Caused quite a stir with our French counterparts. As you know, she was a member of their diplomatic service and then seconded to work for us. Now it seems she wasn't who the French thought she was. Her documents? Forgeries. No one knows where she came from.'

Pickering let it sink in before continuing. 'It doesn't mean a gnat's arse to the French anymore, but it puts us in a very awkward position.'

He felt his strength ebbing away, and he heard his own disembodied voice. 'Then who is Alena?'

'Damned if we know,' said Pickering, retrieving his pipe from the ground. 'It seems someone planted her in the heart of the French diplomatic service.'

'Alena wouldn't do that,' he said.

'Unfortunately, these are the facts,' said Pickering, stroking his beard with the stem of his pipe. 'We are now sure she is a double agent, but who she's working for and what damage she has done to our country is uncertain.'

'And now she's disappeared off the face of the earth,' Ben added, determined one day he would find her wherever she was hiding. 'It's as if she never existed.'

# ALSO BY VIC ROBBIE

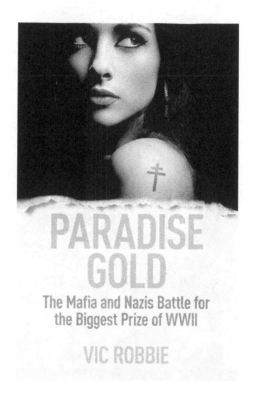

## PARADISE GOLD

### Book 2 of the Ben Peters WWII thriller series

America is facing its biggest threat.

Nazi U-boats are dominating the Atlantic from their base in the Caribbean. And the US government has joined forces with the Mafia to stop Germany from stealing a fortune in gold. Caught between ruthless Germans and Mafia assassins, only American agent Ben Peters knows the Nazis' terrifying plans for America, but first, he has to deal with two beautiful and dangerous women who will do anything to achieve their goals. Award-winning author Vic Robbie continues with his blend of fact and fiction. A pulsating spy thriller that is a roller-coaster read.

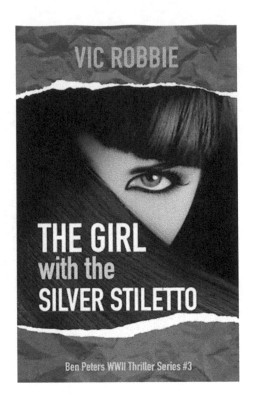

**THE GIRL with the SILVER STILETTO**

**Book 3 of the Ben Peters WWII thriller series**

Could you murder a child to save your own life?

At the end of World War II, Natalie is given an ultimatum. Execute the boy or die. Her only alternative is to hand him over to the Nazis. Why do the Nazis want the boy and who is he? As the suspense builds, the action races across three continents, from London to New York to California to Buenos Aires, and American agent Ben Peters stands alone against evil and his former lover.

# ENJOY THE BOOK?

Thanks for reading *In Pursuit Of Platinum,* and I hope you enjoyed it. If you did, I would be grateful if you could help other like-minded readers discover it, too. Reviews are vitally important in encouraging readers to find new books and also for authors to expand our readership.

Good and honest reviews are like a massive pat on the back to an author and I appreciate your comments and help in getting my books noticed.

If you care to spend a few minutes to leave a review, that would be great. And it doesn't have to be long.

Thanks for your help.

# ABOUT THE AUTHOR

Vic Robbie lives in England and spends time in California. An author of fiction and non-fiction, his work as a journalist has been published worldwide. He has worked as a writer, columnist and editor for newspapers and magazines in the UK, US and Australia. His first book in the Ben Peters thriller series, *In Pursuit Of Platinum*, reached #2 on Amazon's best sellers list for War stories and #3 for Spy stories. He also founded and edited *Golf & Travel* magazine and the *PGA Official Yearbook*. A golfer of little skill, he has also run several marathons, including New York and London, for charity.

www.vicrobbie.com
vic@vicrobbie.com

# ACKNOWLEDGEMENTS

Every book starts and ends with the author but along the way there are a host of people who have played a part in some way for a work to come to fruition, and this book is no exception. Without their support and expertise, the project would have been to no avail.

First, my thanks as ever to those who fuelled me with their encouragement – Christine, Gabrielle, Kirstie, Nick, Maia, Jed, Archie and Isla.

John Peacock for being an important sounding board and saying the right things at the right time. David Legg, author of *Consolidated PBY Catalina: The Peacetime Record*, for explaining the technicalities of the Catalina flying boat and how it operated. Several modifications were made to the Catalina in the story and if there are any errors, they are of my making and not David's. Francisco Corrêa de Barros, of Palácio Estoril Hotel & Golf in Estoril, for his amazing tales of intrigue at the hotel in wartime. Barry Sutherland, of the Bentley Wildfowl & Motor Museum, for his help with classic Bentleys.

And to the platinum experts at Johnson Matthey for explaining everything about the rare metal and its usage in 1940, and also those at the Banque de France.

And finally to all the brave people who fought tyranny in the Second World War and won.

# JOIN ME ON A JOURNEY

Whether writing or reading a book, it's often an exciting journey, taking you to different worlds and meeting new people. Please sign up to my reader's list and join me on a special journey. I've already met many new readers and friends around the world through my books and I look forward to engaging with you, too. You can get special offers and news about what's happening in the book world. And the chance to win some amazing prizes. You won't be spammed, I promise you.

Please visit my website www.vicrobbie.com for more information.

9 780957 346406